GOG
&
MAGOG

GOG
&
MAGOG

THE DEVIL'S DESCENDANTS

JERRY POLLOCK

SHeCHinaH Third Temple, Inc.

This is a work of fiction although one may find historical truths within the pages of my book if, like me, one chooses to believe in God, angels, the Hebrew prophets, and the Garden of Eden. Similarity to events in the future history of humankind is purely coincidental.

ISBN, Softbound Edition: 978-09723866-1-6
EAN-13: 9780972386616
Library of Congress Control Number: 2011900947

Publisher's Cataloguing-in Publication

Pollock, Jerry J. (Jerry Joseph), 1941-

   Gog & magog : the devil's descendants / Jerry J. Pollock. - Boynton
Beach, FL : Shechinah Third Temple, Inc., c2011.
       p. ; cm.
       ISBN: 978-09723866-1-6
   Bible-Prophecies-Fiction. 2. Devil-Fiction. 3. Good and evil-
Fiction. 4. Judgment of God-Fiction. 5. End of the world-Fiction.
6. Apocalyptic literature. 7. Political fiction. 8. Suspense fiction.
I. Title.

PS3616.O5696 G64 2011   2011900947
813.6-dc22   1104

Book Design: Create Space
Cover Design and Author Photo: Magnus Andersson

GOD to Noah
Genesis VIII:21

*"The imagery of man's heart is
evil from his youth."*

Daniel's Vision
Book of Daniel 7:7-8

*"It was different from all the beasts
that preceded it and it had ten
horns. I was studying the horns,
and behold! Another horn came,
a small one, came up among them,
and three of the ten horns were
uprooted before it, and behold!
eyes like human were in this horn
and a mouth speaking haughty words."*

My Marcia

*I am your Adam and you
are my Eve, and we shall
dwell only in the goodness
of the Garden of Eden,
for our souls are one
with God.*

My Creator

*I pledge myself with all my
being and all my love
to You. I ask that You be with
me and guide me always.*

❧ PUBLISHER'S NOTE ☙

The *Hebrew and Christian Bibles* speak about a glorious Messianic Age at the End of Days. Since we humans have a barbarous nature, as God tells Noah after the Flood, it is unlikely that we shall enter this second Garden of Eden together in peace and harmony. The visions of Daniel and the biblical prophecies of the Hebrew prophets, Joel, Ezekiel, and Zechariah, predict an apocalyptic ending to our world with fire and brimstone in the wars of Gog and Magog.

The author's aim in writing this political suspense novel has been to provide an entertaining tale, blending fact with fiction in order to enlighten the reader about possible future events. However, whatever story the author has created in his imagination, the reader has his free will to disbelieve. The interpretations of biblical visions and prophecies cited in Gog and Magog are entirely the author's.

For further correspondence, contact Shechinah Third Temple, Inc:

Tel: 561-735-7958
Fax: 561-738-1535
Email: jerrypollock@bellsouth.net
Web: www.shechinahthirdtemple.org
www.thirdtempleinfo.com

⊶ ACKNOWLEDGMENTS ⊷

My Creator for His blessings. He continually inspires me to be truthful and honest in my heart and guides me in my quest for spiritual wisdom.

My wife, Marcia, my soul mate and queen.

My personal angels, whom I would like to believe are the archangels, Michael and Gabriel.

I thank Tracee, whose primal therapy advice has continued to help me find inner peace, long after I stopped seeing her.

My son-in-law, Magnus Andersson, of Innervision Design, is once again responsible for the beautiful cover design. He gives me much more than his wonderful creativity.

I gratefully acknowledge the tremendous help and support of the Create Space Team. At all steps in the process of helping me create a professional book, they provided superior input and expert suggestions.

1

FALLEN ANGEL

A muscular angel impatiently stomps his right foot on the marble floor of a courtroom that measures sixty feet in length by forty feet in width. The courtroom is lined with six stained-glass windows, three on each side.

A biblical scene of Moses leading the Israelites out of Egypt during the Exodus decorates the domed ceiling. A mahogany lectern stands in the center of the room. A sealed scroll made of papyrus rests on it.

The muscular angel angrily paces back and forth in the empty room, awaiting his fate. He is eight feet tall, and his muddy-gray body is sculpted to perfection with gargantuan bulging muscles. Not a scrap of hair adorns the angel's scalp. Instead ten black horns shaped like sperm whale teeth, each measuring four to six inches, jut out from his oversized head.

The angel's eyes are a crimson red, and vomit drools from the right side of his mouth. He has a ski-shaped nose that emits fire, and his protruding chin bears a deep indent at its center. Two snakes emerge and then retreat from his pointy ears. His forked tongue moves in and out between rusted iron teeth.

As the angel looks up to stare at the ornate fresco on the ceiling dome, his six wings flap in blazingly rapid rhythms, while his entire face contorts in twisted rage. Two wings extend on each side of his body, above and below his arms. And two wings, each three feet in length, flap behind his creaseless back in a motion resembling an engine-propelled moth. When the beating stops, black and yellow tarantulas appear on the angel's moth wings.

In a booming, echoing voice, the muscular angel speaks.

Satan: They dare keep Satan waiting…waiting…waiting.

A second angel flies into the room through the closed entrance door of the courtroom. Satan clenches his fists and expands his chest. This angel, too, is eight feet tall and wears a cloak of white transparent silk. As he lands beside Satan, they bump each other's bodies and glare at one another with eyes that do not blink.

The second angel's body is sapphire blue. His face is like the appearance of lightning, his eyes are like flaming orange torches, and his arms are like the surface of burnished copper. He wears an orange skullcap on his smooth head to match the color of his eyes.

There is a white circular halo surrounding this fierce-looking angel, and he has wings, but only two, one on each side. His body is hairless, a perfect copper tone in color.

Satan: I thought it might be you, Gabriel. You dare be my accuser in this kangaroo court.

Gabriel: The time will come, Satan, when we shall face each other in mortal combat.

Satan: No angel can best me in battle. I do not fear God. He is a useless deity. The day will come when I shall kill you and conquer even Him.

Gabriel: The Ancient One employs scum when it suits His purpose. You have brought shame to Heaven and are a deplorable traitor to your fellow angels. You seek only to destroy the goodness of all that God stands for, and you do your utmost to thwart His plans for the Creation of a new world filled with human, animal, and plant species. There is only darkness within the confines of your abhorrent soul.

Satan: A curse on all of you God-fearing good angels. I prefer evil. The more demonic, the more I thrive.

Gabriel: Be careful what you wish for. I intend to see that you burn in hell.

A third angel flies into the room and stands opposite both Satan and Gabriel. Like Gabriel he has two white wings. His platinum body sparkles with diamonds, and he stands six and a half feet tall.

His face is golden, and his soft, gentle, blue eyes match the hue of the heavenly sky, visible through the narrow windows of the courtroom. A purple crown, studded with rubies and yellow topaz, adorns his head, and a mauve cloak is wrapped around his platinum diamond body.

Satan: Michael, I knew that you would come. Are you to be my executioner?

Gabriel: I'm ready to proceed, Archangel Michael.

Michael: And you, Satan?

Satan: This tribunal has no jurisdiction over me. I am equal to you in stature. You are not my judge and jury.

Michael: I have my instructions from the Ancient One. He alone rules supreme. We are but His servants.

Archangel Michael proceeds to the lectern and unties the gold ribbon wrapped around the scroll. He waves the scroll in front of Satan.

Satan: I suppose God wrote my death sentence on that worthless piece of parchment that you are dangling in front of my eyes.

Michael: Unfortunately God has spared you.

Gabriel: But Satan has conspired against God. I come to this tribunal seeking justice and the death sentence for this unscrupulous evil angel.

Satan: Then you'll have to kill me yourself, Gabriel.

Michael: You are accountable, Satan.

Satan: To whom? Surely not to you or Gabriel.

Gabriel flies headfirst at Satan, and a three-minute kung fu martial arts battle ensues in midair in the courtroom. Michael, stunned, tries to stop the fight, but is unable to separate the eight-foot angels, who are pounding each other without mercy. As they trade blow for blow without resolution, each takes a deep breath and then readies himself to continue. At that precise moment, further combat is interrupted by a loud thunderous noise. The three angels freeze in place.

God's voice fills the chamber. He is not seen.

GOD: You are accountable to me, Satan.

Michael and Gabriel: The Ancient One.

Satan's wings become coated with a honey-like gooey substance. He tries to fly, but his six wings become stuck together.

Satan: Damn You! I shall get even with You, deity.

GOD: But not as an angel. From this point forth, you are a Fallen Angel and are banished forever from Heaven.

Henceforth, Satan, I deem you the Devil. In My mercy and kindness, because I created you and all the angels, I grant you human life until the time of Gog and Magog.

Satan: Do not let me live, deity, for the time will come when I shall wreak havoc on Heaven. Beware to all who dare oppose me.

GOD: Be gone, Devil. I expel you to Planet Earth.

Before Satan can respond, he is twisted into a ball and rolls through the courtroom cedar doors, which open onto ethereal space. Satan falls downward from Heaven to Planet Earth, screaming expletives as he descends.

God, unseen, addresses Gabriel and Michael.

GOD: Satan will serve as the evil inclination in my newly created humans.

Gabriel: But why create a human species if You already know that they are imperfect and will fill their Divine Souls with evil?

GOD: Because just like good and evil are two sides of the same coin, so are imperfection and perfection. Man will live for almost six thousand years as imperfect, and then I shall create perfection at the End of Days in the time of Gog and Magog.

Michael: Is Satan aware that he will be your instrument to bring the evil inclination into the human heart?

GOD: His ego will never allow such thoughts. He believes that he is the creator of all evil. Not I.

Gabriel: Perhaps you are yielding too much freedom to Satan, Ancient One. How will humans be able to handle the evil inclination within their Divine Souls? Only sparks of goodness spring forth from the Divine Soul.

GOD: I shall create a separate animal soul for evil and good within humans. This animal soul shall have free will to make good or bad moral choices. Sin shall accompany bad choices, but I shall allow ample opportunity for repentance during the human lifespan.

Michael: Shall Satan have an animal soul?

GOD: Yes! But there shall be only evil in Satan's animal soul. Without goodness in his animal soul, Satan shall not be able to activate the sparks of goodness in his Divine Soul to connect to the goodness in his animal soul. I know what you are thinking. Why should Satan have a Divine Soul? Because in My mercy and kindness, all humans shall have the opportunity for goodness. I welcome all sinners to repent at any time and return to Me. Humans shall be able to defeat their evil inclination, if they so choose. I shall grant men and women free will and lead them in the direction they wish to go. Come! Let us depart.

The angels, Michael and Gabriel, disappear into space.

2

GARDEN OF EDEN

A man and woman, Adam and Eve, frolic about naked in a magnificent garden, the Garden of Eden. Both the man and the woman are in their early twenties and are beautiful to the eye.

The garden is a lawn of perfect green, with flowers of every color imaginable. Plants fill their shrubbery with sensuous vegetables, and there are multiple species of fruit trees, with multi-colored leaves that match the colors of the flowers.

Babbling brooks flow under small bridges. Birds chirp and rabbits and deer free from Lyme disease scamper about, while frogs croak and turtles peer out from logs in ponds filled with lily pads. Beautiful butterflies symphonically flap their wings and glide from flower to flower.

In the Garden's center stand two large trees. One tree, the Tree of Knowledge of Good and Evil, has luscious fleshy figs the size of golf balls growing on it, and the other tree, the Tree of Life, has black seedlings the size of peppercorns hanging like clusters of grapes from the branches that rise toward Heaven.

All of a sudden, a gentle but assertive voice is heard.

GOD: My children! All your wants and needs are provided for in this Garden of Eden, but you must not eat the figs from the Tree of Knowledge of Good and Evil, or the black seedlings from the Tree of Life.

Adam: But why not, my Lord?

GOD: Because, Adam, your Divine Soul and Eve's Divine Soul know only goodness. Eating the figs from the Tree of Knowledge will contaminate your soul's goodness with evil.

Eve: But isn't knowledge good?

GOD: Yes, but the wrong kind of knowledge can be harmful and lead you astray.

Adam: And what of the seedlings of the Tree of Life?

GOD: The black seedlings are called manna. The manna endows eternal life to those who eat the seedlings. You have not yet earned the right to eternal life. Only the angels, who have been with me since I created the universe fourteen billion years ago, have eternal life.

Eve: How can we earn the right to eternal life and to fly with the angels?

GOD: By following my instructions not to eat from either Tree. You must never eat from the Tree of Life until I have given you My permission.

Adam: Come, Eve. It's time to go. We shall obey You, Lord of Hosts.

Adam grabs Eve's hand as they run merrily through the Garden, laughing in delight.

Just outside the Garden of Eden, Satan touches down on the ground in a clearing in a forest. He unravels himself from his cannonball position and stands up unscathed. He walks upright, stops by a pool of water, kneels to wash himself, and stares at his reflection. He reacts gleefully.

Satan: I'm no longer that dashing evil angel, Satan. Instead, I'm a handsome young man.

8

Just then, Satan hears voices. He walks to a black-coated iron gate and peers through. He sees Adam and Eve in the Garden of Eden. He licks his chops as he takes in the beautiful full-bosomed Eve, but is totally perplexed when he sees Adam. Satan whispers to himself so that Adam and Eve cannot hear him.

Satan: I look exactly like this human creature. I'm even naked like him. God has surely played some kind of evil trick on me. A thousand curses on Him. I must draw closer to hear what they are saying.

Satan quietly opens the gate and moves closer to Adam and Eve, who are walking toward him. Adam and Eve approach the Eastern Gate leading out of the Garden into the forest. The Gate stands eight feet tall, and the entire Garden of Eden is enclosed by an eight-foot stone fence. Eve is about to open the gate, but Adam grabs her arm and pulls her back. Adam cautions Eve.

Adam: We dare not go any further. We are too close to the forest and will soon leave the protection of the Garden of Eden.

Eve: Don't be a sissy, Adam. Let's go through the Eastern Gate and explore the forest.

Adam: No, Eve. We are safe here where God provides for all our needs.

Eve: I'm bored, Adam. If you are not going to leave the Garden, then let's at least eat the figs from the Tree of Knowledge and maybe even the black seedlings from the Tree of Life. God doesn't have to know.

Adam: But He will. God knows everything. Come, let's leave.

Adam departs. Eve reluctantly follows. Satan mumbles to himself.

Satan: So this is God's plan. The creation of spiritual human beings who have no evil. I shall forever be God's foil and destroy His human race by creating evil and desire in his favorite creatures. Hmm! I wonder if God left me with any of my magical angelic powers.

Satan breathes deeply.

He becomes a Serpent, not realizing that God has transformed

him. He appears as a black cobra with a red forked tongue that juts in and out and emits a loud hissing.

Serpent: I still have my evil powers. I shall approach Eve when she is alone.

The Serpent slithers along the ground, tracking Adam and Eve's movements. It notices that Adam and Eve split up, and it sees Eve, alone, picking flowers near the Tree of Knowledge. Eve reaches for a large yellow plum growing on one of the nearby smaller trees and bites into the fruit. The Serpent confronts Eve.

Serpent: Hello, Eve. Are you enjoying the plum?

Eve is unfazed and doesn't ask how the Serpent knows her name.

Eve: Oh, yes! The yellow plums in the Garden of Eden are as sweet as honey.

Serpent: But didn't God say: "You shall not eat of any tree in the Garden of Eden"?

Eve: Of the fruit of any tree of the Garden, we may eat. But of the fig tree, the Tree of Knowledge of Good and Evil, in the center of the Garden, God has said, "You shall neither eat of it, nor touch it, lest you die."

Serpent: You shall not surely die, for God knows that on the day you eat of the Tree, your eyes will be like God, knowing bad and good.

Eve: Perhaps you're right, that the fruit is good for eating. The figs are a delight to my eyes, and I shall indeed sample the fruit.

Eve picks a fig from the Tree of Knowledge, bites into it, and calls for Adam, who is nearby. Adam hears Eve and responds.

Adam: Eve, I'm coming.

Adam arrives at the Tree of Knowledge and glances at the Serpent, then sees Eve with a fig in her hand.

Adam: What have you done? You have disobeyed God.

Eve stares curiously at Adam's naked body. She smacks her lips and looks at him, up and down, from head to toe. She then speaks.

Eve: This talking Serpent must surely be sent by God. For it has convinced me to eat a fig from the Tree of Knowledge. Oh, Adam, the fig is an aphrodisiac. I want you. Come, let us lay together, my darling.

Adam ignores Eve's overtures. He sighs at what Eve has done.

Adam: It is forbidden. Now you will surely die. You have ruined everything.

Eve starts to cry.

Eve: The Serpent has told me that I shall not die. You don't love me.

Adam: Of course I do. Give me a bite of your fig.

Adam eats the remainder of the fig. Suddenly his eyes fix on Eve's breasts and curvaceous body. He clutches her.

Adam: You're beautiful, Eve.

Eve: I feel sexually aroused by you, Adam.

Adam examines himself.

Adam: I feel ashamed of myself. I'm embarrassed.

Eve: I was never aware of my nakedness until I ate the fig. This Serpent has deceived me. Oh, God!

The Serpent makes a laughing, hissing sound. Adam and Eve grab giant green leaves from a nearby tree and cover their nudity. Then they hear the Voice of God. They run away and try to hide. God, invisible, speaks in an angry assertive tone.

GOD: Adam, where are you?

Adam and Eve come out from their hiding places, wearing the giant leaves to cover their shame.

Adam: My Lord, I heard the angry sound of You in the Garden, and I was afraid because I am naked. So I hid.

GOD: Who told you that you are naked? Have you eaten of the Tree that I commanded you not to eat?

Adam looks over at a crying Eve and stutters in fear.

Adam: The wo…woman you ga…gave to me – she ga…gave me the fru…fruit of the Tree and I ate.

God turns to Eve.

GOD: Eve, what's this you have done?

Eve: The Serpent tricked me, and I ate.

The Serpent tries to slither away, but is frozen in place.

GOD: Eve, this Serpent is the Devil, Satan. He is pure evil. If you associate with evil, you also become evil. It is too late to turn back. Evil is now within you and Adam.

God next addresses the Serpent.

GOD: Satan, you have acted cowardly by disguising yourself as a Serpent to entice Eve to eat the fruit of the Tree of Knowledge. Upon your belly shall you crawl from dusk to dawn, and be upright as a man during all the daylight hours.

The Serpent tries to hiss, but his speech is impaired. God continues to scold the Serpent.

GOD: I will put enmity between you, Satan, and the woman, and between her offspring and your offspring. At the End of Days, in the time of Gog and Magog, an offspring of Eve will pound the head of an offspring of yours. And in turn, Satan, your offspring will bite at the heel of Eve's offspring.

Adam and Eve stand with their heads down toward the earth.

GOD: Adam, because you listened to the voice of Eve and ate of the Tree, through suffering shall you eat of the barren ground all the days of your life. For dust you are and to dust shall you return. And you, young woman, your punishment shall be horribly difficult pregnancies that shall cause you great pain. Now be gone. I want you out of my sight. You too, Serpent.

Adam and Eve leave as the Serpent slithers away in the opposite direction toward the Eastern Gate of the Garden of Eden. The angels, Michael and Gabriel, appear. God speaks to them in a somber voice.

GOD: Behold! Man has become like one of us, knowing good and evil. Lest he eat manna from the Tree of Life and live forever, I must banish Adam and Eve from the Garden. Escort them out the

Eastern Gate, and station your Cherub angels there. Have them place the flame of the ever-turning sword at the gate, to guard the way to the Tree of Life.

Two Cherub angels take up their positions on both sides of the Gate. A fiery four-foot sword spins around freely in the air. As Adam and Eve pass through the Eastern Gate into the forest, they look back with tears in their eyes. The Garden is but a blur, and all that is visible is a pink halo surrounding the Cherub angels.

3

THE FOREST

A dam and Eve are lying naked on a leaf-covered bamboo bed in their forest tent. They are making rapturous love under a sheepskin blanket. They finish their climactic intercourse, and Eve rests her head on Adam's shoulder. Adam gently wraps his arm around Eve and holds her close. After several moments of blissful silence, he looks into her quiet eyes and speaks lovingly.

Adam: I must go into the forest and hunt game for our dinner.

Eve: Return quickly, my love, for I thrive in the safety of your arms, with your warmth encircling me.

Adam: I promise to return before dusk.

Eve: We have failed God. We can never fail each other. I love your tenderness. You are so gentle and kind with me.

Adam: Yes, I, too, long for our magnificent days in the Garden. Our life is difficult, but at least we are together.

Eve: I hope that this time I shall become pregnant. I want desperately to give you the child you so deserve.

Adam dresses in his loincloth. He takes his spear and as he exits the tent, he blows Eve a kiss and says good-bye. Outside in the forest, the Serpent is upright and watches Adam leave. It mumbles to itself.

Serpent: This is my chance. It's the light of dawn, and I can transform myself into human form and seduce Eve.

The Serpent breathes deeply and appears as Adam, dressed exactly like him. Meanwhile, Eve has fallen asleep in her bed. Satan enters the tent and startles Eve.

Eve: Back so soon, my love. Did you forget something?

Satan alters his vocal chords, but he cannot quite match Adam's exact voice.

Satan: I've had an insatiable lust for you, ever since I first saw you in the Garden of Eden.

Eve: You don't sound like Adam. Who are you?

Satan: Why, I'm Adam, of course. I swear it by God.

Satan removes his clothes, gets under the blanket, and begins to rape Eve.

Eve: You're hurting me, Adam. You're not your gentle self. Stop!

Satan ignores Eve and pushes more forcefully, harder and harder. He climaxes, then abruptly gets up and leaves the tent without another word. Eve remains in bed trying desperately to comfort herself but cannot. Finally she gives out a shrieking primal scream.

It's late afternoon, and Adam is whistling and briskly walking through the forest, holding two dead rabbits over his shoulder. He approaches home and hears whimpering coming from inside the tent. He pushes aside the opening and is surprised to see Eve still in bed. He sees tears in her eyes, kneels beside her, and then speaks.

Adam: What's wrong? Did something happen in my absence?

Eve: You raped me before you left this morning.

Adam: I did no such thing. I have just returned. I have rabbits for dinner.

Eve gasps. She holds her head between her hands and cries. Adam dries her tears. Eve speaks, but she is barely audible.

Eve: Oh, my God! It was Satan. He came into the tent after you left. He was your identical twin. He was dressed exactly like you, but he didn't sound like you.

Adam: He impregnated you with his sperm.

Eve: What shall we do?

A voice is heard within the tent, but no one is seen.

Adam: It's God. He's here.

GOD: You will bear twin sons in a difficult labor. One from Satan and the other from Adam. You will call the firstborn son Cain. He will be a farmer and will be evil from his youth, like his Devilish father. The other shall be a shepherd and will be all good, because he is the seed of Adam. You will call the good son Abel.

Adam: Will Satan come back?

GOD: No! Satan shall never bother you again. Within six thousand years, a demonic human being, an offspring from Satan through your son Cain, will arise. This modern-day Cain will plot with Satan and Cain's father to lead the world to Armageddon.

Eve: And what of my son, Abel?

GOD: Your son, Cain, will murder your son, Abel.

Eve: Oh, no! O my Lord, you shall have inflicted the harshest punishment upon me, for I shall be left childless.

GOD: What's done cannot be undone. Cain's sin will be atoned for when the Third Temple is built at the End of Days. At that time you, Adam, and your dead son, Abel, will be resurrected to live again in the Messianic Age. I shall banish Cain from the forest, and you and Adam shall immediately have a third son, Seth. From Seth all humankind will descend. In the distant future, a good son will arise from Seth's lineage. His name will be Abel, like the biblical Abel, and he will also live in modern times, along with the modern-day Cain. Abel will fight this twentieth-century Cain in the End Times to decide the fate of humanity in the final battle between good and evil.

4

ANCIENT BABYLON

Daniel, clean-shaven and dressed in a light-brown animal skin, playfully skips stones in the river. He wears a gold Jewish Star around his neck and a black onyx ring on his right index finger. Exiled with the brightest of Jerusalem's youths by king Nebuchadnezzar of Babylon, Daniel, at twenty, has become a rising star, a senior advisor in a foreign government. Yet he refuses to compromise his belief in God, spending quiet time reflecting at the river.

One day Daniel looks up at the sky, and he sees an eight-foot-tall angel flying toward him. The angel's face has the appearance of white lightning; his eyes are like flaming torches. His body is sapphire blue, except for his arms, which are like the surface of burnished copper. Two white wings extend from each side of the angel's body. He wears an orange skullcap, and a white halo surrounds him.

He lands on the riverbank near Daniel, who collapses to the ground and places himself in a prostrate position, trembling in fear. The angel walks to Daniel's side and waves his right hand over him. Daniel slowly rises to his knees onto the palms of his hands, and then stands erect, facing the angel. Daniel avoids looking at the angel.

Suddenly the angel takes human form, transformed into a handsome middle-aged man with blond hair, and sporting a blonde goatee. This human angel wears a white biblical robe with a blue sash and has the pinkest of skin. His feet stand in plain sandals that you might see on the simplest of men. The white halo surrounding the man is the lone vestige from the angel's transformation to human form.

Daniel opens his eyes and sees the majestic-looking man. Daniel feels calm over his entire being and stops shaking. The angel addresses Daniel in a mighty voice.

Gabriel: I am Gabriel, the Angel of Fire and War, sent to you, Daniel, by your God and mine. Fear not, as I have come on a holy mission from the Ancient One.

Daniel trembles on hearing Gabriel's voice. He again falls to his knees and prostrates himself.

Daniel: I am not worthy, dearest angel.

Gabriel: Arise, Daniel. You are a servant of the Lord.

Daniel, his head bowed down, stands. Gabriel speaks in a tranquil voice.

Gabriel: God has chosen you to have visions of the future in your dreams.

Daniel: Oh, great angel! I have had many visions. The worst is the dream of a beast of horrific evil.

Gabriel: Describe him.

Daniel: He had six fiery eyes, six wings, and six toes. There were ten black horns jutting out of his huge head, and two snakes emerged and retreated from his pointy ears. His forked black tongue moved in and out between rusted iron teeth. There was vomit spewing out of his mouth, and fire was smoking from his nostrils. He was your size, and he had an enormous muscular body. In my dream, I heard him speak. He said that his descendants would rule the world.

Gabriel: You have accurately described the Devil, the Fallen Angel, Satan.

Daniel: In my dreams, he calls himself Samael.

Gabriel: Yes, Satan goes by many names. Samael is the Angel of Death. When Satan was an angel in Heaven, God was preparing him to be His ultimate death poison for the humans He was about to create. Satan currently serves this purpose on Earth. Daniel, your dreams foretell different prophecies still to come in the modern world. The Ancient One has instructed me to tell you to seal the book. No man may know the meaning of your dreams until the time is right for revelation. Go now and take your rest.

Daniel: But there is more to the dream of the horns of the beast.

Gabriel: In days yet to come, Daniel, the rest of your dream shall be revealed. Speak of it no more, as danger lurks even here on this riverbank. You shall awake at the End of Days to face your Maker. All humanity shall be judged by God in the End Times to determine who shall sow tears and who shall reap the rewards of the Messianic Age. The second Garden of Eden is coming, when eternal life is promised for those who are written in the Creator's book. Those who are not shall be resurrected to face intolerable pain that they shall be forced to endure forever.

Gabriel flies off into ethereal space. Daniel picks up a stone and throws it in the river. He smiles, as he looks heavenward and voices praise to God.

Daniel: Thank you, my Creator, for sending me Your glorious angel. I shall seal the book, as You command.

5

2,500 YEARS LATER

1975

The Cathedral of St. Matthew in Washington, D.C., over-flows with smiling faces. It's Christmas Mass, and the church is decorated with the festive green and red of the holiday season.

Unnoticed sitting in a pew on the aisle close to the front of the church is a strikingly handsome man of about thirty years of age. He is not Catholic, not even just a non-believer. This man is unshakably anti-God, and he is there solely to observe.

What's strange about this man is that he seems identical to Satan. Yes, that same Satan who raped Eve in the forest outside the Garden of Eden almost six thousand years ago. But this man can't be Satan, unless he has preserved his age the same all these years.

The man is six feet tall and has jet-black hair and unusual eyes. Unusual because the eyes are a brilliant pitch black, and because you feel undressed when he looks at you.

His intoxicating toothy smile, however, disarms your fear when your eyes make contact with his. For some reason his ears don't seem to fit his facial features; they stick out at an angle from his head. Even in the black suit he is wearing, one can tell that this man is sculpted and toned...and could inflict mortal harm if he punched you with the full force of his muscular body.

White snowflakes are falling outside the church, where a table has been set up with Santa Claus collecting donations. Inside Christmas Mass is about to begin, as the choir takes its place on stage. At the podium the bishop also takes up his position, signaling quiet to the crowd. A sister, dressed in her nun's habit, faces the choir and raises her hand. Organ music fills the church and awakens the reverie of the congregation.

The man in the black suit seems bored, but he perks up when he beams in on two young pretty girls in the choir—Daniela Corsini, age fourteen, and Elizabeth Corsini, age twelve. The choir begins to sing.

Choir:

O come all ye faithful. Joyful and triumphant.
O come ye, O come ye to Bethlehem.
Come and behold him born the king of angels.
O come let us adore him. O come let us adore him.
O come let us adore him. Christ the Lord.

The congregants smile, and the man in the black suit notices a man and a woman, the girls' parents, in the front row. The sister leading the choir turns and moves center stage. She thanks the worshippers and then introduces Elizabeth Corsini.

Sister: Ladies and gentlemen, Elizabeth Corsini will now sing "Ave Maria." Elizabeth leaves the choir and stands by herself facing the churchgoers. She begins singing in a beautiful soprano voice that resonates throughout the church.

Elizabeth:

Ave Maria gratia plena. Maria gratia plena,
Maria gratia plena. Ave ave Dominus.

Dominus et-cum. Benedicta tu in mulierbus.

Et benedictus. Et benedictus

Fructus ventris. Ventris tui Iesus. Ave Maria.

Elizabeth finishes singing, bows in a modest curtsy, and returns to the choir. She smiles at her sister. Daniela smiles back, but hides her clenched fists.

Both girls look out into the pews and see their parents, who are restraining themselves from clapping. The bishop continues the service and offers a sermon on good and evil. Afterward the Corsini sisters join their parents outside the church.

Everyone is congratulating Elizabeth on her singing. The man in the black suit offers his hand to Elizabeth. They shake and Elizabeth feels a cold chill running down her body. She withdraws her hand, and immediately warmth returns, as the man introduces himself.

Leamas: My name is Leamas. Dear Elizabeth, you sang beautifully. You brought tears of joy to my Divine Soul.

Elizabeth is trembling inside. She tries to hide her fear from Leamas.

Elizabeth: Thank you.

Leamas smiles and walks away.

Elizabeth: That man scares me.

Corsini Dad: He seems harmless and was just praising you for your singing. Kids, you both sang beautifully.

Corsini Mom: Elizabeth, your "Ave Maria" was wonderful. Daniela, you also sang splendidly.

Daniela: Thank you, Mother.

Daniela turns to Elizabeth.

Daniela: You were cool, sis.

Elizabeth moves toward her sister to give her a hug. Daniela raises her right hand and fakes a sneeze.

Daniela: Achoo! Achoo! Sorry. Can we go for ice cream?

6

1980

The senior class celebrates graduation in their red caps and gowns. Elizabeth stands at the podium. Daniella, their four-year-old brother, and her parents sit in the audience. A large banner across the back of the dais reads Elmont High.

Elizabeth: I'm truly honored to be your valedictorian. I'll try my best to prove my worthiness in the years ahead. Congratulations, graduates.

Graduates scream. The audience claps and whistles.

Elizabeth: Congratulations, parents. Congratulations, grandparents. We couldn't have done it without you.

Graduates stand and clap. Elizabeth motions them to be seated.

Elizabeth: And thank you, teachers, principals, and all of Elmont High's supporting staff.

More clapping.

Elizabeth: I want to make this short and sweet, so I'll offer a quote from the Book of Job. "Days speak and a multitude of years teach wisdom." I hope that we all gain wisdom in the years ahead, and I hope we rock and set the world ablaze. Let's rock, graduates.

Graduates shriek. Audience joins in.

Elizabeth: Ladies and gentlemen! I give you the class of 1980.

Graduates toss their caps into the air. Elizabeth leaves the stage and finds her parents. She gives her little brother a hug, while her sister, Daniela, turns away and frowns. Leamas is looking on from a distance and notices the painful gesture. He smiles to himself. Daniela turns back and gives Elizabeth a huge grin.

Daniela: Congratulations, sis.

Corsini Mom: My two beautiful girls.

Corsini Dad: Beautiful and smart.

Corsini Mom: Daniela is at Harvard, and now, Elizabeth, you'll be going to Barnard.

Corsini Dad: And I'll be going to the poorhouse.

Daniela walks over to Elizabeth and gives her a bear hug, lifting her off the ground and squeezing tightly. Elizabeth winces, but says nothing. She stares at Daniela. Daniela smiles. So does Leamas.

7

1985

The incubator facility in the obstetric ward at Mount Sinai Hospital in Manhattan is crowded with babies. One baby in particular is getting a lot of attention, although it's lunchtime and no one seems to be around. His name tag reads Abel Slobodkin, and he is wide awake, while all of his fellow babies are fast asleep. Abel is looking into space, where three female Cherub angels are circling his crib and entertaining him. The angels repeat in unison.

> *Female Angels:*
>> Could this be the one?
>> Could this be the one?
>> Could this be the one?

Abel gurgles, and the three cherub angels smile back. They then disappear, and Leamas cautiously enters the room. He is dressed in a surgical gown and walks directly to Abel's crib. He peers down, and Abel smiles up at him.

Leamas laughs aloud and talks to the baby.

> *Leamas:* So you're God's hope to save the world.

Leamas reaches down into the tiny incubator crib and pinches baby Abel hard on the cheeks. Abel starts to wail as Leamas leaves the area belly laughing. A bruise quickly forms on Abel's face.

A male nurse hears the cry and comes to the rescue. Closer inspection reveals that the man dressed in the traditional white nurse's uniform is the angel Gabriel in human form. The human Gabriel has blonde hair, a blond goatee, and a distinguishing orange skullcap.

Gabriel picks up the baby and starts singing to Abel to calm him down. Just then Isaac and Rebecca Slobodkin pass by the window and wave to Gabriel and Abel. Gabriel quickly touches Abel's cheeks, and the sore disappears. He brings Abel over to his parents, and they wave to him, as Abel smiles at them.

Gabriel: Look, Abel. It's your parents.

Gabriel gently takes Abel's hand and waves. Isaac and Rebecca wave back. Isaac turns to Rebecca.

Isaac: God's gift to us, Rebecca.

Rebecca: I'm so happy, Isaac. I feel blessed.

Isaac speaks in Hebrew and then translates for Gabriel, whom he is unaware speaks fluent Hebrew.

Isaac: Baruch Hashem! Praise God!

8

1988

The Barnes & Noble bookstore is crowded with buyers and browsers. Senator Malcolm Yale Macorley is signing his new book, *The Way Forward.* The senator looks up at a well-dressed, attractive woman. The senator at thirty has a stunning appearance. As he gazes at the woman in front of him, he thinks to himself: I have a huge ego. My smile is unbeatable, my personality gregarious, and I can charm the pants off you, beautiful lady, because that's what I do with good-looking women.

Senator Macorley: Your name, beautiful lady.

Elizabeth pauses and looks directly in the senator's sexually active eyes and makes a flippant remark.

Elizabeth: Twenty-nine. Make it out to an admirer, Senator.

Senator Macorley: And who is this admirer I'm talking to?

Elizabeth: Elizabeth Corsini.

Elizabeth then adds,

Elizabeth: Shrink. I hope that you have no bias toward psychiatry, Senator. Some people really get turned off. They look at us as if we're quacks.

Senator Macorley: Never trusted shrinks, but I'll make an exception in your case. Is next Friday okay for dinner? I'd love to tell you more about my book.

Elizabeth pulls out a business card and hands it to the senator.

Elizabeth: Your appointment is for five p.m.

Senator Macorley: What makes you think I need shrink therapy?

Elizabeth: All you charismatic creatures are hiding something.

Senator Macorley: OK, I'll do it on one condition.

Elizabeth beckons the senator to stretch across the desk. She whispers in his ear. The man with the black eyes, a few feet back in the line, is the only one to hear Elizabeth's secret words.

Elizabeth: I agree. Dinner and sex afterward.

Senator Macorley laughs uncontrollably. Elizabeth also laughs.

Elizabeth: You know, Senator, if I had the power to foresee the future, I'd predict that you'll be president.

Senator Macorley: You read my horoscope.

The senator signs Elizabeth's book and hands it to her. He covers her hand with his and holds on noticeably too long, as people waiting in line stare at the duo. Elizabeth blushes and pulls her hand away.

Elizabeth: Good luck with the book, Senator.

Elizabeth walks away without turning back. The senator's eyes follow her wiggle as she disappears from view. He signs several more books until the man with the jet-black hair and brilliant black eyes is standing in front of him. Leamas also asks the senator to stretch across the desk. The senator obliges, as if he is following a command and not a request. Leamas whispers in his ear. The senator's face pales, trying to digest what he just heard. Leamas repeats his words.

Leamas: I can't offer you sex like Dr. Corsini, but I can make you president.

Senator Macorley is rarely taken off guard. He quickly recovers and utters a feeble response.

Senator Macorley: Who are you?

Leamas: My name is Leamas. Some heavenly beings think I'm the Devil, but I'm just a good Samaritan. I can do anything and everything for you, like make you president. However like all good things, there is no free lunch.

Senator Macorley: And your price?

Leamas: All in good time, when I feel I can trust you. Here's my business card with cell phone number.

Leamas abruptly departs without a signed book. The senator glances at the card. The card is black with yellow lettering. It reads—

Leamas, alias Satan, alias the Devil
Anacostia National Park
Cell Phone: 666-666-6666

Senator Macorley: It's impossible. That's not a proper number.

The senator pulls out his own cell phone and dials the 666 number on Leamas's business card. An unexpected voice comes on at the other end.

Leamas: Mr. President. How nice to hear from you so soon. I'll see you at your office at three, before your sexual interlude with Dr. Corsini.

The phone goes dead. The senator makes another call to his oldest friend, Jason Smithies.

Smithies: Hello, Malcolm.

Senator Macorley: I want you to check someone out. His name is Leamas, and his phone number is 666-666-6666.

Smithies: Leamas must be the epitome of evil. The numbers 666 are the Mark of the Beast.

Senator Macorley: I'm not surprised. Leamas claims he's the Devil. He just offered me the presidency.

Smithies: And in return?

Senator Macorley: My soul.

9

1994

Elementary schoolteacher Leamas walks around the classroom handing out the fourth-grade students' geography test papers. He stops at Abel Slobodkin's desk, momentarily stares, then continues passing out the student exam scores. Leamas returns to his desk at the front of the room and sits, placing two unclaimed test papers in front of him. Leamas looks up at the class and speaks.

Leamas: There are two papers without the student's name. Please come up and claim your exam results.

Abel sits, too terrified to move. He watches to see if anyone goes up to Mr. Leamas's desk. Nobody does. After a couple of minutes of silence, Leamas repeats his command.

Leamas: For the second time, please come up and claim your geography scores.

Again nobody walks up to Leamas's desk, as Abel is frozen in place. Leamas is about to speak when one of the students yells out that Ronald is absent.

Leamas: Thank you, Earl. Okay, one of these papers belongs to Ronald. The other I believe belongs to you, Abel.

Abel sheepishly walks up to Mr. Leamas's desk. He observes that one exam paper shows a blank map of the United States with a red zero marked on it, while the other map is partially filled out with state capital names and has received a red forty result.

Abel is about to pick up the map with the zero, his paper, when Leamas takes Abel's chin and forces Abel to make eye contact with him. Abel looks into Leamas's black piercing eyes. Leamas nods and Abel turns away, picking up Ronald's test paper with the red 40 score.

Leamas grabs Abel's wrist, releases it, and beckons Abel to take his seat. Abel returns to his seat with Ronald's paper and rubs his sore wrist. Leamas looks across the room at him and smiles. Tears stream down Abel's cheeks.

10

2014

Leamas, sporting a black goatee and black mustache, addresses ten applicants sitting at desks with exam booklets in a room inside the FBI Building.

Abel Slobodkin stares at the examiner and immediately recognizes his fourth-grade teacher from twenty years ago. He shakes his head, wondering to himself how Leamas has not aged. He still looks thirty years old. Little does Abel know that Leamas was the one who pinched him when he was a baby, and whose age has not changed since then and since the biblical time of the Garden of Eden with Adam and Eve.

Abel is also clueless to Leamas's true identity: the Devil, alias Satan.

Abel says nothing and tries to keep his composure as Leamas glares into his eyes. Leamas smiles and makes an announcement to the candidates.

Leamas: You are the ten finalists for admission into the FBI. You have been chosen from a pool of hundreds, so you should be proud of yourselves. Unfortunately only one of you will be selected, based upon the highest score on this examination. You will have thirty minutes to complete your answers. The question is in two parts. Good luck.

The students nod, but Leamas only makes eye contact with Abel. Abel turns ghost white.

Leamas: Here's your question. If you were plotting the destruction of the United States, what would your plan be? And as an FBI agent, how would you prevent your suggested plot?

The students all begin writing, except for Abel, who is in a frozen panic state. He doesn't seem to be prepared for the question. Leamas looks over at him.

Leamas: Is anything wrong, Mr. Slobodkin?

Abel: I'm feeling ill, sir. I have a stomach virus, and I need to visit the bathroom. Badly!

Leamas: Then go. But remember, you're on your honor. The bathroom is just outside this room.

Leamas smirks.

Abel exits the FBI examination room and enters the men's room. He sits in a stall, takes off his right shoe, and pulls out a piece of paper from the removable sole insert. He studies the paper, tears it up into pieces, vomits, and then flushes the pieces down the toilet. Abel breathes deeply and returns to the testing room.

Abel enters the examination room, avoiding eye contact with Leamas. He sits at his desk and begins writing. Leamas makes a sarcastic comment.

Leamas: Did you find what you were looking for, Abel?

Abel: I feel better. Thanks.

Time passes, and candidates start handing in their papers. Abel is the last one in the room. Thirty minutes to the second, he gets up and walks over to Leamas, handing him his answers. He turns around and starts walking toward the door, but before he can exit, Leamas calls to him. Abel freezes, his heart racing, and then he turns around, dreading that he has been found out and that he has failed in his mission.

Leamas: Would you have a seat up front, Slobodkin? I want to look over your answers.

Abel has no choice but to obey Leamas. Leamas peruses Abel's answers and comments.

Leamas: Your answers are rather clever. Where did you learn about Gog and Magog and the destruction of the world?

Abel feels temporarily relieved.

Abel: I was brought up Orthodox and attended Jewish religious school at a yeshiva in Brooklyn.

Leamas: Do your parents, Isaac and Rebecca, still live on Eastern Parkway near the Chabad Center?

Abel: Yes! How did you know that?

Leamas: I make it a point to know everything about everyone. That's what the FBI is all about. You have to be ruthless to be an FBI agent, and you have to kill without reason. Can you do that, Abel?

Abel: Yes, I can.

Leamas: Good, because I'm recommending you for admission into the agency.

Abel: Thank you, sir.

Leamas: Don't call me sir. You know who I am. And now would you care to admit you have sinned, like you did twenty years ago on your fourth grade geography test?

Abel: Who are you, Leamas?

Leamas: Why, I'm the Devil, of course. Some people call me Satan, and I have other names like Beelzebub.

Multiple Leamas clones suddenly appear throughout the room. All are laughing, and Abel is frantically trying to figure out where the real Devil is.

Before he can turn in the right direction, Leamas lands a sucker punch on Abel's chin. He then picks Abel up with one hand by the scruff of his neck and tosses him hard against the wall. Abel winces in pain, favoring his left shoulder. Leamas laughs in multiple voices.

Leamas: Oh, this was so much fun. Let's do it again. And by the way, you can report back to your Jewish friends. But don't worry; your secret is safe with me—for the time being, anyway. Tomorrow you will have to pass a physical and be officially sworn in as an FBI agent. So get that shoulder repaired. Failure to report will cost you admission. Sorry to put a crimp in your plans. Maybe your God can help you? You'll be working directly with Daniela Corsini, the deputy FBI director.

The multiple Leamas clones disappear. The lone remaining Leamas picks up the applicants' papers, walks past Abel, and exits the room laughing.

Abel sits quietly against the wall, nursing his separated right shoulder. The pain is too much for him and he lets out a cry of helplessness. He then picks himself off the floor and grimaces, gritting his teeth. In a determined voice, he utters, Next time, I swear I'll be ready.

An invisible gentle voice appears in the room. Abel is terrified. He glances around, but sees no one.

Gentle Voice: I am your Guardian Angel.

Abel feels warmth in his separated left shoulder, and in an instant, his shoulder is repaired. The gentle voice is gone.

11

2016

President Malcolm Yale Macorley addresses the nation from the Oval Office. His speech is being broadcast live on network and cable TV. The president appears calm and deliberate and exudes his boyish charm to the American people.

President Macorley: It's my personal belief that a woman has the right to choose. I believe in the Almighty God, and if He wanted all babies to be born, there would not be any miscarriages. To play Devil's advocate in favor of the right-to-life argument, I have reservations on aborting a fetus, except in cases of rape, incest, and danger to the mother's life. Why? Because humanity may lose a potentially great leader had he or she been allowed to live.

The president continues his speech. Jason Smithies, the president's chief of staff, and Roger Arnold, the deputy chief of staff, sit on Queen Anne chairs in Smithies' office. Both men are a decade older than the president.

In their sixties, with silver-gray hair, they are distinguished looking, as career politicians are expected to be. Smithies turns away from the TV screen and makes eye contact with Arnold.

Smithies: I just love to see the president being decisive on the issues.

Arnold is thinking that he wants to impress Smithies, but Smithies reaction is just the opposite.

Arnold: Yes! The president sure knows how to wow the nation. He has even more charisma than former Presidents Obama and Clinton.

Smithies frowns and responds to Arnold's comment.

Smithies: I meant it sarcastically. We can't have the president go on national TV and bullshit the public with his wishy-washy opinions. You always were an ass kisser, Roger. For once in your life, tell me what you really think.

Arnold: What I think?

Smithies is boiling. He jumps up and stands directly over Arnold.

Smithies: Yes, goddamn it! That's what you're being paid for.

Smithies closes his fist and taps it on Arnold's head.

Smithies: Hello! Anyone home?

Arnold is bewildered. He whispers a feeble response.

Arnold: I think…uh…uh…I think the president hit another home run.

Smithies' face and neck turn beet red.

Smithies: You're as passionate as a toad. Even a blind man would be fucking more objective than you, Roger. The president just fucking struck out. He came off like God's gift to humanity, as he always does. That's what we want, but he can't keep fucking showing it to the public. You need to start rolling your marbles, Roger, or quit the game and go home.

Smithies sits down, grumbling and shaking his head. He turns to the television. Arnold sheepishly follows suit and squirms in his chair, trying to become invisible. President Macorley picks up his rhetoric.

President Macorley: I will not be satisfied until every American who wants to work has a job. I will not stop until every American has affordable health insurance. I will weed out the fat cat corporate corruption and the greed in every nook and cranny of our society. My foreign policy will move the world toward peace. Before God I pledge that I will not bow down to the dogs of war.

The speech ends. Jason Smithies enters the Oval Office. He sighs and gives the president a high five. The president lights up a cigar.

Smithies: You kicked ass tonight, Mr. President.

President Macorley: Yeah! I'm the only one who can save the country from itself.

Smithies: The Republicans know sweet "f-a."

President Macorley: Sweet "f-a?" Cut the Canadian lingo, Jason.

Smithies: Sweet fuck all, Mr. President.

The president smiles and looks down at his cigar.

President Macorley: The perks of the job. We have no relations with Cuba. Yet I can get Cuban cigars with the snap of my fingers.

Smithies: If Kennedy hadn't botched the Bay of Pigs a half century ago, we'd own the damn island and have the Hispanic vote in our pocket.

President Macorley: We still will. I'm moving along with my plan to offer amnesty to illegal immigrants.

Smithies: That's been tried before. No president has succeeded.

President Macorley: If history has taught us anything, it's that great leaders are not born great. They rise to greatness. Besides, I have an ace up my sleeve.

Smithies: An ace?

President Macorley: Yes, the ace of spades—the Devil card in the deck. Jason, you have to think beyond your human brain. I keep telling you that.

Smithies: With all due respect, Mr. President, I keep repeating to you that my human brain is all I have.

President Macorley: That's why I'm the president and you're not. To change the subject, have you made any headway on the Elizabeth Corsini issue?

Smithies: We've initiated the foolproof plan that you suggested.

The president puts out his cigar in the ashtray.

President Macorley: Good! Keep me posted. The First Lady is waiting. We'll continue this conversation later. Oh, one more thing, Jason. My son, Cain, just graduated Yale Law School.

Smithies: Is that how you got your middle name, Yale?

President Macorley: Yes. Now Cain has followed in my footsteps, as I knew he would when he was born twenty-six years ago. I want you to be his special mentor. Teach him everything you know and groom him for your position, as you're retiring at the end of my first presidential term. Don't tell him that he'll be chief of staff when I'm reelected.

Smithies: It will be my pleasure, Mr. President.

Smithies departs. Macorley picks up his secure red line and dials the 666 number. There is a pickup on the other end.

President Macorley: Hello, Leamas.

It's evening, and the president doesn't realize that God has cursed the Devil so that he is a human by daylight and a serpent at night. The Serpent talks into its rigged phone set up with the same voice as its human counterpart, Leamas.

Serpent: Didn't I tell you never to call me after dusk?

President Macorley: I thought you'd be happy with the news, Leamas. I've taken the first steps in the plan you suggested for accomplishing our future goal of Gog and Magog. My son, Cain Arlis Macorley, will be groomed to be chief of staff when you get me reelected in 2020.

Serpent: And Elizabeth Corsini? Your old flame.

President Macorley: She'll be eliminated, if necessary. However we have her FBI agent sister, Daniela, in a box, so I don't think Liz will be a problem. Daniela is already working with the CIA, as Jason has leaned on her, and hard.

Serpent: Don't fuck it up, Macorley. Or I won't be calling you Mr. President for much longer.

The President hears the line go dead. He breathes a deep sigh of relief.

12

CORSINI SISTERS

E lizabeth and Daniela Corsini are sitting at the bar of the Four Seasons Hotel drinking scotch. They are on their third round of Macallan 12.

Daniela: The damn government. I'll never be able to afford Macallan 18.

Elizabeth smirks.

Elizabeth: Quit your griping, Dannie. I'm paying, and Macallan 12 is pretty damn good.

Daniela: Well, of course, Lizzie. You're the one earning the big bucks as a hotshot psychiatrist.

Elizabeth: You don't have a daughter that you're putting through medical school.

Daniela: How is Sophia?

Elizabeth: As beautiful as we used to be. We're just a couple of has-beens.

Daniela: Speak for yourself. Marshall may one day make an honest woman out of me.

Elizabeth: I would love to be your maid of honor. It's better than winding up an old maid.

Daniela: When are you going to tell Sophia who her father is? For God's sake! You won't even tell me. I keep trying to get you plastered, but three scotches are your limit.

Elizabeth: I can't share with you because you have a big mouth, and the whole town would be talking about Sophia's father instead of the usual political crap. As for Sophia I offered to tell her, but she doesn't want to know.

Daniela: Well, he must have been special because ever since you had Sophia, you've given up on men. You're not that bad looking. Of course, you're not as pretty as me. You know, I haven't forgiven you for our childhood.

Elizabeth: It's not my fault that I'm smarter than you. You got the looks, and I got the brains.

Daniela: Bullshit, Lizzie. You fucking got the looks and the smarts, although I'm pretty good in both of these departments. Your problem is that you're too damned reserved. Men don't come near you because you walk with a pickle up your ass. By the way what happened to your Romeo?

Elizabeth: It was almost thirty years ago…1988. We had a sizzling romance for a year, and then he abruptly broke it off. He married a high-society Delaware chick and immediately had a baby who'd be the same age as Sophia.

Daniela: You need to get out more, Lizzie.

Elizabeth: I have my work.

Daniela: I hose loonies at the hospital. That's work?

Elizabeth: It's true. We're seeing a deluge of psychotic patients. Speaking of which I have to get back. The scotch will give me the courage to face the second half of my day. I'll see you at Mom and Dad's on the weekend.

The sisters click glasses and depart.

13

ESTHER

Esther Hirsch, forties, a curvaceous blonde, wanders around her home in a pink nightgown and pink slippers. She has a hammer in her right hand. She walks into the den, where a stuffed stag's head hangs above the fireplace. On top of the mantle are dolls from different countries.

Esther momentarily remains in the den, observing the eye of the deer. She then leaves the den and enters the living room. She sits down on her knees on the Chinese carpet. Behind her on the wall is an original oil painting of a rabbi painted by an artist named Bromberg.

A framed photograph of Esther and a man with a brown mustache sits on the coffee table, which also has a sculpture of two lovers kissing. Esther removes her watch and places it on the carpet. She then raises the hammer and smashes the watch over and over again. A deep voice is heard, but there is no one else in the room. Esther frantically looks around, but sees no one. She pulls at her blouse and runs her hands roughly through her blonde hair.

Esther:

(deep voice)
Go away. Leave her alone.
Someone fucking help Esther.
She's going crazy.

Esther doesn't seem to realize that the voice is actually coming out of her own mouth.

Esther:

(deep voice)
Fuck you, Esther! Fuck you!
Fuck you!

Esther moves to the corner of the living room, falls to the floor, shivers, and puts her clasped hands on top of her head. She becomes the normal Esther again and speaks.

Esther:

(normal voice)
You're not real.

She gets up, goes to the piano, plays a few bars, and then stares into space with a wild look in her eyes.

Esther:

(deep voice)
Who then are you
fucking talking to?

The real Esther emerges.

Esther:

(normal voice)
If you're real, tell me
a name I've never
heard before.

Esther flips back into non-reality. She has that glazed look in her eyes.

Esther:

(deep booming voice)
"Samuel."

Esther:

>(normal voice)
>I don't know any Samuel.

Esther:

>(deep mocking voice)
>Sure you do.

Esther:

>(normal voice)
>Samuel was my grandfather's
>name, but we called him
>Sam, Zady Sam. He was
>never called Samuel.

Suddenly the psychotic Esther jumps up and laughs. She takes her right index finger and rubs it back and forth over her left index finger. She speaks rapidly.

Esther:

>(deep taunting voice)
>Esther needs help! Esther
>needs help! Shame, shame
>on Esther.

14

PSYCHOSIS

E sther, shaking, clasps her hands while sitting on a hard chair in an examination room of the emergency room of Washington Central Hospital. Next to her is Dov Hirsch, Esther's husband, and the man with the brown mustache in the photograph at the Hirsch home.

Dr. Corsini enters wearing a white coat. She carries a clipboard and greets Dov and Esther. Dr. Corsini is wearing a gold necklace supporting a large gold cross. The doctor introduces herself.

Elizabeth: I'm Dr. Corsini.

Dr. Corsini extends her arm to Dov. Dov shakes her hand.

Elizabeth: What's going on?

Dov: My wife, Esther, is hearing voices.

Esther: Doctor, just give me a shot, and I'll be on my way.

Elizabeth: Anything else beside the voices? Are you seeing strange things or people, Esther?

Esther looks at Dr. Corsini. She stands, grabs at Dr. Corsini's lab coat, and speaks rapidly, her eyes darting about the room.

Esther: Yes, I see someone trying to kill me. I saw them in the waiting room. They were all looking at me.

Esther suddenly gets in Dr. Corsini's face and makes direct eye contact.

Esther:

(deep voice)
Why are you fucking
staring at me, Doctor?

Dr. Corsini, surprised, turns to Dov.

Elizabeth: Mr. Hirsch, I need to admit your wife to our psychiatric ward.

Dr. Corsini reaches for her clipboard. She turns to Esther, who has quietly sat down and looks perfectly normal.

Elizabeth: You need to be hospitalized, Esther. Sign this paper that you agree to be admitted voluntarily.

Dr. Corsini tries to hand the clipboard to Esther. Esther suddenly jumps up and knocks the clipboard out of Dr. Corsini's hand.

Esther:

(deep voice)
Get that fucking paper
away from me. I'm not
going into your fucking
psycho ward.

Esther turns to Dov.

Esther:

And fuck you, too, Dov.

In the blink of an eye, Esther pushes Dr. Corsini aside and makes a beeline out of the examination room. She reaches the emergency room waiting area, with Dr. Corsini and Dov in pursuit. Dr. Corsini yells to the security guards.

Elizabeth: Stop her.

The guards catch her just before she can exit to the outside and escape into the parking lot.

Security Guards: We got her, Doc.

Patients waiting to be seen, look up in shock. The security guards drag a screaming and kicking Esther back to the examination room.

The guards hold her down on the gurney, and Dr. Corsini pulls up Esther's skirt and gives her a shot in the buttocks. Esther immediately conks out. Dr. Corsini turns to Dov Hirsch.

Elizabeth: Mr. Hirsch, we have no choice but to admit your wife involuntarily. Come by tomorrow morning and we'll talk further.

Esther is strapped down and rolled into the elevator on her way to the psychiatry ward. Dr. Corsini follows while Dov departs the hospital. A very tiny smirk forms on Dov's mouth.

15

DOV

A burly man greets Dov as he enters Washington Central Hospital. They momentarily look and smile at each other, nod, and go their separate ways.

Dov finds his way to the psychiatry ward and enters the secretary's waiting room. Lynn, twenties, greets Dov and waves him on into Dr. Corsini's private office.

Elizabeth: Mr. Hirsch, I'm afraid Esther may have bipolar disorder.

Dov clears his throat, and then speaks in a gravelly voice.

Dov: My apologies, Doctor. I'm really upset about my wife.

Elizabeth: Understandably. Are you familiar with manic depression?

Dov: Esther is forty years old. There's no history of bipolar disorder in her family.

Elizabeth: Bipolar disorder is hereditary only half the time, according to identical twin studies. Furthermore, although most patients acquire the illness in their teens and twenties, and as young as eight years old, a smaller group of patients can acquire the disease at age forty and even older. Let me show you a graph.

Dr. Corsini attempts to hand the graph to Dov, but Dov pushes the paper away. The graph shows two bell-shaped curve peaks, a larger first peak for the younger population and a second smaller peak for Esther's age group.

> *Dov:* I know what the graph means.
>
> *Elizabeth:* Esther may be a Bipolar Type I.

Dov snickers and sarcastically says,

> *Dov:* Medical psycho babble. When can I take Esther home?
>
> *Elizabeth:* She needs treatment. Time to heal.
>
> *Dov:* I need to see her.
>
> *Elizabeth:* Perhaps in a couple of days. We need to stabilize her. Keep her quiet.

Dov bangs his hand on Dr. Corsini's desk.

> *Dov:* I insist that you allow me to see my wife. Now!

Elizabeth speaks assertively.

> *Elizabeth:* You insist? As long as your wife is in my care, I'll be the judge of what's best for her. Do I make myself clear?

Dov nods angrily.

> *Elizabeth:* By the way what happened to your right hand?

Dov glances down at his hand. It's covered with a large gauze bandage.

> *Dov:* It's nothing. I was peeling potatoes for my wife, and the knife slipped. Wait a minute. Why the fuck am I telling you?
>
> *Elizabeth:* Pretty big bandage for a potato cut.

Dov gets red with rage and then gives Dr. Corsini a phony smile.

> *Dov:* Is there anything else, Doctor? I'd like to get the hell out of here. With all due respect, of course.
>
> *Dr. Corsini:* Perhaps it's best that you do leave.

Dov gets up and storms out of Dr. Corsini's office without saying good-bye. He ignores Lynn, mumbling to himself as he leaves the psychiatric ward.

Dr. Corsini shakes her head and quietly talks to herself.

> *Elizabeth:* Nothing like a royal schmuck to make my day.

16

MARSHALL

Marshall Lamster and Elizabeth Corsini eat popcorn and watch the ending of the 1940s' movie, *Casablanca*.

Elizabeth has kept both her age and figure well. She's as vibrant as she was when she was a young girl having a fling with the president, then Senator Malcolm Yale Macorley of the great State of Delaware. Marshall is handsome in his own right, distinguished looking with a touch of gray, and in his mid-to late-fifties, about ten years older than Elizabeth.

At the end of the movie, actors Humphrey Bogart and Claude Raines are walking together in the Casablanca night air. Humphrey puts his arm around Claude and utters that famous last line:

Humphrey Bogart:

"Louis, I think this is the
beginning of a
beautiful friendship."

Lights come on. Marshall and Elizabeth leave the theater with the other patrons, talking about the movie.

Elizabeth: Humphrey and Claude are just like us, Marshall.

Marshall: We're much more than friends, Liz.

Elizabeth: I wish circumstances were different.

Marshall: Me, too.

Marshall imitates Humphrey Bogart in one of his great scenes with Lauren Bacall.

Marshall: "Here's looking at you, kid."

Elizabeth laughs and grabs Marshall's arm.

Elizabeth: You do a great Bogey, but I can't go to your place tonight. I have to bone up on personality disorders.

Marshall: I see psychotics in my line of business. Do you want to trade notes?

Elizabeth: Actually, I might need your help. I'll let you know after I see my patient tomorrow.

17

BIPOLAR DISORDER

D r. Corsini hits the intercom. Lynn responds to the buzz.

Lynn: Yes, Dr. Corsini.

Elizabeth: Lynn, have one of the nurses on the ward bring Esther Hirsch to my office.

Esther is lying listlessly on her bed. The room is sparse. Only a single bed, metal chair, and a wall closet next to the bathroom are in evidence. The ward nurse enters and taps Esther on the shoulder.

Ward Nurse: Esther, the doctor wants to see you in her office. Please follow me.

Esther gets up and does what she is told. As they pass through the psychiatric ward, male and female patients are milling about. Some patients look reasonably normal, but others give away their mental illness with their lifeless eyes, downturned heads, and incoherent mumblings. The mix is understandable, as these poor individuals are the dregs and lost souls of normal society.

Lynn looks up as Esther enters Dr. Corsini's office.

Lynn: The doctor will see you now. Right through that door. You needn't knock. The doctor is expecting you.

Dr. Corsini is sitting at her desk looking at files. A framed picture of the president, against a backdrop of the American flag, hangs on her wall along with her diplomas.

The office is ten feet by fifteen feet and except for the metal desk, a four-drawer filing cabinet, and a four-foot freestanding bookcase lined with psychiatry and medical books, the room holds no other furniture, not even a couch.

Esther sits in one of the two inexpensive, uncomfortable wooden chairs opposite Dr. Corsini's cushioned armchair. The buttocks-unfriendly chairs are standard government issue and are meant only for short meetings with patients and parents, so that Dr. Corsini can get through her overloaded day.

Esther trembles with anxiety as she speaks.

Esther: Will you help me, Doctor? Something terrifying has been happening to me.

Elizabeth: Do you remember how you got here?

Esther: The last thing I remember was hammering my watch and hearing the voices.

Elizabeth: Can you still hear the voices?

Esther: Yes! Yes! Can you please get rid of them? They terrify me and won't leave me alone. I can't get any peace of mind while the voices constantly bombard my every thought. I know, I just know that they're trying to kill me.

Esther suddenly looks up to the ceiling and closes her eyes. Her face becomes distorted, and her teeth grind noisily.

Esther:

(deep boisterous voice)
We're still fucking here, Esther.

Elizabeth: What was that?

Esther:

(normal voice, eyes
blinking rapidly)
What was what?

Dr. Corsini stares astonishingly at Esther.

Elizabeth: Are you aware that your voice just changed?

Esther: My voice didn't change.

Dr. Corsini reaches over the desk and strokes Esther's hand.

Elizabeth: We've given you medication. You won't hear the voices in a couple of days. I promise.

Esther, panicking, screams out.

Esther: They're still here. They're not going away.

Elizabeth: They will.

Esther lunges over the desk and pulls at Dr. Corsini's watch. Dr. Corsini stops her from breaking the band.

Esther: The watch was evil. It had to be destroyed.

Elizabeth: Tell me about the watch.

Esther: We were eating chili at our favorite restaurant, the Hard Times Café on King Street in Alexandria.

* * *

Dov and Esther laugh, eat chili with corn bread, and drink beer. Dov removes a wrapped box from his front pants' pocket and hands it to Esther. Esther opens the box.

Dov: Happy birthday, darling.

Esther: Oh, Dov! It's beautiful.

The watch has a blue strap with a square, circle, triangle, and diamond at each directional pole of its white face. The symbols on the watch face are blue like the strap.

* * *

Esther comes back to the present. She gets up out of her chair and paces nervously.

Esther: At first I loved it.

Elizabeth: What changed?

Esther: By the next day, after an evening of celebration, my whole world turned inside out. Each symbol on the watch gave me a different evil power.

Esther closes her eyes and is having a flashback of herself sitting in bed in her house, as Dr. Corsini silently observes.

* * *

She moves her right index finger from symbol to symbol, vertically, horizontally, and crisscrossing in different directions. Her eyes take on a wild, angry look, and her teeth jut out over her upper lip.

Esther:

(deep male voice)
This triangle is the Messiah.
No, it's the square. No, I'm
the circle. I'm the Messiah.
Dov's the diamond. He's
the Messiah. No, he's the Devil.
Dr. Corsini walks around the desk and shakes Esther.
Elizabeth: Esther, wake up.

* * *

Esther's eyes blink, and she gradually relaxes her muscles. Dr. Corsini touches her gently, like a mother caring for her daughter. She speaks very softly to Esther.

Elizabeth: Was your birthday about a week ago?

Esther: Yes, how did you know?

Elizabeth: It's typical to experience mania accompanied by psychosis for a week or so—and sometimes longer—in bipolar disorder before a doctor makes the diagnosis.

Esther, clearly agitated, begins pacing again back and forth in the office. Dr. Corsini allows her to do so.

Esther: I'm not insane. Am I, Doctor?

Elizabeth: No, you don't have a distorted perception of reality. You're right with me in the here and now. You know that the voices are not real. The insane live their psychosis. It's part of their everyday "normalcy."

The intercom buzzes.

Lynn: I have your sister on line one.

Dr. Corsini picks up the phone and listens. The pink hue leaves her face in a matter of seconds and takes on the appearance of an albino. She wretches a dry heave.

Elizabeth: I'm sorry. I must go.

Before Esther can respond, Dr. Corsini runs out of the office into the cool Washington weather without her coat. Esther and Lynn are left dumbfounded.

18

FAMILY LOSS

D aniela and Elizabeth sit in the Mount Olivet Funeral Parlor
by themselves, trying to comfort each other.

Daniela: They never had a chance, Lizzie. It was a head-
on collision.

Elizabeth: Oh, Dannie, our parents were the best.

Daniela: I'm glad they'll be buried in a mausoleum in the garden. It's such a peaceful and beautiful location.

The sisters walk over to the open caskets of their parents.
Both cry. Elizabeth turns to Daniela and hugs her.

Elizabeth: We only have each other now.

Daniela: Is Sophia coming home from medical school?

Elizabeth: Yes. She'll be home tonight in time for the funeral
tomorrow. Thank God this is her last year, and she'll be interning
right here at Washington Central Hospital. I need her to be with
me. I'm lonely.

Daniela: I miss her, too. Will she specialize after she graduates?

Elizabeth: Obstetrics and gynecology. She is looking to meet
her Sir Lancelot and wants to start a family right away.

Daniela: You know, I am mentoring a nice, bright young man whom I like a lot and think would be good for Sophia. He's a couple of years older than she and has a great future at the FBI. He's also a lawyer.

Elizabeth: What's his name, and more importantly, what's his religion?

Daniela: Abel Slobodkin, and he's Jewish. His parents, Isaac and Rebecca, are Orthodox Jews living in Brooklyn. They were originally from Poland and were able to survive the war by pretending to be Christian children, making their way to Israel, where they met. Abel's father, we understand, was in Israeli politics before coming to the United States. The parents spent their years in Brooklyn in the eighties and had Abel late in their lives. Abel's schooling was all in New York; he graduated from NYU and did law at Columbia.

Elizabeth: Mom and Dad would have never approved. Neither would the sisters who schooled us. But if you're going to marry out of the faith, a Jewish husband would be a good choice. Look at me—I've already got my daughter marrying and converting. Would his parents consent?

Daniela: From what Abel tells me—very doubtful. They would be grieving as we are, like it was Abel's funeral.

Elizabeth: We had such high hopes and aspirations. They seem to have disappeared with the years, and now with Mom and Dad gone, I'm beginning to see a gray world. It has to get better. It just has to.

Daniela: Don't worry, sis, I promised Mom and Dad that I would always protect you. We'll both be okay.

19

CAIN

Cain Arlis Macorley is sitting with his father in the Oval Office. The president offers Cain a cigar. Cain declines and the president lights up a Cuban.

President Macorley: I heard about the Corsini parents. Tell me again why that was necessary?

Cain: We needed to send Daniela a message. She's been threatening to terminate our covert operation. She doesn't know about the hit on her parents, but she suspects.

President Macorley: You can't be a vigilante, Cain. Jason informed me that the other Corsini sister problem is not going away. These Corsinis are a thorn in my side.

Cain: I can fix that if you like.

President Macorley: Are you listening to me? It's not the right time. I want to give Jason's plan a chance to work.

Cain: Okay, Pop. You're the president.

President Macorley: You're young, Cain. You need to learn *savlanut.*

Cain: What the hell is that?

President Macorley: The Hebrew word for patience.

Cain: I didn't know you spoke the Hebe's lingo.

President Macorley: I don't, but as King Solomon said in his Book of Proverbs, "The kisses of the enemy are deceptive." And as *The Godfather* wisely told us, you keep your friends close and your enemies closer.

Cain: Gog and Magog, Mr. President?

President Macorley: It's coming, Cain. But it won't happen until I'm reelected.

Cain: And how do you know you'll be reelected?

President Macorley: Let's just say that I'm a snake when it comes to politics.

Cain: I'm just like you, Dad. It's our family genes.

President Macorley: Of course! We're both descendants of the Devil. Will you excuse me, son? I have to use the red phone.

Cain clasps his hands in a prayer-like mode and makes a Namaste greeting to his father. The president smiles as Cain departs. The president calls Leamas, who is roaming around Anacostia National Park, disgustingly eating a live rabbit.

Leamas: That son of yours could turn out even more evil than you, Mr. President. Maybe I'm backing the wrong Macorley. I liked his cold-blooded assassination of the Corsinis' parents. That will give God something to think about. I intend to foil His Lordship's plans. Next on my agenda are Abel Slobodkin and Sophia Corsini. That would be the *coup de grace*, the ultimate blow to God.

President Macorley: Might I suggest we wait for a while. At least until I solve our current problems.

Leamas: But of course! You're the president. However, speed it up. Unlike you I don't have *savlanut*.

20

TWO DAYS LATER

Dr. Corsini and Esther sit together.

Elizabeth: My parents were good people.

Esther: Don't you think you should take some time off?

Elizabeth: My work is the best thing for my grieving. My daughter was home for the funeral, and she got me settled down and back on track. Enough about my personal problems. These sessions are about you, not me. Tell me what other strange things happened to you the past week.

Esther focuses on the picture of the president hanging on the office wall.

Esther: There was a painting.

Elizabeth: A painting?

Esther: Of a rabbi. Dov and I are Jewish.

* * *

Esther goes into a trance, visualizing herself back in her home a week ago. She is staring at the oil painting of the rabbi. She focuses on the artist's name—Bromberg. She picks out four selective letters of the name and separates these four letters from the remaining four letters. The four letters seem outside her head, hanging directly in her line of vision, but her eyes remain closed. In her stupor, she blurts out aloud.

Esther: The artist's name is Bromberg.

Elizabeth: Tell me what you see, Esther.

Esther: I see an "o," "g," "r," and "e" in a diagonal line. Wait! Now the letters are moving and are vertical.

Elizabeth: Those are four letters in Bromberg, the name of the artist. They are spelling out the word "ogre." An ogre is a hideous folklore monster.

Esther: Wait! Wait! The rabbi is changing into a horrifying, ugly, wrinkle-faced monster. I'm scared, and I'm running into the kitchen. I reach under the sink and pick up a can of Lysol.

Esther makes motions with her body as she describes her flashback.

Elizabeth: And then what happened?

Esther returns to the present, opening her eyes.

* * *

Esther: I ran back to the living room to the rabbi's portrait. The monster was still there, so I sprayed Lysol all over the painting. I saw the droplets of liquid running down the monster's face, but the painting didn't change. I couldn't get rid of the monster. I'm sorry, Dr. Corsini. The painting was evil.

Elizabeth: It's okay, Esther. You're safe now. Was there anything else evil in the house?

Esther contracts her body. She stops breathing and then loudly exhales her trapped breath.

* * *

Esther is staring at the head of a deer she purchased at a garage sale. The head is hanging over the fireplace in her family room. The deer is looking at her with its evil eye. She feels its eye piercing her soul even when she isn't in the room. She can't stand it anymore, so she runs to the linen closet and takes out one of her white bed sheets. She stands about five feet from the deer and tosses the sheet toward its stuffed head. But she misses, and the sheet falls as if it is floating to the floor. Fear grips her as she crawls on her hands and knees to retrieve the sheet. The evil eye is still glaring at her. She gets up and moves closer, and when she is about three and a half feet away, she throws the sheet on the deer's head. This time she is successful. She momentarily relaxes the tension in her body, but her mind is overwhelmed with thoughts of the deer's eyes.

* * *

Elizabeth: And now?

Esther: It's not bothering me.

Elizabeth: What happened when Dov came home and saw the sheet?

Esther: He made light of it and even mockingly said, "Redecorating, are you, Esther?

Elizabeth: How long have you and Dov been married?

Esther: About six months.

Elizabeth: Do you work?

Esther: Yes. I'm an investigative reporter for an Internet political blog. I majored in journalism with a minor in biology.

Elizabeth: Do you still have the painting and deer head?

Esther shakes her head in a no response.

* * *

She drifts backward in time, closing her eyes and remembering.

She sees herself driving to the shopping mall next morning and throwing the painting and deer's head into the dumpster. She drives away and returns home. After several hours, she realizes what she has done, so she returns early evening to retrieve what she had thrown away. She looks around to make sure no one is watching and climbs into the dumpster, scraping her knee, but the dumpster has already been emptied. Tears stream down her face. She opens her eyes.

* * *

Elizabeth: And was Dov nonchalant about this as well?

Esther: Yes. I was scared to death about his reaction. All he said was, "I never really liked that deer." Not a word about the painting. I felt guilty and ashamed.

Elizabeth: Of your actions?

Esther: The wine cup belonged to my Zady Sam, my maternal grandfather.

Esther sheds tears. Dr. Corsini passes her tissues and reaches across the desk, clasping Esther's free hand.

Elizabeth: I'm so sorry, Esther. This is a good place to stop for today. I'm meeting my sister at my parents' house.

Esther thanks Dr. Corsini with a hug and departs the office. Dr. Corsini picks up her briefcase, inserts Esther's file, and leaves to meet Daniela.

21

DANGER LURKING

Daniela is already there, waiting for Elizabeth. They kiss and hug as Elizabeth silently observes the photos of her family scattered about the downstairs and on the walls ascending up the stairway to her and Daniela's bedrooms. This was the house in Silver Springs where the sisters grew up. She has many fond memories of her childhood. Tears come to her eyes as she looks at the pictures of her parents. She is totally taken by surprise at Dannie's first words.

Daniela: It wasn't a head-on collision, Lizzie. It was a tractor trailer that rear-ended Mom and Dad off the road.

Elizabeth is stunned. For a moment no words come out, and then…

Elizabeth: What?

Daniela: Our parents may have been murdered. That's my hunch, anyway.

Elizabeth: Have you talked to the truck driver?

Daniela: He's nowhere to be found. Vanished into thin air. Apparently, he's not the real driver. The real driver was tied up at a weigh station. He said that he couldn't identify the person, because this mysterious man mugged him from behind and bopped him on the head. He was unconscious when a patrolman found him. In all the confusion of the crash, no one got a good look at the killer.

Elizabeth: I thought I was…

Elizabeth gasps.

Daniela: Tell me, sis…Remember, I'm the FBI. Were you going to say, "I thought I was safe?"

Elizabeth: I just got frightened. What if it was one of my patients?

Daniela presses Elizabeth.

Daniela: Who?

Just then a rock shatters the living-room window. Daniela picks up the rock and sees a folded note attached by an elastic band. She pulls out her gun, runs through the front door, and spots a red Cadillac speeding down the street. The car is too far for her to make out the license plate.

She renters the house with the note in hand, unfolds it, and reads aloud.

Daniela: "You're next, Corsini."

Elizabeth is in shock.

Elizabeth: Oh, my God, Dannie! Nobody knows we're here. What's going on?

Daniela appears cool and collected, almost aloof.

Daniela: I wonder if the note was meant for you or for me, or perhaps both of us.

22

NIGHTMARE

Dr. Corsini is back at work. Esther is sitting opposite her. Dr. Corsini's mind wanders back to the rock thrown through her parents' living-room window. Esther was the only one she told prior to leaving for Silver Springs to meet with Daniela. Something is bothering her.

Elizabeth: Is Dov violent, Esther?

Esther: He's the sweetest man.

Dr. Corsini gives her a questionable look.

Elizabeth: You haven't answered my question.

Esther blushes, gets out of her chair, and turns her back to Dr. Corsini.

Esther: He's never laid a hand on me, but he does have a temper.

Elizabeth: What did he do to his hand?

Esther turns, hesitating.

Esther: He'd be very upset with me if he knew that I told you.

Elizabeth: Everything discussed between you and me in this office is confidential. The only way Dov would find out would be if you elected to tell him. If Dov is violent, then telling him would be foolish and dangerous.

Esther: I need to begin with an upsetting conversation that Dov and I had just before I became manic.

* * *

Dov and Esther are eating dinner at home.

Esther: I had the nightmare again.

Dov has a wild look in his eyes. His face goes red.

Dov: I told you I didn't want to hear about your damn beast again.

Dov gets up, walks over to Esther, and raises his hand to strike her. He stops suddenly, still holding his fist up over his shoulder, and runs like a madman out of the kitchen to the front door. Esther immediately rises and runs after him. In horror she watches incredulously as he smashes his fist through the pane of glass in the door.

Esther freezes as Dov turns to her with blood pouring profusely onto the foyer floor. Dov yells a profanity and starts walking quickly through the living room, dining room, and kitchen, purposely dropping blood everywhere. Meanwhile Esther finally reacts and rushes to the linen closet to grab some towels.

Dov is standing in the kitchen with a raging, piercing look in his eyes. He then miraculously calms down.

Dov: Oh, honey. I'm sorry for the mess on the carpet. I'll help you clean it up.

Esther places Dov's bleeding hand under the faucet and washes it. She wraps a light towel around his bloodied hand and leaves him there while she goes to the bathroom for hydrogen peroxide, Neosporin ointment, and bandages.

* * *

Dr. Corsini listens intently to Esther's flashback.

Elizabeth: What do you think triggered such a violent response?

Esther: Even before all this happened, I've had this recurring dream. When I try to tell Dov about it, he refuses to listen. Well, I tried one time too many, and he blew his cork, and went stark, raving mad.

Elizabeth: Tell me about your dream.

Esther: It seems to be triggered when I see the president on TV.

Elizabeth: The president! How odd!

Esther: Yes! Our president, Malcolm Yale Macorley.

Elizabeth: Can you describe to me exactly what you see in your dream?

* * *

Esther: I see a beast with ten large horns, and then an eleventh smaller horn emerges through the beast's head, knocking off three of the larger horns. The beast is a fire-breathing black dragon swimming in a stormy sea. The three dislodged larger horns fall into the sea and disappear.

* * *

Esther shakes uncontrollably.

Elizabeth: Like rotten teeth falling out of your mouth. Why does your dream sound familiar? And why does it bother Dov so much?

Elizabeth pauses and then changes the conversation.

Elizabeth: What were you working on before all of this horror?

Esther: Mostly the ramifications of the world economy on our global foreign policy.

Elizabeth: Hmm. It doesn't seem like your work could be connected to your nightmare.

Esther tilts forward and clutches Dr. Corsini's hand.

Esther: Am I losing my mind?

Elizabeth: When you came into the emergency room, we sedated you and gave you a shot of Haldol to break the psychosis. I also prescribed lithium, a mood stabilizer, and Xyprexa, an antipsychotic, which you've been taking for the last three days. These drugs treat bipolar disorder, a mental illness in which the patient displays symptoms similar to yours. Quite often the manic psychotic state is, however, followed by clinical depression.

Esther: Sounds heavy on drugs. I don't take drugs.

Elizabeth: We'll need to monitor your lithium levels in the hospital and when you leave. We do this through blood tests. The drugs are necessary to get you feeling better.

Esther: I'm not crazy about needles.

Elizabeth: Having made you aware of a potential manic depressive diagnosis, I don't see any signs of depression. My gut feeling is that you'll make a quick recovery.

Esther: Is that the diagnosis, doctor—bipolar disorder?

Elizabeth: It looks that way, but I can't be certain. Why don't we stop for today, so you can get some rest?

Esther hugs Dr. Corsini and exits the office. Dr. Corsini pulls out her Dictaphone machine and speaks into it.

Elizabeth: Esther is a pleasant woman. I am treating her for bipolar disorder, although she doesn't have up and down mood swings. Even on her second visit with me, she seems to have stabilized. This is highly unusual, if she were truly mentally ill. Her psychosis may have been drug induced. Her dream is perplexing, and I worry about her husband.

23

FOCUS GROUP

Elizabeth relaxes on her couch. She's watching TV and has a glass of red wine in one hand while she pats her white Maltese, Muffin, with her other hand. She puts her glass down and lights up a cigarette.

Elizabeth's apartment is exquisitely decorated with paintings, sculptures, and fine contemporary furniture. On the coffee table, there's a framed picture of the president, signed "Love, Malcolm."

Elizabeth addresses Muffin.

Elizabeth: What do you think, Muffin? How could our handsome, loving president trigger Esther's nightmare?

Muffin barks, gets up on his back paws, and licks Elizabeth's face. Elizabeth kisses Muffin's fluffy white hair. On TV a focus group is discussing the president. Thirty people form the group. They are sitting in three ascending rows, bleacher style. The group is composed mostly of seniors, with and equal number of men and women. Each person wears a name tag.

Moderator: How many of you believe the president is fighting for you? Raise your hands.

The vast majority of hands go up.

Moderator: How many of you believe the president is just another politician who doesn't care about the will of the people? That he's only concerned about being reelected?

Only two hands go up.

Elizabeth: You see, Muffin, how the political winds can shift.

Muffin barks. Elizabeth continues.

Elizabeth: For a long time, the Republicans in Congress had the upper hand. Now our beloved president is more popular than the tooth fairy.

The moderator points to a balding man in the front row whose name tag identifies him as Bert.

Moderator: Bert, how do you feel about the president?

Bert: He's the first politician who does not speak with a forked tongue. He's the most transparent president we've ever had.

Moderator selects an elderly woman wearing a wig.

Moderator: And what about you, Melanie? Do you think that the president is doing a good job?

Melanie: Yes. I voted for the president and continue to believe in him. It's the Congress that I'm fed up with.

Moderator: Any reservations at all, Melanie?

Melanie: He's too nice.

A young man, Bruce, wearing a soldier's uniform holds up his hand.

Moderator: Bruce, you were one of the two who weren't happy with the president.

Bruce: Actually I've had a change of heart listening to all the good comments about him.

Moderator: Enough to vote for him next time?

Bruce: I'm fifty-fifty right now, but leaning toward him. I'll have to see what he does in the next three years, especially with his foreign policy initiatives.

Elizabeth switches off the TV.

Elizabeth: I've heard quite enough, Muffin, for one night. How about you?

Muffin looks up and barks.

Elizabeth: The public has a blind eye when it comes to their president. I know him for the callous bastard that he really is. He'll crush anyone and throw him under the bus if he stands in the way of his ambitions. Somebody has to stop him before he destroys the country with his socialist Marxist policies. Let's go to bed, Muffin.

Muffin follows Elizabeth to bed.

Elizabeth: Oh, Muffin, good news. Sophia completed her medical schooling early. She'll be home in a couple of days. It will be so good to have her back.

Muffin: Woof! Woof!

24

ANGELS

Next morning, Elizabeth is driving in her car on her usual route to work. She stops at a light and looks straight ahead. She is taken aback when she sees a ray of white sunlight and a ray of blue light shining through her front window in the shape of a hybrid-colored upside-down "V."

Elizabeth: How strange! I wonder how that's possible?

She drives on further and comes to a halt in the busy traffic of the capital. This time the rays reverse, with white and blue on the opposite side.

She continues and comes to another stoplight. She is amazed as she now visualizes two blue rays coming in through her front window. She tries to touch the rays with her hands, but comes up empty-handed.

Elizabeth: God in Heaven! What are these magnificent blue rays?

She continues driving and two blurry figures with wings flash in front of her car. She rubs her eyes.

Elizabeth: This can't be. My eyes are playing tricks on me.

She looks through the window, and the winged creatures are still there. They smile at her and disappear into space. Elizabeth cautiously smiles.

    Elizabeth: I saw angels. I can't tell Dannie, because she'll be jealous. I can't tell anyone, or they'll lock me up in my own loony bin.

25

CODE NAME DANIEL

Esther and Dr. Corsini stroll in the courtyard adjacent to the psychiatric ward. The area encompasses about seven thousand square feet and is lined with trees and shrubs, except for a small cement area where male patients are shooting hoops.

What's odd about psychiatric wards is that most patients and staff smoke. Even if you don't, you find yourself bumming cigarettes to be a part of something when the rest of the world looks down on you and believes you are part of nothing.

Elizabeth: Cigarette, Esther.

Esther: Sure! I didn't know you smoked, Dr. Corsini.

Elizabeth: An old flame of mine introduced me. I know it's a bad habit, but it's only once in a while. How are you doing, Esther?

Esther: I can't believe it's been only three days, Dr. Corsini. I feel like a new woman. The voices are gone, as you promised. I'm so grateful.

Elizabeth: I've changed my mind on the diagnosis. I don't feel you have bipolar disorder.

Esther: What, then?

Elizabeth: Something else seems to have induced your psychotic state. Hallucinogenic drugs can do this.

Esther: I told you. I don't do drugs.

Elizabeth: Still I'd like to run further blood tests.

Esther: When will I be able to leave the hospital?

Elizabeth: Day after tomorrow. But for a while, I'd like to meet privately with you on a weekly basis. I must confess that I'm troubled by your husband's behavior. Putting one's hand through a glass pane is not normal.

Esther: But the violence only emerged in connection with my nightmare.

Elizabeth: Nevertheless you need to be on your guard.

Esther: You're frightening me.

Elizabeth: Tell me a little bit about your ancestry and background. Psychiatric disorders run in Jewish Ashkenazi families because relatives marry each other.

Esther: Oh, you mean like first cousins. According to the DNA analysis report of my brother's cheek cells from a company called World Family DNA, my maternal and paternal grandparents may have been related to each other. My grandparents were all born in the Ukraine near Kiev. The company told me that it would be better to submit a male relative's scraped cheek cell sample rather than my own. My brother, who was killed in a car crash a few months later, agreed. I don't really understand the genetics.

Elizabeth: Well, I do. My PhD was in genetics, and coincidentally I submitted my brother's DNA to the same company. Let me try to explain as simply as I can.

Esther: Please.

Elizabeth: The male YDNA has sixty-seven markers, with each marker being different, because each marker has a different sequence and length of the four nucleic acid bases making up the DNA. Everyone in the world has the same sequence of nucleic acid bases at each marker.

Esther: I follow you so far.

Elizabeth: If you look at each marker, the world population has a different number of repeats. For example at marker number thirty-five, your brother might have twenty-three repeats of a particular DNA sequence and length, and my brother might have ten repeats on his YDNA at this marker. Our brothers, and you and I, are clearly not related, but someone who is very closely related to your brother would also have the same twenty-three repeats at marker thirty-five. If we looked at, say, marker ten, which has a different number of nucleic acid bases and a different sequence than marker thirty-five, we could perform the same analysis. And so on for all sixty-seven markers.

Esther: Now you've lost me.

Elizabeth: It's really quite simple. Looking separately at the repeats of all sixty-seven markers, someone in Poland or Spain or anywhere in the world might be an exact match to your brother or might be a close match. Instead of twenty-three repeats, the person from Poland or Spain might have twenty-two or twenty-one repeats, indicating a mutation or a double mutation. If two people are zero to seven mutations different in all sixty-seven markers examined, then they share a common ancestor in the not-too-distant past. Actually, the whole world is related to a lesser or greater degree.

Esther: Really! The whole world is related?

Elizabeth: You can do something similar for the female ancestry through an examination of the mitochondrial DNA. Males can get both their YDNA and mitochondrial DNA analyzed, while females unfortunately are only able to determine their mitochondrial DNA, so it was better for you to submit your brother's cells for DNA quantitation rather than your own. Of course anyone related to your brother is related to you.

I coincidentally submitted my brother's DNA before he died of leukemia, because he wanted me to look into our Italian ancestry. He died much too young, at age nineteen.

Esther: Oh, I'm so sorry to hear about your loss, Dr. Corsini.

Elizabeth: Thank you. Tell me, Esther. What was your motivation for sending off your brother's sample for genetic analysis?

Esther: I know this sounds stupid. I wanted to know if Dov and I were related. I made it a condition of marrying Dov that he needed to submit his oral cells for DNA testing. He reluctantly agreed because he was eager to become my husband.

Elizabeth: Quite unusual in our modern world for a husband and wife to be related. How did you meet Dov?

Esther: I was a student majoring in journalism at American University when I met Dov in an elective biology class I was taking at George Washington University. He was in his junior year in biochemistry at George Washington.

Elizabeth: Go on.

Esther: We lost track of each other for a period of fifteen years. And then I unexpectedly met him at a reception for journalists at the White House.

Elizabeth: Didn't you tell me the other day that Dov was a toxicologist? What was he doing at the White House?

Esther: Come to think of it, that question never came up in our conversation. It probably got lost in our excitement of meeting up again after fifteen years.

* * *

I remember spotting Dov at the reception. Dov looks handsome in his blue blazer and khaki pants. I go over to him to say hello, and he recognizes me immediately. He hugs me, and we start to chat when two distinguished, charming gentlemen wearing tuxedos come over to talk to Dov. Dov shakes their hands and introduces me.

Dov: Esther, this is Jason Smithies, the White House chief of staff, and his deputy, Roger Arnold.

Esther: It's an honor, gentlemen.

Esther gives her hand to Jason Smithies, who kisses it softly, while Arnold reaches over and gives her a peck on the cheek. Smithies compliments Dov's choice.

Smithies: My God, Dov. She's beautiful. You're a lucky man. When did you say you we're going to marry this delightful woman?

Esther: We just met up again after fifteen years, Mr. Smithies.

Smithies: Please call me Jason.

Arnold looks Esther up and down.

Arnold: And call me Roger.

Roger Arnold looks deeply into Esther's eyes.

Arnold: Dov would be wise to hang onto you. He's a lucky man.

Fifty feet away, the burly man who was seen at the hospital entrance when Esther was admitted, waves to Dov to come over.

Dov: Esther, I'm going to leave you for a couple of minutes. Don't let these fine gentlemen steal you from me. I think the old goat Roger is ready to seduce you.

Dov snickers to Smithies and Arnold, who laugh at Dov's comments. Dov then departs and walks over to the burly man. Esther turns to Roger Arnold.

Esther: Who is Dov talking to, Roger? That man is awfully heavy on his feet.

Arnold checks with Smithies with a questionable glance. Smithies answers for Arnold.

Smithies: He's actually enormous. His name is Frankie, Frank Kavorsky.

Arnold can't help himself. He chimes in.

Arnold: We call him Tubs.

Smithies: If you'll excuse us, Esther, something's come up, and we have to leave.

Smithies and Arnold kiss Esther. She grabs a glass of champagne and a mushroom tart off a waiter's tray and wanders over toward Dov. She stops and turns her back toward them. They fail to notice her, as they are engaged in what appears to Esther to be a serious conversation.

Kavorsky: Dov, the White House began a new covert operation, Code Name Daniel.

Dov: I'm all ears, Frankie.

Kavorsky sips his drink, stuffs in three Swedish meatballs from his plate, and notices Esther. He alerts Dov, who turns around to see Esther close by.

Dov: We'll pick it up later.

Dov leaves Kavorsky and goes over to Esther.

Dov: Hi! It's a boring party. Let's get out of here.

Esther: I thought you'd never ask.

The two walk arm in arm out of the White House. Esther speaks to Dr. Corsini.

* * *

Esther: Dov knew all these important people.

Elizabeth: Code Name Daniel sounds like some kind of CIA operation. Esther, I'm seeing Dov tomorrow, as I wanted to have a final conversation with him before you leave. Dov is dangerous, and you need to be on guard.

Esther gets up and leaves. Dr. Corsini pulls out her Dictaphone machine. She speaks into the microphone.

Elizabeth: Patient seems essentially cured. It is troubling that she may have had a drug-induced psychosis. Patient claims to have not taken mind-altering drugs, and I believe her. She has no reason to lie. I'm almost afraid to release her to her husband, given the possibility of foul play. First the nightmare triggered by seeing the president on TV and now a secret White House operation, Code Name Daniel. What's next in this bizarre tale!

Elizabeth puts her microphone away, and then a smile shines on her face. She thinks to herself.

Elizabeth: I need a break. Thank God, I'll be seeing Marshall tonight. And the day after tomorrow, Sophia comes home for good.

26

MARRIED CHEATER

E lizabeth passionately kisses Marshall Lamster in their room at the Four Seasons. They finish making love and lie in bed. She pushes him away as he reaches for her.

Marshall: What gives? We just made incredible love.

Elizabeth: I needed to come after a stressful few days, but I don't need you now that I had my orgasm. You lied to me about being divorced from your wife.

Marshall: My wife and I are separated, though we still have frequent sex. Sex was the only good part of our marriage.

Elizabeth: My mama warned me about all the married cheaters. And she would roll over in her grave if she knew I was romantically involved with one. Besides, you're fucking my sister.

Marshall: Please make sure that Daniela doesn't find out. She has fingernail claws the size of my hand, and she wouldn't hesitate to use them on me.

Elizabeth: It's over, Marshall.

Marshall: You Corsini sisters are impossible. You're the founding members of *Ball Crushers Incorporated.*

Elizabeth: I'm ashamed of myself. I betrayed my own sister at your Christmas party.

Marshall: That's when I had you for the first time. God, you were great…

Marshall drifts off in a flashback two months before.

* * *

A lit Christmas tree, decorated with red and gold ornaments of bells, wreaths, and Santa Clauses, stands about six feet tall in the home of Marshall Lamster. Neatly wrapped presents lay under the tree for the attendees of the party. Daniela, still very much attractive and flamboyant, grabs onto her sister, Elizabeth, and leads her to Marshall.

Daniela: Elizabeth, I want you to meet God's chosen gift to women, Marshall Lamster. Marshall, this is my sister. I call her Lizzie. And beware, she's a psychiatrist.

Marshall gives Lizzie a prolonged kiss on the cheek.

Marshall: You're definitely not an Elizabeth or a Lizzie. I crown you Liz. And with the exception of Daniela, you're the most beautiful woman at this boring party.

Daniela: Pay this man no heed. He shovels bullshit faster than Popeye can eat spinach.

Marshall: Would you care to analyze me, Dr. Corsini?

Elizabeth wobbles and is about to need to sit down, when Marshall reaches over to support her.

Elizabeth: Sorry! I'm afraid I've had more than my limit. My sister keeps spending your money by filling up my glass. I feel a bit tipsy and unlike Dannie, I don't like being out of control. After all I'm a shrink.

Marshall: Even shrinks have to eat.

Elizabeth: Touché, Marshall.

Daniela steps in between Marshall and her sister.

Daniela: I see where this is going. Is the president coming, Marshall?

Marshall: He promised he would try to make it for a few minutes, if his schedule allowed it.

Elizabeth is taken aback.

Elizabeth: President Macorley is coming here? Tonight! You know I feel more than a little drunk, and I wouldn't want to make a bad impression on the president.

Marshall: Have you ever met the president?

Elizabeth coughs, looks down at the floor, and then looks up directly in Daniela's eyes.

Elizabeth: Not socially.

Elizabeth pauses.

Elizabeth: I cannot tell a lie. I actually met him at one of his book signings when he was a Delaware senator.

Daniela: Was that a slip of the tongue, sis? Have you met the president previously on a professional basis?

Elizabeth is obviously surprised by the inference and now must lie to protect herself.

Elizabeth: Of course you're joking, Dannie. Wow! Now I feel really drunk. I'm sorry, but I have to leave before I puke all over my sister.

Daniela: God forbid. Am I my sister's keeper?

Marshall: Pretty corny, Daniela. I'll drive Liz home. Everyone is so drunk that they won't even care if their host is here or not.

Elizabeth: Thank you, Marshall. I would appreciate that.

Daniela: Give Muffin a kiss for me. I'll see you and Sophia on Friday afternoon. And as for you, Romeo, keep your hands to yourself and your penis in your pocket.

Marshall: You know I'm only loyal to you, Daniela. Whoops, I let the cat out of the bag.

Elizabeth: Keeping secrets, Daniela?

Daniela: The apple doesn't fall far from the tree, Lizzie. Why are men so dumb?

* * *

Marshall and Elizabeth chuckle, thinking back on the Christmas party.

Elizabeth: I betrayed my sister that night you took me home. You took advantage of my being drunk. We made lustful love in my apartment, and it was wonderful. God forgive me.

Marshall: Yes, it was glorious, just as it is now. Do you really want to give up what makes you happy?

Elizabeth: You're a sweet man, and I love you dearly as a friend. But I'm not in love with you.

Marshall: I don't know if I can bear life without you. I love you, Liz.

Elizabeth: Oh, Marshall! You love me because you feel so alone. I'm not as nice a person as you think I am. Behind this cracking exterior is a dried-up prune who is fast becoming an old lady.

Marshall: I don't care about you getting old and wrinkled. I love you for who you are, and I want to be with you for whatever time I have left on this earth.

Elizabeth: You need to accept that it's over. I'd like to still be friends.

Marshall: Alright, Liz. I'm here if you need me.

Elizabeth: Thanks, Marshall. I need to ask a favor, and you don't have to answer me if it creates a problem for you. What is Code Name Daniel?

Marshall: I haven't the foggiest. Not one of ours.

27

THIRD TEMPLE

The angels Michael and Gabriel are conversing in the Sanctuary of the Third Temple in Heaven.

The sanctuary is thirty-five feet on the short side and extends seventy feet on the long side. The height of the sanctuary reaches more than one hundred feet and is covered with a golden roof. The construction is hollow, like an apartment building without stories.

Located on the marble floor a few feet away from the left side wall and about halfway along the long side is a golden seven-foot menorah bearing seven oil-burning lamps.

Nearby is a golden incense altar and golden showbread table, which has twelve loaves of freshly baked challah bread on it. The showbread table is also seven feet in height and is located a few feet from the right side wall.

The showbread table is the same distance as the menorah along the opposite long side of the sanctuary. The incense altar fills the entire hollow structure with enticing perfumery that titillates the senses. The altar is a bit shorter in height, about five feet tall, and is located between and in front of the menorah and showbread table. The latter houses weekly bread baked on the Sabbath for the Kohanim and Levite priests in the temple.

The walls are gold on cedar. The panels are etched with palm trees and cherub angels so that there is a palm tree between every two cherubs. Each cherub's head has two faces, one human and one lion, that share scalp hair and face in opposite directions.

At the back of the sanctuary is a closed burgundy curtain. Behind the curtain is the Golden Ark of the Covenant, housing the tablets of the Ten Commandments.

A small table with two chairs sits at the very front of the sanctuary. Standing beside the table are Archangels Michael and Gabriel. Both appear in human form, Gabriel with his blonde hair and blonde goatee, and Michael with his red hair and red beard. Both are dressed in white robes with a blue sash. Gabriel is wearing his orange skullcap.

Michael: Earth is such a busy place, Gabriel. People on the go, hurrying like chickens scampering around with their heads cut off. I love the solitude of Heaven.

Gabriel: It's great to be an angel. I love being in the Third Temple. It's where I can really feel the presence of the Ancient One.

Michael: Gabriel, why don't you sit down?

Gabriel speaks in a serious tone.

Gabriel: Michael, you know we angels have no joints. We can only stand.

Michael's mouth forms a sly smile.

Michael: We are in human form. Here, try it out.

Michael pushes a chair to Gabriel, who cautiously lowers himself in a half-sitting position. Michael forces him the rest of the way down.

Michael: We might as well indulge in a little spirits that the priests made from the grapes of Heaven. It's one of the benefits of being human.

Gabriel: You're worse than the Serpent in the Garden of Eden. And I don't think that we should have played those visual tricks in front of Dr. Corsini's car when she was driving to work.

Michael imbibes from his brass goblet.

Michael: You're such a stick in the mud. You need to lighten up a bit. What's the news from Earth?

Gabriel: As humans are fond of expressing, Michael, the oars are rowing and the wheels are turning in God's plan, though Abel has not yet met Sophia. Daniel's ancient dream of twenty-five hundred years ago in Babylon, with the smaller horn displacing three of the larger horns from the beast's head, has taken its first baby step. Dr. Corsini will soon figure out Daniel's dream, and with Esther's help she'll see the relevance to the White House plot of Code Name Daniel.

Michael: Lizzie's life is in danger. We'll need to protect her if she falters. And what of Satan?

Gabriel: He calls himself Leamas, and he has already bought the soul of President Macorley. As destined both Macorley and his son Cain are the Devil's descendants that God spoke about to Adam and Eve. Eve's descendant, Abel, will meet Cain in the final battle of good and evil in the time of Gog and Magog.

Michael: Yes, but first Code Name Daniel must happen.

Michael takes a sip of his wine. He continues musing.

Michael: These earthly beings must not yet know about Gog and Magog. God will give us the signal as to when the events of the final days of humanity will unfold. In due time Abel will figure out that the remaining seven large horns of Daniel's dream represent the seven nations who will attack the State of Israel at the End of Days. At that time our modern-day Abel Slobodkin will clash with Cain Macorley.

God's voice is heard in the sanctuary.

Michael and Gabriel: The Ancient One!

GOD: It is then, Gabriel, that you will fight Satan to the death. Be of courage, my angel, for you must beat the Devil on your own.

I cannot help you win. He has never lost in battle. Never trust Leamas, because he cheats and lies. He will deceive you if he senses any vulnerability within you. There is no truth to him. He is the evil inclination in all humans, but there is no human more demonic than him.

    Gabriel: I relish the challenge, Ancient One. And I will not disappoint You.

    GOD: Michael and you are my most loyal and endearing angels these past fourteen billion years, ever since I decided to create the universe. We are the triumvirate of the spiritual world. We must help the misguided humans, who are all too capable of destroying themselves in the twenty-first century. Now, Godspeed.

    God departs, and the angels become invisible.

28

KAVORSKY

Dov Hirsch touches a large metal button on the wall to the right of the locked door of the psychiatric ward. A buzzer sounds, and Dov pushes the door open. He proceeds to Dr. Corsini's office. Lynn looks up from her desk.

Lynn: Good morning, Mr. Hirsch. Dr. Corsini is expecting you.

She buzzes the intercom. Dr. Corsini responds.

Elizabeth: Yes, Lynn.

Lynn: Dov Hirsch is here. He is requesting to see his wife before he meets with you.

Elizabeth: I'm coming out.

Dr. Corsini greets Dov in the reception area.

Elizabeth: Let's walk to Esther's room. I have some good news for you, Dov. I decided to send Esther home today instead of tomorrow.

Dr. Corsini carefully scrutinizes Dov's reaction.

Dov: Already? Isn't this highly irregular for a bipolar patient?

Elizabeth: She doesn't have bipolar disorder.

Dov: Oh, I see. You think that Esther took psychedelic drugs.
Elizabeth stops, as does Dov. She makes eye contact.
Elizabeth: Did she?
Dov ponders the question, but doesn't answer.

* * *

Meanwhile, Frank Kavorsky, wearing a Washington Central
Hospital gray uniform, enters Lynn's office. He stands upright,
with his stomach protruding far in front of him. A tool bag hangs
from his belt and a name tag is pinned to his shirt. The name tag
reads John Urenko.
Lynn: Yes?
Lynn glances at Kavorsky's name tag with matching picture.
Kavorsky: Hi, beautiful! Problems have been reported with
the phones.
Lynn picks up the receiver.
Lynn: My phone seems to be working. Are you sure?
Kavorsky: Would I be nuts enough to come to the psycho
ward if I wasn't? We're checking all departments to see if we can
determine where the source of the problem is. Let me check your
phone again to be safe.
Kavorsky checks Lynn's phone.
Kavorsky: You're right. It's good. Any other phones?
Lynn: In there.
Kavorsky enters Dr. Corsini's office. He quickly opens her
desk phone and installs an electronic bug. He closes the phone
and returns to the reception area.
Kavorsky: You're all set. No problems. Bye, sweetheart.
Kavorsky exits the psychiatry ward.

* * *

After moments of silence, Dov answers Dr. Corsini.

Dov: You've put me in an awkward position. I make it a habit of not sharing personal information. Esther has taken hallucinogenic drugs like LSD. She regularly smokes marijuana. I can vouch for the pot, because I smoke it with her. Does that answer your question?

Elizabeth: Tell me, Dov. How is it that you know so much about bipolar disorder and drug-induced psychosis?

Dov: I've been a student in one way or another for most of my adult life.

Elizabeth: And the LSD? Where did she get that? It wouldn't by chance have come from your laboratory?

Dov tries to control his anger.

Dov: If you're suggesting that I have access to mind-altering drugs in my job, I resent the implication. I have a high-level security clearance at the CIA, and I would not risk such foolishness. Is there anything else, Doctor?

Dr. Corsini gives Dov a piercing look.

Elizabeth: Did you just say CIA?

Dov, without even blinking, glares back at Dr. Corsini.

Dov: No! I distinctly said EPA. You need to get your hearing checked out.

They enter Esther's ward room. Esther smiles when she sees Dov.

Esther: Hello, Dr. Corsini. Hi, Dov.

Elizabeth: Esther, Dov can take you home today. We needn't wait until tomorrow to discharge you. Make an appointment with my secretary for next week on your way out.

Dov is obviously frustrated.

Dov: Why does she have to come back?

Esther: Dov! What if the psychosis returns?

Dov raises his voice.

Dov: I'm not happy. You don't need therapy. I'll pack your suitcase.

Dov packs up Esther's things, while grumbling under his breath.

Esther: Thanks for everything, Dr. Corsini.

She hugs Dr. Corsini.

Elizabeth: I have some marijuana if you need calming down. I prescribe it strictly for medical purposes.

Esther: No, thanks. I told you. I don't do drugs.

Dr. Corsini makes eye contact with Dov. Neither one flinches.

Elizabeth: Esther, stop by the nurses' station to pick up your prescriptions. And don't forget you'll need to do blood tests to check for lithium levels.

Dr. Corsini exits, leaving Dov and Esther. She returns to her office, where Lynn greets her.

Lynn: A hospital repairman checked out our phones.

Elizabeth: I'll be in my office.

Lynn: He was weird looking.

Elizabeth: How weird?

Lynn: He was enormous.

Elizabeth: Hmm! No, it couldn't be.

Lynn: Couldn't be who?

Elizabeth: Oh, it's nothing. That's the way Esther described a man named Kavorsky in a flashback she was telling me about.

Lynn: The telephone repairman's name was John Urenko.

Elizabeth: Enough of my intuition.

Dr. Corsini enters her office and closes the door. She speaks in a quiet hush, sitting at her desk.

Elizabeth: Something is terribly wrong with Dov and Esther. One of them is lying. My gut strongly suggests that it's Dov. He's not normal.

Meanwhile Dov and Esther are close to exiting the psychiatric ward. Dov stops near the bathrooms and takes a stance, standing with his feet apart.

Dov: Excuse me, honey. I have to call the office. Why don't you use the bathroom before we drive home? We'll smoke a joint when we get back to the house.

Esther smiles and enters the women's bathroom. Dov takes out his cell phone and dials.

Dov: Hello, Kavorsky. Did you insert the bug? Yes...Excellent!

29

WHITE HOUSE GARDENS

President Macorley and Jason Smithies walk together in the White House Garden. Cain observes them through an inside window.

Cain: I wonder what they're talking about. I don't see why the president doesn't confide exclusively in me. I'm much brighter than Smithies and more ruthless. He isn't cruel enough, which is not acceptable in politics.

President Macorley: You know, Jason, God did not create one useless thing in this world.

Smithies: I didn't know you were a believer, Mr. President.

President Macorley: I'm not.

Smithies: You lost me.

President Macorley: Do you believe in angels, Jason?

Smithies is surprised by the president's question.

Smithies: Huh?

President Macorley: I just read this sparkling quote of Michelangelo. When they asked him how he produced such beautiful sculptures, he replied, "I saw an angel trapped inside the marble, and I carved to set her free."

Smithies: Don't go religious on me, Mr. President.

The president ignores the inference.

President Macorley: Is Code Name Daniel in place?

Smithies: Yes, it is. When enacted the Europeans will have no choice but to recognize you as the leader of the free world.

President Macorley: Good work, Jason. Once we get through Code Name Daniel, we'll be able to initiate Gog and Magog and bring humanity to its knees. The entire global community of nations will beg for my leadership to save the planet.

Smithies: One problem. I don't trust either one of the Corsini sisters. They could gum up Code Name Daniel.

President Macorley: Let me show you how we get rid of female pests. You see that beautiful monarch butterfly on the flower. Watch what happens.

Smithies watches. The president removes his jacket and swats the butterfly, crippling its wings. He then laughs.

President Macorley: God would never approve of maliciously hurting any of his creatures, like I just did. You see what I think of God.

The president belly laughs. Jason shivers at what just transpired. Cain is watching and smiling.

30

HALLUCINOGEN

Daniela props her feet on the desk in her FBI laboratory office, surrounded by low-temperature freezers, analytical weighing balances, ultra centrifuges, and various high-tech instruments. A state-of-the-art mass spectrometer occupies the center of the thousand-square-foot space.

Daniela's ten-by-ten cubicle is in the back of the lab. The office has government-issued metal furniture consisting of a desk, file cabinet, and a bookcase. Abel is with her and remains silent while she browses files in her computer. She looks up at Abel.

Daniela: No record of a man called Leamas working at the FBI. You say this happened when you were admitted to the FBI three years ago, when Leamas proctored the exam?

Abel: Yes.

Daniela: People do have aliases in the FBI. Perhaps you heard his name wrong.

Abel thinks back to Leamas as his fourth grade teacher and his cheating on the geography test.

Abel: No! I'm absolutely sure that Leamas was his name.

Daniela: My niece, Sophia, will be here with her mother in about five minutes. I'd like you to take her to lunch while I discuss some private business matters with my sister.

Abel seems reluctant.

Abel: I have a ton of work to catch up on. I'd like to oblige, but…

Daniela: It's not a request, Abel. Besides, it will do you good to take a break. You might even enjoy it. My niece is gorgeous, and she's smarter than both her mother and me. She just completed medical school and is back in the capital to do her internship and then a residency in obstetrics at Washington Central Hospital. Her mother is a psychiatrist at the same hospital.

Elizabeth and Sophia walk past an oil painting of Marshall. The painting frame reads Marshall Lamster, FBI Director. Elizabeth naughtily smiles at the painting. They walk to an open elevator and take it to the basement. They enter Daniela's laboratory and walk into the office without knocking.

Elizabeth: Your aunt still dwells in this dungeon.

Daniela gets up and gives Sophia a great big hug and kisses her sister.

Daniela: I'm so happy to see you, Sophia. I can't say that about your mother. Abel, this is my sister the shrink, Dr. Elizabeth Corsini, and this is my pride and joy, my niece, Sophia, the number one ranking student in her medical class.

Sophia: You're embarrassing me, Auntie.

Abel can't take his eyes off Sophia.

Abel: It's a pleasure to meet you both.

Daniela: Abel is going to take Sophia to lunch while you and I, Lizzie, have that heart-to-heart talk.

Sophia: I'd be delighted.

Daniela: Why not go to Sophia's favorite haunt, the Ritz Carlton? Abel, put the tab on my expense account. What good is being the associate FBI director and working your balls off, if you can't treat your favorite niece to a welcome home lunch?

Elizabeth: Don't mind your aunt's crude language, Sophia. I've given up trying to reform her.

Sophia: I love Auntie's character. Is the Ritz okay with you, Abel? It is my favorite place.

Abel: Yes, everything except for who is picking up the check for lunch. I insist on paying.

Elizabeth: Chivalry still exists in this corrupt town. I'll see you later, darling. Bye, Abel. My intuition tells me that I'll be seeing more of you.

Daniela: You and your intuition. You've been talking about your smarts since we were kids. Put a damper on it.

Sophia kisses her mother and aunt, and heads out with Abel. Abel takes Sophia's hand outside the FBI, and there's immediate electricity between them. They both notice the warm energy in their palms and smile at each other.

Daniela: How's the shrink business?

Elizabeth: Tolerable, Daniela. Tolerable.

Daniela: Now, what's all the hurry about this patient of yours?

Elizabeth: I have an unusual situation. Her name is Esther Hirsch. She's made a Guinness record book recovery from a psychotic episode. At first my diagnosis was bipolar disorder, but my intuition told me it was a drug-induced psychosis. Esther claims she doesn't take drugs, but her creepy husband, Dov, begs to differ.

Daniela: And your so-called intuition tells you that the husband is lying. Correct?

Elizabeth: I'm not sure on this one. The whole situation is fishy, but I definitely suspect foul play by the husband.

Daniela: Let's get a cup of coffee in the FBI's finest. I'll even spring for a croissant. If we're lucky, they'll still be some uneaten by the vultures around this joint.

Elizabeth: Your office is dingier than mine. Yes, let's get the fuck out of here.

Daniela: Why, sis! How unbecoming for a lady.

The sisters laugh and head for the elevator up to the first floor. As they sit in the cafeteria and nibble on their croissants, they fail to notice a burly man, Frank Kavorsky, observing them from a corner table.

Daniela: Have you checked out all the common mood-altering drugs that could induce psychosis?

Elizabeth: That's the first thing I did. Nothing shows up in Esther's blood.

Daniela: Maybe we should check her blood here at the FBI. She doesn't have to know.

Elizabeth: Well, I would obtain her consent.

Daniela: Sounds just like you. Morally correct Lizzie. Except with men, of course.

Thoughts are racing around in Elizabeth's brain. How could Daniela have found out about her affair with Marshall?

Elizabeth: Marshall told you. I'm so sorry, Dannie.

Daniela: Marshall didn't tell me shit. You forget. I'm more of a slut than you. I see in you what's already inside of me.

Elizabeth: If it's any consolation, it was a short-lived fling. I broke it off.

Daniela: You've been besting me since we were kids. And you've done it again with my man, Marshall. If it weren't for Mom and Dad and my promise to protect you, I don't know if I could love you as much as I damn well do.

Elizabeth begins to bawl.

Elizabeth: I'm so sorry, Dannie. I don't ever want to hurt you. Please forgive me.

Daniela sees the tears in Elizabeth's eyes.

Daniela: That's another thing that always bothered me when we were kids. You could always get to me with those tears. All my anger would melt seeing you bawling, and it still does now. OK, Lizzie, you're forgiven. But if you're going to hurt me, let me know ahead of time. I hate these fucking surprises you pull on me.

Elizabeth: Promise.

Elizabeth dries her eyes and gets right to the point.

Elizabeth: Are there any hallucinogens that can't be detected in the blood or saliva?

Daniela thinks to herself. Why not tell her.

Daniela: I guess I can share. I wouldn't be breaching any security issues, because the CIA has openly disclosed information on these hallucinogens to the press.

Elizabeth: Funny, but Dov mentioned the CIA in a slip of the tongue.

Daniela: There are two new powerful hallucinogens. The Chinese have developed them for military purposes. The drug pharmacology is based upon mescaline, the Native American peyote. Only these new chemically synthesized hallucinogens are one hundred times more potent than peyote. If you ingest even the tiniest amount of these compounds, you will hear voices that command you to kill yourself. Not unlike the voices bipolar and schizophrenic patients hear.

Elizabeth is obviously stunned at Daniela's disclosure.

Elizabeth: Oh, my God! That's exactly what happened to Esther. That son of a bitch, Dov. I've never heard of mind alteration to the degree you're describing.

Daniela: Here at the FBI, we've chemically synthesized these hallucinogen compounds, but we can't detect them in the bloodstream because only miniscule amounts are needed for the hallucinogenic effect.

Elizabeth: Who in the United States has these peyote hallucinogens?

Daniela: Besides the FBI? The CIA, of course. Let's go back to the lab.

Kavorsky continues to observe them, as they head back to Daniela's office. On the way, Elizabeth asks for a special favor.

Daniela: I know that look. You want something from me that will make me uncomfortable.

Elizabeth: You know me so well. Do you still have contacts at the CIA?

Daniela: This better be good, Lizzie. I tread lightly when I ask for favors from the CIA.

Elizabeth: I want to know if a man named Frank Kavorsky is CIA. And the same for Dov Hirsch.

They return to the office. Daniela picks up her phone and dials.

Daniela: Jenny, can you run a check on a Dov Hirsch and a Frank Kavorsky?

Jennifer lays down the phone and hits the computer keyboard. Meanwhile, the sisters keep talking.

Elizabeth: Have you ever heard of Code Name Daniel?

Daniela: Can't say that I have.

Jennifer speaks.

Jennifer: Negative on Hirsch. Positive on Kavorsky. He's the new CIA liaison to the White House. Is that it?

Daniela: Code Name Daniel. Is it a CIA operation?

Momentary silence. Jennifer is frowning, unseen on her end of the conversation.

Jennifer: You know better than to ask about CIA operations.

Daniela: Can you tell me anything?

Jennifer: Off limits, kiddo.

Jennifer abruptly hangs up the phone, without saying goodbye.

Daniela: Jennifer can be pretty stoic, but it sounds like Code Name Daniel is a CIA operation.

Elizabeth: From what Esther told me, it's also a secret White House operation. But it makes no sense. Even if Dov works at the EPA and is linked to the CIA, how and why is Esther being targeted? One more question, Dannie.

Daniela: You're pushing it, Lizzie. I feel the branches of our family tree shaking.

Elizabeth laughs.

Elizabeth: Is it possible that your hallucinogen would show up in detectable amounts in a patient that was on another mind-altering drug?

Daniela: I know where this is going. Like lithium for instance.

Elizabeth: Exactly! Lithium can raise the concentration of hallucinogens in the bloodstream.

Daniela: Alright, Lizzie. You were always the scholastic genius in the family. I'll see what I can do. Let me know when you can send over a sample of Esther's blood.

Elizabeth: It's great to have Sophia home.

Daniela: Yes. And my intuition, which I barely exercise because yours always dominates, tells me that Sophia and Abel will hit it off.

Elizabeth: What do you know about this young man?

Daniela: A model FBI agent. Under my tutelage he'll go far. I'm his mentor, and I'm grooming him. He seems to have fine qualities, and unlike me, is humble. The only weird thing was today when he asked me about an ageless man named Leamas, who admitted him into the FBI about three years ago. According to FBI records, Leamas doesn't exist. I have to check further on this, as this character Leamas is bothering me too.

Elizabeth: I'm glad I'm not the only one seeing supernatural beings.

Daniela immediately raises her voice.

Daniela: What do you mean?

Elizabeth: I might as well tell you. We share everything. Right, sis?

Daniela hesitates. She knows the sisters keep secrets from each other.

Daniela: Of course. Don't keep me in suspense.

Elizabeth: The other day while driving to work, I swear I saw angels in front of me.

Jealousy is written all over Daniela's face. Her defenses take over.

Daniela: Shit! You're out of your fucking mind, Lizzie. Get the hell out of here before I incarcerate you.

The sisters hug and kiss. Elizabeth departs. Daniela's true feelings come out.

Daniela: Angels! Could it be true? Damn that Lizzie. I haven't seen shit, and I fucking pray every night to Jesus.

31

SOPHIA

Abel and Sophia are sitting on a couch in the Ritz Carlton Hotel drinking freshly juiced custom-made strawberry mango margaritas made from Silver Patron tequila, Grand Marnier, and frozen limeade, and then sweetened with stevia in place of sugar. They are working on their second round while nibbling on cashews and a chicken quesadilla.

Sophia is strikingly beautiful at five feet seven inches. Her skin is olive and her eyes emerald green. Her jet-black hair is freely swaying, and she sparkles as she smiles. Her voice gives off the most rapturous philharmonic sound, and her fragrance is incredibly stimulating to Abel's sexual organs. The air coming out of her nostrils has the most delightful aroma, and her skin is soft and cuddly like an infant. She is the epitome of perfection.

Sophia is every man's dream girl. She's not self-centered or over the top. Her defenses are refreshingly invisible, while her conversation is both engaging and stimulating. Best of all she makes you feel truly alive and important.

Abel: I've been looking for you all my thirty-three years.

Sophia laughs.

Sophia: That can't be, Abel. I'm only twenty-nine.

Abel: You take my breath away. And to think that I told your aunt that I was too busy to take you to lunch. I'm ready to give up work altogether and spend all my time with you.

Sophia: I have a career. It's just beginning. I've never had time for romance, and I can't start now.

Abel: Surely you must have had multiple suitors pursuing you.

Sophia: They all wanted to take me to bed.

Abel: I don't! I want to marry you.

Sophia: I know your type. I marry you and then you never let me out of bed.

Abel laughs.

Abel: And it doesn't bother me that you're smarter than me. My ego can take it.

Sophia: I haven't felt so good and relaxed in years, but next week I start my internship. Then all bets are off.

Abel: It sounds like you could have gone anywhere and had your pick of internships and obstetric residencies.

Sophia: I needed to be with my mother. I never knew my father, nor do I desire to know who he is, although my mother wanted to tell me. My mother has unselfishly sacrificed. She means everything to me.

Abel: My parents had me when they were in their golden years, and they have become religious. They're Orthodox Jews and attend the Chabad Lubavitch Center in Brooklyn. I hardly get to see them.

Sophia: And what would they say if they knew that their son was making overtures of love to a nice gentile girl?

Abel: Oy veh!

Sophia: There's a translation for oy veh in Italian. It means, "no way."

Abel: They would disown me. I wouldn't be their son. Unless...

Sophia: Unless what?

Abel: Unless this shiksa named Sophia became Jewish through an Orthodox conversion.

Sophia: What's a shiksa?

Abel: Boy, you really have led a sheltered Catholic life. A shiksa is a non-Jewish woman desired by a Jewish man.

Sophia: I'm not totally ignorant. I know I would have to study Torah and go to the mikvah. I kind of like that you're so upfront and transparent, Abel. It's refreshing.

Abel: Jewish men make good husbands—at least they used to. They don't stray. And they don't drink to get drunk. I stereotype when it's to my benefit.

Sophia: Do you believe in God? I heard that only about thirty percent of Jews believe. And you are an FBI agent now, and unlike your parents you don't lead a religious life.

Abel: I keep breaking the Ten Commandments, but I do believe and trust in and love the Creator.

Sophia: Would you lie to me, Abel?

Abel is taken back. Of course, he would lie.

Abel: Wow! Where did that come from?

Sophia: God values truth in one's heart most of all.

Abel: If I said no, I'd be lying that I wouldn't lie. It's the nature of my job. In truth I would have to lie to you.

Sophia: Thanks for the honesty. But lying is a deal breaker for marriage. Let's just have fun and enjoy.

Abel: And now I have a question for you, Sophia.

Sophia: Uh-oh! I opened up a can of worms.

Abel: If I told you something that no one else knows except my contacts, would you keep it confidential? You especially couldn't tell your aunt, as it would endanger my life. Not even your mother. Could you do that? If you could then I would never have to lie to you.

Sophia is perplexed. She thinks long and hard.

Sophia: Yes, I could keep that kind of secret.

Abel: Then someday I'll tell you. The truth is that I can't tell you now because then your life would be in danger. There would be one secret between us, at least for the time being. I've never said what I just said to anyone.

Sophia: For a first date, this conversation has all of a sudden gotten very heavy. Do you have anything to lighten the mood?

Abel: Did you just say first date? Does this mean you'll see me again?

Sophia: Yes, I want to. I really want to.

Abel pulls out a crumpled piece of paper from his wallet.

Abel: I wrote this short poem when I was twelve. I've been waiting to read it to the girl I actually called Sophia in the poem.

> The mist rose off the water white
> The sun did shine with all its might
> A sound of music in the tree
> Was whispering gently, I love thee
> Oh, Sophia, darling, you are mine
> In my heart, until the end of time.

Sophia: It's beautiful, Abel. Can I have it?

Abel: You're my soul mate. The poem belongs to you.

Their lips meet in tenderness and in love.

32

CAR ACCIDENT

Esther speeds down city streets.

Esther:

(deep echo voice)
Now's your chance, Esther.
Do it now…now…now.
End it now…now…now.

Esther panics in her normal voice.

Esther:

(normal voice, crying)
I can't stand it.
Help me! Please help me!
I need help.

E sther turns down the wrong way on a one-way street into oncoming traffic. Her car hits one car, then a second. Esther's car folds like an accordion, as an ambulance and police car rush to the scene. Esther is pulled out, and seems miraculously okay. She is taken to Washington Central Hospital.

Dr. Corsini rushes in, speaks to a nurse, and is directed to a curtained area where Esther is lying on a hospital gurney with an intravenous feed. Her eyes squint open when Dr. Corsini gently touches her shoulder.

Elizabeth: I just heard about the car crash and hurried right over.

Esther: Hello, Dr. Corsini.

Elizabeth: You're going to be fine, Esther. God is watching over you.

Esther: You have to believe me. I never did anything like this before.

Elizabeth: I believe you, but you need to tell me what happened before you left for work this morning.

Esther snivels.

Esther: Nothing. Dov gave me my usual glass of orange juice with an English muffin.

Elizabeth: Esther, we've drawn your blood, and I'd like to send it over to the FBI for analysis.

Esther: The FBI! Why? What's wrong? What did I do?

Elizabeth: Just trust me and sign this paper.

Esther: What does it say?

Elizabeth: That you voluntarily agree to be committed to the psychiatric ward.

Esther: I trust you, Dr. Corsini, but I have such anxiety when the outside door locks, and I'm trapped inside. Anytime that door opens, I want to make a mad dash to escape out of the ward. I feel like I'm in prison.

Elizabeth: You won't be a real patient. We'll just be pretending, so we can keep you safe. You'll even be able to leave the psychiatric ward with me on my outings, as long as we know there is no danger.

Esther smiles and signs the admission paper in front of her. She hands it back to Dr. Corsini.

Dr. Corsini doesn't realize that Kavorsky is planning to set up a surveillance van close to the hospital, so that he can observe her comings and goings.

Elizabeth: Good girl. I'll make the arrangements for admission into psychiatry. Bye, Esther. I'll see you soon.

Esther: Bye, Dr. Corsini. And thank you.

Dr. Corsini nods and then returns to her office. She picks up the phone and dials.

Elizabeth: Hello, Daniela. Esther has been in a car crash. Emergency services drew her blood, and I'll send it over to the FBI immediately for analysis. Can you contact the DC police and find out if they are investigating the accident? You can…thanks.

33

PANDAS

Dov and Kavorsky are standing in front of the Washington Zoo special exhibit. Both panda bears are in view and are entertaining the crowd.

Kavorsky: Chinese pandas. What's the matter? We can't afford our own?

Dov: Frank, I don't trust that bitch, Dr. Corsini. She got Esther admitted again.

Kavorsky: Don't worry. I have her phone bugged, and the van will be in place today. Corsini is small potatoes. Code Name Daniel has finally been officially activated. It's been a long time in coming. My contact in the White House doesn't know what the fuck he's doing.

Dov: Can you tell me who's heading up the operation?

Kavorsky: I don't know. Nor do I care to know. It's safer not to ask too many questions when you work for the CIA.

Dov: Did you hear the news?

Kavorsky: Yeah! The president got a peace deal in the Middle East between the Israelis and Palestinians.

Dov: Another crowning achievement for the leader of the free world.

Kavorsky: You have to expect the unexpected in this life. Why do I get the feeling that there are some surprises coming down the road? Let's be extra careful on this one, Dov. Trust no one.

Dov: What about you, Frank? Would you double-cross me?

Kavorsky: Are you kidding me? I take my secrets to the grave. You and I are like blood brothers.

Dov: Can I slit your throat to seal our pact?

Kavorsky squirms. Dov laughs.

Dov: Hey! Lighten up. It was only a figure of speech.

Kavorsky tries to smile but can only frown.

Kavorsky: Honor among thieves, Dov?

Dov: More like, It's better that your buddy dies and you survive if you're both in a foxhole under fire.

Kavorsky: You got the expression wrong. It's, "There are no atheists in foxholes."

Dov: And we're both atheists. Aren't we, Frank?

Kavorsky: Remember what Tonto said to the Lone Ranger. Fuck you, Ke-mo sah-bee. You're on your own, white man. Me, Indian, me safe. You, dead man.

This time it's Dov's turn to squirm.

Dov: Okay, enough with the jokes. Let's bury the hatchet. I'll pledge my loyalty to you if you'll do likewise, Frank.

Kavorsky: Agreed. Let's shake on it.

Both men try to get the best of each other, as they shake hands with all their strength. But it's a standoff. They both half-heartedly laugh, and go their separate ways.

34

THREATS

Jason Smithies is talking to Daniela in his White House office.

Smithies: Have you got it under control, Daniela?

Daniela wants to tell Smithies to go fuck himself, but knows she can't do that.

Daniela: Yes.

Smithies: I wouldn't want to see anybody get hurt. Especially, family.

Daniela feels enraged.

Daniela: Is that a threat?

Smithies: Just do your job.

Daniela: I will. But you keep your goons away.

Meanwhile Elizabeth is back in her office when a call comes in from Dov. Elizabeth reluctantly picks up the phone.

Dov: You had better release my wife, Corsini.

Elizabeth: Is that a threat, Dov?

Dov: Take it any way you fucking like.

Dov slams down the receiver. Elizabeth mutters to herself.

Elizabeth: What a shithead.

A second phone call comes in. It's Daniela.

Daniela: Hello, Lizzie. Can we meet at the Washington Monument in an hour? It's safer to talk in public.

Tourists mill about, shoot photos, and ride the elevator to the top of the monument. Daniela greets Elizabeth.

Daniela: I made contact with Detective Larson of the DC police. I'm afraid it's bad. They found marijuana and LSD inside Esther's night table. It gets worse.

Elizabeth: Son of a bitch. How did they get a warrant so quickly to search her house? It's a setup.

Daniela: They also found an ounce of cocaine. The Drug Enforcement Agency is now fully involved and is threatening to charge her with illegal possession.

Elizabeth: Shit! Esther's being framed. We need those lab results. You have to find the hallucinogen.

Daniela: I'll do my best. Go back to the hospital, and I'll be back to you within two hours. And, sis, say a prayer.

The Corsini sisters depart for their offices.

35

CONFRONTATION

The intercom buzzes in Dr. Corsini's office.

Lynn: Mr. Hirsch is here to see you.

Dr. Corsini tenses up.

Elizabeth: Send him in, Lynn.

Dov enters and immediately displays his temper. He waves his fist at Dr. Corsini. His neck and face are beet red. The angels Michael and Gabriel appear, but are invisible to Dov and Dr. Corsini.

Dov: You bitch. You have no goddamn right to commit my wife to your nut ward.

Elizabeth: My nut ward is where you belong.

Dov lunges toward Dr. Corsini, but is pushed back into the chair by an invisible force. It is Michael who forces him back. Dov appears bewildered and frightened and then mumbles.

Dov: What the fuck! What was what?

Dr. Corsini senses the confusion but is also ignorant of what just transpired. Dov recovers his composure and restrains himself from attacking Dr. Corsini. He stands and waves his arms around his body in a defensive posture, trying to hold his ground.

Dov: You have no idea who you're dealing with. I could have you squashed in a fucking heartbeat.

Dr. Corsini, too, gets out of her seat, comes around the table, and stands toe to toe with Dov, showing no fear.

Elizabeth: Like you tried to do with Esther.

Dov laughs nervously and holds his hand up to strike Dr. Corsini, but once again he is propelled backward, almost tripping. He is stunned but is able to maintain his balance. He now sits down calmly but doesn't respond to Dr. Corsini's accusation.

Dov: I could kill you right now. But I enjoy your pushing my buttons. It makes the game all the more interesting.

This time Dr. Corsini gets angry. She points her finger at Dov and raises her voice.

Elizabeth: This is no game. You're a snake whose rattling days are over.

Dr. Corsini glares at him.

Dov: I'd be shitting my pants if I were you. I have powerful friends.

Elizabeth: To hell with you and your friends.

Dov: I happen to know the law on patient rights. My wife signed in voluntarily. That means she can leave in seventy-two hours if she signs an "intent to leave" paper.

Elizabeth: What makes you think she'll do that? I've told her that you want to harm her.

Dov cannot control his anger. He makes one last attempt to grab her. Once again he is pushed back into his seat, trembling. This time, however, Dr. Corsini sees two blurry figures with folded wings. Both Dr. Corsini and Dov are aghast with surprise.

Dov: Is this room rigged with ghosts? Esther has big problems. Without my help she'll be rotting in a prison cell, indefinitely.

Elizabeth: Get out of here, Mr. Hirsch, or I'll have you escorted out. You're a scumbag, and you don't deserve Esther.

Dov: So long, psycho lady. I know where you live, and I'm going to set fire to your apartment with you and your ugly mutt in it.

Dov exits. Dr. Corsini smiles.

Elizabeth: I have two guardian angels protecting me.

The phone rings. It's Daniela.

Elizabeth: Hello, Dannie.

Daniela speaks rapidly into her phone.

Daniela: Hello, Lizzie. The Air and Space Museum at the Smithsonian. It's important.

Kavorsky is listening in his surveillance van to Dr. Corsini's conversation with Daniela. Dov enters the truck.

Kavorsky: This might be a good time to scare her off. There she is. She's heading for the Air and Space Museum.

Dov: I'm on her.

Dov puts on his disguise, departs the van, and hails a cab to the Smithsonian.

Michael and Gabriel change into human form and hail their own cab. They converse in the back seat.

Gabriel: Do you have any money?

Michael: I come prepared for all contingencies. Driver, follow that yellow taxi just ahead.

They close the glass partition, so the driver cannot hear their conversation.

Gabriel: That Dov is a nasty sort. He has no scruples.

Michael: He's very dangerous, and I'm afraid he means harm to the good doctor. We'll have to stop him.

Gabriel: Fear not, Michael. I shall do what Esau's angel did to Jacob while they were wrestling.

Michael: Oh, you mean dislocate his hip. Remember, it was Jacob who defeated the angel. Jacob fought on, even with a dislocated hip.

Gabriel: I promise. All will be well.

Michael: Kavorsky meant for Dov only to scare the doctor, but Dov is so enraged that he means to kill her.

Gabriel: He reminds me of Leamas, a sociopath devoid of feeling.

Michael: Humans don't really know angels. They don't realize that God gave us emotions.

Gabriel: We angels also are made in God's image.

36

AIR AND SPACE MUSEUM

Daniela and Elizabeth meet up at the museum. A crowd of visitors are browsing around the exhibits.

They don't see a strange-looking man observing them. He is bundled up with a coat and scarf, which is unusual since it is not cold outside. He wears a Scottish hat and sports a full gray, scraggly beard. You can't see his sky-blue eyes due to the sunglasses he wears.

Daniela: Sorry to drag you out, but it's safer to talk in a crowd. We barely saw it on the mass spectrometer. It's definitely the Chinese peyote hallucinogen.

Elizabeth: Oh, Daniela, what a relief. That prick Dov Hirsch was just in my office threatening me.

Daniela: I'll have him picked up, and we'll read him the riot act. That will keep you safe for a while, but we can't hold him very long.

Elizabeth: Be careful, Dannie. Dov is a sociopath.

Daniela: Geez! We've got so many whackos in this town. I'll call Detective Larson and fill him in.

Elizabeth: Thanks, Dannie. Finding the peyote drug should help clear Esther from the drug charges, and put the focus of the investigation on Dov.

Daniela: I hope this will give you the time you need with Esther to figure out Code Name Daniel.

Elizabeth: I can't for the life of me decipher Esther's dream.

Daniela: You're a shrink, sis. It will come to you. By the way Marshall was pissed as hell on learning that the CIA might be running still another rogue operation. He used an analogy that cracked me up.

Elizabeth: Oh yeah, what was that? I could use a laugh.

Daniela: He compared the FBI to the CIA. He said the FBI was like horse manure that is spread thinly on the soil for farming. The manure doesn't smell when used in this productive way. But if you gather up all the manure on the farm and put it in a large pile, you have the CIA. It looks like shit, it smells like shit, and it is shit.

Elizabeth laughs.

Elizabeth: You made my day. Give my best to the director.

Daniela: Keep the faith, Lizzie. I've got to get back to the FBI. I'll talk to you later.

Daniela leaves. She is followed by the strange-looking man with the Scottish cap, who waits outside. Elizabeth spends several minutes in the museum looking at the airplanes on display.

She then exits the museum and walks leisurely on the Smithsonian Mall. Archangel Michael walks invisibly beside her. About twenty-five yards behind her walks the strange-looking man with the gray beard and sunglasses under his Scottish cap. He has a knife hidden under his coat sleeve and is intent on killing her within the next few minutes.

The man breaks into a marathon walk. When he is less than ten yards away, he removes his knife from his coat sleeve. Suddenly Gabriel, in human form, comes out of nowhere on a Schwinn racing bike, which he purposely loses control of. The bike plows into the man at high speed and knocks him over.

The man twists his ankle and dislocates his hip as he falls to the ground. Gabriel gets off his bike and disappears into the crowd before anyone notices. He becomes invisible.

Everyone around is looking at the man lying on the ground in obvious pain, clutching at his hip. Elizabeth turns around to see what's going on, hearing the commotion behind her. As she turns she sees a man about thirty with piercing black eyes and jet-black hair helping the strange-looking man up onto his feet.

The thirtyish man firmly grabs the fallen man's hip and forces it back into its socket. The bearded man feels immediate relief and thanks the handsome stranger who alleviated his pain.

Dov: Who are you, kind stranger?

Leamas: Why I'm the Devil, of course.

Dov, still in shock from the fall, hurriedly limps away, like a deformed man walking on a peg leg. Satan turns back to see Elizabeth in the distance. He uses all his eye strength to faintly make out an outline of two forms walking on either side of her. He correctly surmises that they are God's angels, Michael and Gabriel.

Satan: My time will come. I'll have the last laugh.

Elizabeth hails a taxi, leaving Michael and Gabriel alone on the Mall.

Gabriel: I feel no pity for Dov. He has no conscience and would have committed murder if I hadn't stopped him.

Michael: Yes, sometimes good force is necessary to combat evil force. Dov is fortunate that you only maimed him. You could just as easily have killed him.

Gabriel: The only one I want to kill is Satan.

37

GENETICS

Lynn buzzes the intercom.

Lynn: Dr. Corsini, Esther Hirsch is with me and is anxious to see you.

Elizabeth: Send her in.

Esther: Dr. Corsini, I'm afraid.

Elizabeth: You're safe now, Esther. I suspect it was Dov who tried to kill you. He slipped something into your orange juice yesterday morning, causing your car accident.

Esther: Well, it's Dov who I want to talk to you about.

Elizabeth: Let's go out. I feel cooped up, and anyway I need to run an errand. I have to get a new gold chain for my cross. We Catholics take our religion seriously.

They are driving in Dr. Corsini's car. Esther has a memory flash.

* * *

Esther is drinking her orange juice. Dov approaches and asks her for his DNA analysis. He is agitated and hostile.

Dov: Where the fuck is it?

Esther: I swear! I gave you your DNA report.

Dov: You're a fucking liar.

* * *

Esther: He went on a rampage, running all over the house, continually cursing, opening drawers, and throwing my collectibles on the floor. He then ran over to me and grabbed my wrist, squeezing tightly until I pleaded for mercy from the pain.

* * *

You're hurting me, Dov. Please let go. I don't have your genetics analysis.

Dov: You lying bitch.

* * *

Esther: I clenched the fist of my free hand and struck Dov in the face with all my strength. He winced in pain and let go of my wrist. He then slapped me hard on the cheek and left the house in a rage. This is not the man I married.

Elizabeth: I'm afraid it is. Do you have Dov's DNA records?

Esther: Yes, I retrieved Dov's and my DNA analyses from a secret place in the house and stuck the reports in my purse this morning.

Elizabeth: Go on.

Esther: Well, my science background finally came in handy. Before I had breakfast, I compared Dov's and my brother's DNA. One of the genetic markers is different. How can this be, according to your previous explanation to me?

Dr. Corsini pulls into a parking lot of a strip mall in front of the Capital Jewelry Exchange. Esther and Dr. Corsini enter the building. They continue talking.

Elizabeth: Did your brother and Dov both do the sixty-seven genetic markers on their YDNA?

Esther: Yes, I upgraded to the full analysis on both.

Elizabeth: Which is the genetic marker in question?

Esther: Marker sixty-six.

They pass rows of small jewelry booths full of diamonds, rings set with precious stones, watches, earrings, necklaces, pins, and bracelets. They arrive at a booth, where an elderly bald man is busy polishing a ring.

Elizabeth: Hi, Angelo.

Angelo turns and smiles and reaches over the counter to clasp Dr. Corsini's hands.

Angelo: Elizabeth. How are you?

He turns toward Esther.

Angelo: My favorite psychiatrist. Your name, beautiful lady?

Esther: Esther.

Angelo: A wonderful Italian name. Any repairs, Doc?

Elizabeth: A battery for my watch.

Angelo: I'll be right back.

Angelo leaves the booth and walks down the aisle to a jewelry repair booth. Esther digs into her purse and hands Dr. Corsini two pieces of paper. Dr. Corsini lays both papers on Angelo's counter.

Elizabeth: Yes, you're right. Your brother and Dov have different nucleic acid sequences on the YDNA at marker sixty-six when they should be identical. If you look at the asterisk at the bottom of the page, the company states that this is a genetic anomaly not seen in their database of two-hundred thousand submissions.

Esther: This is why Dov was so anxious to get his DNA analysis back.

Dr. Corsini further examines Dov's marker sixty-six sequence.

Elizabeth: This is scary. If you look at the first letter only of each amino acid that corresponds to every three nucleotide bases of the fifteen bases at marker sixty-six, you get s–a–t–a–n.

Esther: Spelling "Satan." Dr. Corsini, thank God for your genetics background.

Elizabeth: Well, I cheated a bit, as we don't know where the nucleic acid sequences actually begin in this type of analysis. Even so there must be some mistake. Someone is playing a practical joke on us.

Esther: But it's here in black and white.

Elizabeth: We've opened up a can of worms. Who would believe such wild claims of Satan in the DNA? Besides, Satan doesn't exist.

Esther: I'm not so sure about that. The other night Dov was mumbling in his sleep. He kept saying, "Thanks for your help, Devil."

Angelo returns with Dr. Corsini's watch.

Angelo: Let me polish it up for you.

Angelo turns on the buffing machine and polishes the band of the watch.

Esther: Dr. Corsini, I'm terrified. I've been having it every night.

Elizabeth: Your nightmare?

Esther: Yes. It used to be once a week, and now it's more often. The beast with the ten horns and the little horn is becoming more terrifying.

Angelo interrupts the conversation.

Angelo: Here's your watch. Anything else?

Elizabeth: My chain broke on my necklace.

Angelo reaches for a tray of gold chains.

Angelo: This would be perfect for your gold cross.

He puts the chain through her cross and then places the necklace around her neck.

Elizabeth: Thanks, Angelo. It's beautiful.

Angelo: On the house.

Elizabeth: I couldn't. This is expensive. I need to pay you.

Angelo: I'm an old man who doesn't get too many opportunities to see two beautiful women. It's your gift for coming, Elizabeth.

Elizabeth: You're the sweetest man I know. If only I were fifteen years older. Good-bye, Angelo. And bless you.

They leave Angelo and walk back to the car. Once inside, Dr. Corsini shares her thoughts.

Elizabeth: I have a hunch about your dream, which we can discuss back on the ward. I need to contact a friend of mine to see if she can help with this genetic anomaly that you've discovered at marker sixty-six.

38

MUFFIN

Dr. Corsini turns the lock on her apartment door. She enters and finds the entire place ransacked. Her white Maltese, Muffin, barks when he sees her. Someone has tied Muffin to the wooden leg of the couch with a thin rope. Nobody appears to be in the apartment. But then a gray-bearded man dressed in a UPS uniform comes up behind Dr. Corsini and forcefully pushes her down on the living room carpet. She gets up on one knee and looks up, trying to remember where she has seen this familiar strange man. He points his gun at her. Muffin growls.

The angel Gabriel appears in the room unseen. Before he can stop the bearded man, Muffin gets loose and immediately jumps high in the air at the bearded man's arm. The dog bites the man's wrist, just as he fires the gun.

Gabriel observes the bullet veering away from Dr. Corsini. The man screams in pain and also watches the bullet go astray and miss its intended target. He swears and runs out of the apartment limping.

JERRY POLLOCK

An invisible Gabriel pats Muffin, while Dr. Corsini catches her breath. She sits on the couch, and Muffin jumps up and licks her face.

Elizabeth: Oh, Muffin! You're my hero. That's the same man. I recognized him. It's Dov in disguise and he's limping. Dov was the one on the Smithsonian Mall who fell down when a bicycle hit him. Why is he trying to kill me?

144

39

CONFESSION

Daniela is in the Cathedral of St. Matthew confessing her sins to the priest.

Priest: Yes, my child.

Daniela: I have sinned, Father.

Priest: What have you done, Daniela?

Daniela: I've not been truthful with my sister. I'm in love with a married man. And I drink too much.

Priest: You need to cleanse yourself. Say ten Hail Marys and pray to Jesus for forgiveness. He will know what's in your heart.

Daniela departs the church and heads for the Four Seasons lounge. She orders two Macallan 12 scotches and sips her drink, waiting for Elizabeth to arrive.

Daniela: So much for my Hail Marys.

She crosses her heart and then glances heavenward. Elizabeth waves.

Daniela: I took the liberty of ordering. We've done damage control on the drugs in Esther's night table. There won't be any charges. Hey, now that I'm looking at you instead of that handsome bartender, you look a bit shaken up.

Elizabeth: I didn't sleep well last night

Daniela: What happened?

Elizabeth: Dov Hirsch apparently has a one in two hundred thousand genetic anomaly on his DNA. Never mind the science.

Daniela: I wish I had your smarts.

Elizabeth: I deciphered the genetic code at Dov's YDNA marker sixty-six, and the corresponding amino acid message spells the word "Satan."

Daniela: What the hell are you talking about? Have you gone bonkers?

She bangs her fist on the table.

Elizabeth: I'm not kidding, Dannie. This is not a random event. I have another request.

Daniela: Shit, Lizzie! You might as well join the FBI. Raise your right hand, and I'll swear you in. The Bureau is filled with loonies like you.

Elizabeth: You have to lean on Frank Kavorsky, Dov's contact at the White House.

Daniela: Are you nuts? I might as well light up a stick of dynamite and hold it until it goes off. For Christ's sake, Lizzie, Kavorsky is CIA.

Elizabeth: We need Kavorsky's blood sample so we can analyze his DNA markers; in particular, marker sixty-six.

Daniela: Fuck! You're talking about some evil genetic ancestry. You are nuts. I promise to visit you every day as a patient in your own psychiatric ward.

Elizabeth: Humor me.

Daniela downs her scotch in one gulp and then scolds her sister.

Daniela: It's ridiculous that such a logical person can be so stupid.

Elizabeth: This is serious, Dannie.

Daniela: I think I can get clearance from Marshall.

Elizabeth: I owe you.

Daniela: As I'm wasting my time talking to you, my wheels and oars are in motion. We need information as to what Kavorsky knows about the secret operation, Code Name Daniel. That's what I'm going to sell the director on, not your cockamamie theory about Satan.

Elizabeth: Be kind to me. You and I were taught by the nuns before we became corrupt women.

Daniela: The sisters were the only honest people I ever knew. OK, I'm getting you out of my sight before you dump more guilt on me.

Elizabeth: God, I love you, Dannie. Call Marshall as soon as I leave. Bye, sis.

Daniela is left alone in the bar. She covers her mouth with her blouse to muffle her scream.

Daniela: I hate myself.

She removes her cell phone from her purse, dials, and speaks.

Daniela: Hello, Smithies.

Elizabeth, meanwhile, arrives back in her office and finds Esther waiting for her.

Esther: I hope you don't mind. I've been too upset to eat. The dream is hounding me, and I'm frightened.

Elizabeth: You have to eat. I'm hungry too.

Dr. Corsini taps the intercom.

Elizabeth: Lynn, can you rustle us up some sandwiches? Esther, if my memory serves me right, the Book of Daniel in the Old Testament talks about a dream that Daniel had in ancient Babylon about a beast with ten large horns.

Esther: Was it like my nightmare?

Elizabeth: It was your exact dream. But we have to figure out how it is connected to Code Name Daniel. Someone in the CIA and possibly the White House is trying to kill you, because you somehow stumbled upon their plan through your dream. It all sounds so bizarre.

Just then the phone rings. It's Daniela.

Daniela: Lizzie, Dov Hirsch is dead. He was shot in the head. They found his body behind a trash can near the Washington Monument.

Elizabeth: Shit, Dannie! I have Esther here with me.

Esther: What is it?

Elizabeth: I was just told that Dov has been murdered.

Esther breaks into tears.

Esther: No! No! I know we had our problems, but he didn't deserve to die. I loved him.

Elizabeth: It's a cruel world, Esther. Your husband tried to murder you, and there's some kind of sick justice that it was he who was killed.

Esther: But why?

Elizabeth: I don't know.

Esther: Was it my fault?

Elizabeth: Of course not. I'll have Lynn take you to your room so you can get some rest. When you feel well enough, we'll continue with your dream. I'll get more details from Daniela, and you can make arrangements for Dov's funeral

Esther departs with Lynn and Dr. Corsini's phone rings. It's Daniela.

40

COCKROACHES

Daniela speaks rapidly into the phone. Elizabeth tells her to slow down.

Daniela: Meet me in the Smithsonian Museum of Natural History at the cockroach exhibit.

The sisters examine the cockroaches under one of the glass cabinets.

Daniela: Detestable little creatures. Did you know that cockroaches are one of the oldest living species?

Elizabeth: I have this feeling you have something you want to tell me about human cockroaches.

Daniela: The entire human race is fucked up. Frank Kavorsky has the same genetic anomaly at marker sixty-six as the recently departed Dov Hirsch. I almost laid an egg. Kavorsky was told by a higher-up in the White House to eliminate Hirsch.

Elizabeth: Any idea, who?

Daniela: Roger Arnold, the deputy chief of staff, but Arnold denies the accusations vehemently. Marshall gave the okay on immunity for Kavorsky if he gave us something substantial on Code

Name Daniel. Kavorsky threw us a bone and said that it was a secret White House operation and not an independent CIA directive.

Elizabeth: I'll bet Marshall was pleased as punch.

Daniela: The director was pissed as hell that it wasn't a CIA rogue plan. He was ready to let the pit bulls loose. Anytime the FBI can get a leg up on the CIA, that's like winning the Army-Navy football game.

Elizabeth: Did Kavorsky say whether the president was involved?

Daniela pauses and makes eye contact with Elizabeth.

Daniela: I didn't know you had a crush on the president.

Without flinching Elizabeth responds to Daniela's unexpected curiosity.

Elizabeth: All I meant by my comment is that the country has already gone through the scandals of Presidents Clinton and Nixon. We certainly don't need another one to set us back.

Daniela: You're quick on your feet, sis. Anything new on your end?

Elizabeth: I'll be with Esther at the art fair. Why don't you join us, and maybe we can solve the riddle of her dream and its relevance to Code Name Daniel.

Daniela: My cockroaches at the FBI are calling. I think I will meet you at the fair. I'm curious about your patient. She seems too nice.

41

REVELATION

Esther and Dr. Corsini are strolling in the street, looking at the different exhibits of paintings, sculptures, handicrafts, baskets, and knickknacks.

Esther: Before all this happened to me, I was writing a piece for our political blog. I titled my article, "The Downfall of the United States."

Elizabeth: That's not so far-fetched.

Esther: You didn't let me finish. I'm thinking now that my title should be, "The Downfall of the United States and the Rise of the American President."

Elizabeth: Does this have anything to do with the story of Daniel's dream in the Old Testament?

Esther: The Italians don't have the market on the Bible. We Jews can teach you a thing or two. The Book of Daniel was about the apocalypse, the End of Days.

Elizabeth: Don't keep me in suspense, Esther.

Esther: The beast in my nightmare is a sea dragon with ten horns, and then a little horn emerges.

Elizabeth: Probably the leviathan in the Bible. Daniel had the same dream, only his beast was not a dragon but was just as fierce, and it too had the ten horns and the little horn. What are you trying to say? For Christ's sake just say it.

Esther: I think the president metaphorically is the little horn, the final beast. Code Name Daniel is a covert operation in the White House to make the president the ruler of the world, the Messiah. The president will become a hero to the entire world, even if America is on its way down.

Elizabeth: I think I know where you're going with this. President Macorley is the little horn, and he displaces three of the larger horns from your dragon's head. These larger horns represent nations or groups that the president defeats.

Esther: Exactly! The three large horns that fall off of the dragon's head when the little horn emerges are Al Qaeda, the Taliban, and then either Iran or more likely an easier Muslim country to defeat like Yemen.

Elizabeth: My God! You stumbled upon their secret operation through your dream. That's why your life is in danger.

Esther: Do you think the president is aware of his entire messianic destiny?

Elizabeth: I'm sad to say that I do. I've been at the practice of psychiatry for twenty-five years, and I've never seen a president who needs love and approval the way Malcolm Yale Macorley does. He seems mild mannered, but he is thin-skinned when it comes to anyone criticizing him.

Esther: It seems as though you know him personally.

Elizabeth ignores Esther's comment and switches subjects.

Elizabeth: I've treated patients by regressive therapy. Anytime I see the extreme need for approval, it never fails that it is a result of parental deprivation of love. You have to remember that the president was essentially abandoned by his parents at a young age and was then raised by his grandparents.

Daniela approaches and greets Esther and Dr. Corsini.

Elizabeth: Esther, this is my sister, Daniela Corsini.

Daniela: I have some news for Esther. Frank Kavorsky was found dead in his apartment. His neighbor discovered him with a rope around his neck hanging from a hook in the ceiling. It was set up to look like suicide, but with Esther's husband also dead, it's very unlikely. Esther could be next. More news. Roger Arnold just a few hours ago implicated his boss, Jason Smithies in a White House covert operation, Code Name Daniel.

Elizabeth: It's getting awfully close to the president.

Daniela: In another bizarre event—within the last half hour in fact—Arnold's car exploded in his driveway with him in it. Somebody's doing his best to tie up all the loose ends.

Elizabeth: I guess they made the connection between Esther's dream and the Book of Daniel, like Esther and I did moments ago.

Daniela: Are we back at religious school, Lizzie?

Elizabeth: We haven't filled you in yet, Dannie. You remember your Old Testament.

Daniela: Are you kidding me? The nuns used to whack us with a ruler across our knuckles if we didn't know our Bible.

Elizabeth: Esther has had the same dream as Daniel.

Daniela: As I recall Daniel's dream, a little horn emerges in the fourth beast's head and knocks off three of the ten larger horns. Are the horns supposed to represent something that I should know about that's relevant to what's going on?

Esther: The three large horns knocked off the beast's head by the little horn represent Al Qaeda, the Taliban, and either Yemen or Iran. With regard to Iran, we don't know how the political winds will shift in regard to Iran abandoning its nuclear weapons program.

Daniela: We've left the military option on the table, thank God, if Iran doesn't comply with our diplomatic failures. If we destroy Iran, then I would agree it's the third large horn. My gut tells me that it's more likely to be Yemen. Regardless the inescapable conclusion is that the president then becomes the little horn.

Elizabeth: I guess that means that we're all in danger.

Daniela looks over at a clown passing candy and balloons out to children at the art fair.

Daniela: I love clowns. Wait…He's got a gun.

The clown pulls out a revolver from his suit and points it at Dr. Corsini. Daniela reacts immediately, pulling out her gun and firing before the clown can get off his shot. The clown falls to the ground, blood flowing everywhere. Dr. Corsini is aghast, but Esther seems remarkably calm. Daniela leans down beside the dead man.

Daniela: Would you check his pulse, sis?

Elizabeth kneels down and feels the pulse in the clown's neck.

Elizabeth: He's dead. Do you know him, Dannie?

Daniela: No, I don't. But I'll check him out at the FBI.

Elizabeth: Could this be one of Dov's or Kavorsky's cohorts?

Daniela: More likely it is one of Jason Smithies' goons, particularly since Dov and Kavorsky and Arnold were in my estimation eliminated by Smithies. You're in real danger, Lizzie. And so is Esther. I'll do my best to protect you. However I can't be with either one of you twenty-four/seven.

Elizabeth: What do you suggest?

Daniela: We need a bargaining chip, but we don't have anything to bargain with.

Elizabeth: Dannie, can you get Esther back to the hospital? I need to do some serious thinking about all this. I'll be back to you with my thoughts.

Daniela: Are you sure you're alright?

Elizabeth: I'm fine. I'll meet you at the Hirshhorn Museum tomorrow when it opens at ten a.m.

Elizabeth is driving in her car when she hears her cell phone ring on her Bluetooth. She pulls over to the side of the road on the shoulder. The phone display reads, Private Caller.

She stares at the dashboard and lets the phone ring.

Ring…ring…ring…ring.

The phone stops ringing as her answering message comes on. Before the message is completed, the phone call is aborted. She takes a long drive out of the city to clear her head and then doubles back to her apartment. Darkness has set on the capital.

At the steps of her brownstone, she glances around and notices a figure across the street by a lamppost. She can't believe her eyes when she sees President Macorley coming toward her. She gasps in fear as he faces her.

Elizabeth: Did the Secret Service drop you?

President Macorley: No. I snuck out alone.

Elizabeth: To see me?

President Macorley: No. To ask you to either give me my file or burn it.

Elizabeth: As a doctor I can't legally do that. I'll lose my license.

President Macorley: I know that. I'm asking as your president, and only this one time am I asking nicely.

Elizabeth: And if I don't?

President Macorley: Let's just say that you will no longer have an important friend in your life, a very important friend. I won't be able to guarantee your safety. Goodbye, Elizabeth.

The president gets into his car and drives away. Elizabeth is standing there in a frozen state, unable to move. She shakes uncontrollably.

42

FILE

Daniela and Elizabeth walk around observing the paintings at the Hirshhorn Museum.

Elizabeth: I was the president's psychiatrist when he was a senator representing the State of Delaware.

Daniela: Why did the president need a shrink? If that ever got out, it would be political suicide.

Elizabeth: The case history is confidential. I can't discuss the medical issues of a patient, even if it's the president.

Daniela: Lizzie, you amaze me. Who cares about the details? The file could buy us paradise.

Elizabeth gives Daniela a hard stare.

Daniela: Only kidding. I'm a devoted public servant. I'll call the White House and tell them we're bringing the president an early Christmas present. Give me the file, and I'll make the arrangements.

Daniela holds out her hand.

Elizabeth: I don't have it.

Daniela: What do you mean you don't have it?

Elizabeth: As soon as Senator Macorley was elected President Macorley, I placed the file in a locker at Ronald Reagan Airport. Locker 492.

Daniela laughs.

Daniela: You're losing your marbles. And the key to locker 492?

Elizabeth: On Muffin's collar. Here's an extra copy of my apartment key.

Daniela: God, you're the smart one in the family. I wouldn't have guessed it in a million years. Your dog's collar. Shit, Lizzie!

Elizabeth: I'll need assurance that the White House will back off and stop trying to kill Esther and me. They've wanted this file for a long time.

Daniela: What are you saying? They've threatened you? Why didn't you tell me, Lizzie?

Elizabeth: Yes, last night and on other occasions. I didn't want to worry you. As long as I had the file, I didn't think they would try to kill me. I was wrong.

Daniela: I can tell the White House that neither Esther nor you ever heard of Code Name Daniel. I don't expect them to buy it.

Elizabeth: Do it. I'm worried about Esther. She's been very fragile since you told us about Dov's death.

Daniela: I'll get the file to the White House within the hour and be back to you as soon as I can.

Elizabeth: Thanks, Dannie.

Daniela exits. Elizabeth smiles and speaks aloud.

Elizabeth: Daniela has always underestimated me.

43

TAXI RIDE

Elizabeth leaves the Hirshhorn Museum and hails a cab. The angels, invisible, hop in with her. The taxi driver turns to Elizabeth.

Taxi Driver: Where to, lady?

Elizabeth: Washington Central Hospital. I hope that your day has been as pleasant as mine.

Taxi Driver: Same old.

Elizabeth: I wouldn't mind the same old.

The driver looks in his rearview mirror.

Taxi Driver: Any reason why someone should be following you?

Elizabeth turns and looks out the back window. So do Gabriel and Michael.

Elizabeth: I don't see anyone.

Taxi Driver: Two cars back. Watch the black SUV with the tinted windows, when I make a turn.

The driver turns right, then left. The black SUV follows.

Elizabeth is alarmed when she sees the car come right up beside the taxi. She screeches to the cab driver.

Elizabeth: I see someone in the passenger seat rolling down their window. Oh, shit! It's a gun.

The window drops further, and Elizabeth recognizes the man with the gun inside the black SUV.

Elizabeth: Oh, my God! It can't be. It's Dov Hirsch. He's supposed to be dead.

Sirens suddenly blare. A police car pulls up behind the black SUV. Elizabeth sees Dov drop the gun on the pavement. Gabriel and Michael give themselves a silent high five. Elizabeth breathes a sigh of relief.

Elizabeth: Please! Just drive me to the hospital.

The taxi pulls up in front of the hospital's main entrance. The angels reach for their wallets, and then realize they don't have any money. Elizabeth pays the driver and exits with the angels.

Elizabeth: Thanks for being so observant. That was touch and go back there. Please keep the change.

Taxi Driver: Thanks for the nice tip. Have a better day, lady.

Elizabeth enters Esther's room. She exchanges no pleasantries and speaks in a commanding voice.

Elizabeth: I need to talk to you. Let's go to my office.

44

THE STING

Esther and Dr. Corsini walk on the ward. A female patient is screaming obscenities, and the nurses and staff are trying to subdue her. Finally one of the nurses gives the patient a needle, and she passes out. Elizabeth addresses Esther directly, without any of her usual compassion or sensitivity.

Elizabeth: You'll be able to pick up the pieces of your life. You're going to be inheriting a lot of money very, very soon.

Esther: I have no idea what you're talking about. Did someone in my family die?

Elizabeth: Your share of the loot when Daniela sells the president's psychiatric file to the highest bidder. What did Daniela promise you?

Esther: I still don't have the foggiest notion of what you're implying. I met Daniela for the very first time today. You introduced us.

Elizabeth: Come now, Esther. The gig is up.

Esther: You need help, Doc. Your ducks are not in order.

Elizabeth: At first you had me fooled, but then I watched your demeanor very carefully and realized that you weren't who you appeared to be. Your remorse for your husband was quite unconvincing, and when Daniela shot the clown at the art fair, you remained as cool as a cucumber.

Esther: You're babbling. And I'm afraid that you seem quite paranoid. Is there anyone you want me to call? You really need professional help.

Elizabeth: I played along, because I wanted to see how far Daniela would go to extract the president's psychiatric file. We've always had this sterling competition since we were kids. And Dannie has always come up second best.

Esther: I have no interest in your family rivalry.

Elizabeth: Come off it, Esther. You've been caught with your pants down. Do you want me to call the police? I wouldn't recommend it.

Dr. Corsini takes out her cell phone and dials. Esther begins chanting her own version of a nursery rhyme.

Esther:

(deep voice)
Little Miss Muffat
sat on her tuffet
eating her curds
and whey.
Along came a spider
and sat down beside her,
and said,
'What's in the bowl,
bitch?'

Elizabeth: Your bowl will be filled with prison food, Esther, for the rest of your days. You can entertain the inmates with your fake paranoia voice.

Esther: I guess there's no harm in telling you. A half a million dollars if we were successful in getting you to give up the file.

Elizabeth: Daniela got you on the cheap. In street dollars the president's file must be worth at least five million. But of course Dov has to get his share, and Frank Kavorsky deserves a little something.

Esther: What good is money to them? They're both dead.

Elizabeth: You can stop acting, Esther. Daniela isn't the only one with contacts in the FBI. The director and I are intimate, and he's shared certain secrets.

Esther: I thought I had you convinced. Before I became a CIA agent, I worked as an actress.

Elizabeth: You were excellent. Almost had me fooled. I would rate your performance as Oscar caliber.

Esther: What tipped you off?

Elizabeth: I kept coming back to your psychosis. You just can't recover as fast as you did. Your paranoia with the voices was marvelous. Incredibly authentic.

Esther: I don't mind bragging. I learned my craft at the Actors Studio in New York.

Elizabeth: I have a surprise for you. We did give you real antipsychotic drugs, but I held back on the lithium. You were swallowing a placebo.

Esther: Why would you do that?

Elizabeth: I needed a way to trap Dannie. The lithium was supposed to allow the detection of the hallucinogen.

Esther: We've underestimated you. You've got talent, Dr. Corsini. I could get you a role on stage if you like.

Elizabeth: You flatter me.

Esther: Well, you sure as hell had me convinced that you believed the Satan genetics. Dov's DNA documents were forged, of course.

Elizabeth: Sorry, dear. I never really bought into your preposterous DNA story. I must say I was a pretty good actress myself. However I'm not one of those people who believe what they want to hear or see.

Esther: The spider in my nursery rhyme was dead on. Did anyone ever tell you that you're a nasty bitch, Lizzie?

Elizabeth: Why, no! Everyone thinks I'm as sweet as apple pie, like you, Esther. Except that your apple is rotten at its core.

Esther: Now, now, Doctor. Sarcasm is unbecoming to your personality.

Elizabeth: Who's the expert geneticist in the group? Is it Dov? Elizabeth looks at her watch.

Dov, limping, barges in on the conversation.

Dov: I've been looking all over for you, only to find you with this bitch.

Elizabeth: Well, well! Mr. Hirsch. Right on time, visiting hours on the ward. You've made a remarkable recovery from the grave. You're not dead after all, and neither am I. No thanks to you.

Dov: The psycho lady. Let's get out of here, Esther.

Elizabeth: Are you a real toxicologist?

Dov: Fuck you.

Elizabeth: I have a job for you: checking out the toxicology of prison food.

Dov: You've got nothing on me.

Elizabeth: Your whole scheme has collapsed.

Dov: Screw you, Corsini.

Elizabeth: How much money were you promised?

Dov looks at Esther.

Esther: The bitch knows.

Dov: Three hundred thousand.

Elizabeth: Are you two married?

Esther: We're a couple.

Elizabeth: Well, you two seem to deserve each other. If I were either of you, I would prepare myself.

Dov: Prepare for what?

Elizabeth: To be shortchanged. There will be no money. The FBI director will be there when Daniela arrives at the airport locker to retrieve the file.

Esther: What will happen to Daniela?

Elizabeth: The director is aware of her talents. I think she'll get a slap on the wrist, but who knows? I plan to make her life miserable for almost getting me killed by your darling Dov.

Dov: I don't like people who think they're smarter than me.

Elizabeth: I can't say that I blame you. I also don't like people who are smarter than me. I was first in my medical school class.

Dov pulls out a gun. Michael and Gabriel fly into the room.

Dov: Let's finish the cunt off.

Elizabeth: I wouldn't do that if I were you.

Dov: Why not? I'd love to see you beg for mercy before I kill you.

Elizabeth: The FBI will be here in a few minutes, so I suggest you make good use of your time.

Dov: She's bluffing.

Elizabeth walks right up to Dov and looks him squarely in the eyes. She takes his wrist and points his gun directly at her face.

Dov: You have balls, bitch. I'll give you that.

Elizabeth: The director knows all about the both of you. He may let you go on your merry way now that he has the file, but homicide means the electric chair.

Esther: Let's go, Dov. She's right.

Esther pulls at Dov's arm, and the duo exits. The angels depart knowing Elizabeth is safe.

Elizabeth takes a deep breath. She then picks up the phone and dials Marshall Lamster.

45

LOCKER 492

Marshall Lamster picks up his ringing cell phone.

Marshall: Hello, Liz. I'm at the airport waiting for Daniela and I'm pissed. Abel Slobodkin is with me.

Elizabeth: What's Abel doing with you?

Marshall softens his tone.

Marshall: I have no choice but to temporarily suspend Daniela for insubordination. Abel will keep her informed about the goings on at the Bureau. Daniela is his mentor, and they trust each other. Besides, I understand that Abel has been seeing Sophia and is almost family. He tells me that he's madly in love with her.

Elizabeth: Please don't rush my life away. Abel and Sophia hardly know each other. Marshall, how long will Daniela be suspended? She's not going to be happy with your decision.

Marshall: I won't tell her, because I want to give her a spanking. It will be a couple of days at most. Any more would be dangerous for my well-being. I have to show Daniela that I'm the boss and that she can't go off half-cocked without keeping me in the loop. I won't call it a suspension, so she won't be embarrassed by her colleagues at the Bureau.

Elizabeth: Thanks for being gentle on Daniela. My guess is that she was under a lot of pressure from the White House. Marshall, the file in the locker is blue.

Marshall: Why in Heaven didn't she come to me?

Elizabeth: I know my sister. She would never have sold the file. Jason Smithies was likely supplying the monies to pay off Dov, Esther, and Kavorsky for their part in the sting operation to get me to give up the file. Their plan was rather ingenious. Trying to persuade me that Dov was slipping the Chinese peyote hallucinogen into Esther's orange juice, causing her to become psychotic.

Marshall: Okay, Liz. But I can't forgive Daniela for not trusting me. Whoops, there she is. Got to go.

Daniela opens locker 492 and removes the blue file. Marshall sneaks up from behind and taps her on the shoulder. Daniela is surprised.

Daniela: Well, hi, Marshall. Hello, Abel. This isn't necessarily the best place to have a business meeting. Let me check my calendar.

Marshall: This isn't funny, Daniela. I'll take the file.

Daniela: Damn that Lizzie. She's outsmarted me again.

She gives Marshall the file and then looks directly into his eyes.

Daniela: You've been balling my sister.

Abel is embarrassed by the revelation. This is Sophia's mother and aunt, and they are both competing for the same man, the FBI director. At least, that's what Abel initially thinks. Marshall and Daniela ignore him.

Marshall: I'm sorry, Daniela. I never meant to hurt you. It happened the night of my Christmas party. If you remember we all were pretty sloshed that night.

Daniela: How could you when you've been fucking me all this time?

Marshall: If it's any consolation, Liz broke it off soon after that night.

Daniela: I guess we're even. You hurt me and I hurt you by not telling you what was going on. But I had my reasons. The White House put pressure on me because I was Lizzie's sister.

Marshall: I was going to ask you to take off work for a couple of days, but let's just forgive and forget. I do care for you, Daniela. The saying is true. There's no fool like an old fool. I was cursed with high testosterone.

Abel: Is something going on at the White House?

Daniela: My sister was the president's psychiatrist when he was a senator from Delaware. I was ordered by the White House to devise a plot to retrieve the file. I recruited a young couple with links to the CIA, a Dov and Esther Hirsch. The covert operation was called Code Name Daniel, and it has global implications beyond the psychiatry.

Abel: Does this have anything to do with Daniel's dream in the Book of Daniel about a beast with ten large horns and a smaller horn that knocks off three of the larger horns?

Daniela: I thought that we Christians had the monopoly on religion.

Abel: You forget we are the Chosen People.

Daniela: Let's not banter over trivial points, Abel. We both own shares in Heaven. Esther had a similar dream to the prophet Daniel's in ancient Babylon. The dream suggests that the president is the little horn who wins victories over Al Qaeda, the Taliban, and either Iran or Yemen. Metaphorically they are the three large horns of the beast in Daniel and Esther's dream.

Abel: And the president then becomes the hero to the world, a global Messiah. Fascinating fiction.

Marshall grows impatient.

Marshall: I hate to break this philosophical discussion up, but I have to get the file to the president.

Daniela: You run along, Marshall. You too Abel. I have my own meeting with destiny.

46

TWIST

Rabbi Adam is over Abel, spotting him as he bench presses three hundred pounds at the Capital Gymnasium.

Rabbi Adam: Aren't you overdoing it?

Abel: On the contrary I need to get a lot stronger if I'm going to have any chance at all with Leamas. He threw me around as if I was light as a feather.

Rabbi Adam: I've been instructed by the prime minister to tell you to cool your relationship with this gentile girl, Sophia.

Abel: I can't do that. I'm in love with her.

Rabbi Adam: Have you spoken to her about the real nature of your work?

Abel: No. It's the one secret I haven't shared with her.

Rabbi Adam: You must not jeopardize your mission. A lot is riding on you, Abel. The future of the homeland is at risk.

Abel: There's news from the White House.

Rabbi Adam: I'll inform the prime minister.

Abel: I learned yesterday about a White House CIA covert operation, Code Name Daniel. Remember Daniel's ancient dream?

Well, it's coming true in modern times. The disruption of three of the large horns by the little horn is a metaphor for President Macorley, who represents the little horn and succeeds in destroying Al Qaeda, the Taliban, and either Iran or terrorist radicals in Yemen.

Rabbi Adam: The prime minister is concerned about the activation of Gog and Magog by the United States.

Abel: Code Name Daniel is the prerequisite for Gog and Magog.

Rabbi Adam: I don't follow you.

Abel: In Gog and Magog, the first phase of the attack on our state is by seven nations. Correct?

Rabbi Adam: Yes, that's true.

Abel: Well, the seven remaining large horns of the beast in Daniel's dream represent the seven attacking nations.

Rabbi Adam: Brilliant, Abel. President Macorley is Gog.

47

LIES AND DECEPTION

E lizabeth pours scotch into two glasses in her office. Daniela bursts in. Elizabeth hands her one of the glasses.

Daniela: A little early in the day for you. I would never have thought it, but you're quite the liar, Lizzie.

Elizabeth: I learned from the best. You, Dannie. I hope that you gave Marshall my love.

Daniela: That damn bastard has no morals. Making love to both of us.

Elizabeth: You have your morality wrong. The infidelity is to his wife. He's still having sex with her, even though they're separated.

Daniela: That SOB liar.

Elizabeth: Let's take a walk.

They walk in the psychiatric grounds courtyard. Patients talk, smoke, or play volleyball. Two male patients are shooting hoops.

Daniela: He's a bastard no matter how you slice it. Did you really go to bed with that moron?

Elizabeth: We were drunk.

Daniela: My downfall for introducing you. I actually care for the asshole.

Elizabeth: I almost told you about the president's psychiatric file. I was pretty plastered that night. You didn't tell me the truth either, but I still love you, even though you almost got me killed with your sting operation. What the hell's the matter with you? You're my sister for Christ's sake.

Daniela: I feel like shit, but the White House left me with no choice. That psycho Dov is another story. I forgive you if you forgive me. Now tell me, where did I slip up?

Elizabeth gives her sister a hug, then separates from her and responds softly.

Elizabeth: You couldn't have known about the lithium. I never gave it to Esther. I gave her a placebo. If she never took lithium, how were you able to detect an imaginary peyote hallucinogen in her bloodstream?

Daniela: Shit, Lizzie. Do you ever play fair? Is that it? The lousy lithium.

Elizabeth: You did make one other mistake. I never explained the details of the genetic anomaly at marker sixty-six, so how could you have analyzed the genetic data in Kavorsky's blood? Yet you knew about it when you called me with the results. And why believe that I would believe something as preposterous as Satan genetics?

Daniela: Dov got me up to speed on the genetics. It was his idea to tease your inquisitive mind so that you would follow through on Kavorsky's blood sample. I didn't know at the time that he was intending to kill you.

Elizabeth: Sociopaths are not too dependable. What will happen to Dov and Esther?

Daniela: I honestly don't know. It was Smithies who told me to recruit Esther from the CIA. Dov really is a toxicologist at the EPA, with connections to the agency.

Elizabeth: Did Smithies also supply the money for the sting operation on me?

Daniela: Yes, but Dov and Esther never knew where the money was coming from. I guess they thought it was from the FBI. There was never any intention of my selling the file for money. I had orders from the White House, which I was instructed not to share, even with Marshall. At all costs I was to retrieve the president's file in exchange for your well-being. I was following orders because I needed to protect you. You're my baby sister.

Elizabeth: I know, Dannie. By the way the file Marshall has in his possession? It's a phony. It belongs to a long-deceased patient of mine whom I saw when I first started practicing psychiatry.

Daniela belly laughs, and Elizabeth joins in.

Daniela: I wouldn't want to be in the room when Marshall and the White House find out that you've tricked them. The president will know immediately that the file is a phony. Why did you give them a fake file?

Elizabeth raises her right hand like she's swearing on a Bible in court.

Elizabeth: I took the Oath of Hippocrates when I completed med school: "Do no harm." I can never reveal doctor–patient conversations, except when a patient dies or in cases of wrongdoing. The president's file was neither of those situations.

Daniela: Aren't you harming the president?

Elizabeth: I'm sure you would agree that wouldn't be such a bad outcome. The truth is that I'm actually protecting the president. You know as well as I that you can't trust anyone in this town. I might release the file if I saw that the president was taking the whole country down with him.

Daniela: Oh, you mean his Messiah complex and Code Name Daniel. Where's the file, sis?

Elizabeth: In an unnumbered account in Switzerland out of harm's way. You can inform the director and the White House.

Daniela: I have no choice.

Elizabeth: If anything unforeseen should happen to me, then my instructions to the head of the Swiss bank are to release the file in its entirety. Kind of like the Wiki papers. The Swiss are pretty honorable human beings when it comes to money.

Daniela: I've got to hand it to you, Lizzie. You've thought of everything. Even a fail-safe insurance policy for yourself. There's only one problem.

Elizabeth: What's that?

Daniela looks at her watch.

Daniela: Marshall told me that he was going to call me about now.

Daniela's cell phone rings. Ring...ring...ring...ring. She hits the speaker button.

48

DOUBLE CROSS

Daniela shrugs her shoulders as if saying, "I really don't want to take this call."

Daniela: Hello, Marshall.

Marshall: Director Lamster in public, Daniela.

Daniela smiles at Elizabeth.

Daniela: Yes, sir. Oh, Marshall, I'm with Liz. You're on speaker.

Marshall: Good. Liz needs to pay us a house call. Bring her with you to headquarters. No, make it the Four Seasons lounge. Thirty minutes. And Daniela, come with alacrity.

Daniela: Oh, Marshall, such big words for a big man with a big…Do they still comp you at the bar? And…

Marshall interrupts.

Marshall: Cut the bullshit, Daniela. The president is not happy. Marshall abruptly hangs up.

Daniela: Marshall must really be pissed off. He didn't even say goodbye.

Elizabeth: We'll grab a cab to the hotel. The Four Seasons is my favorite haunt.

Daniela: How can you be so glib?

Elizabeth: I have to practice what I preach.

Daniela and Elizabeth proceed to the lounge. They spot Marshall Lamster and walk over to his table.

Marshall: Shit! I'm outnumbered by Corsinis.

He picks up his glass and chugs his drink as the sisters sit. He knows what's coming.

Daniela: And exposed for what you are, you creep. Making love to both of us at the same time.

Marshall: And to my wife. I'm quite a sex machine. Pretty good for an old fart.

Elizabeth: Have you no morals, Marshall?

Marshall: What happened to the good guy–bad guy routine? Never mind. I'll get to the point.

Daniela: Not without buying us a Macallan 12, you cheapskate.

Marshall: Your routine never changes, Daniela. Drinks are on the way. There's the waitress now.

The waitress brings three scotches to the table. Everybody takes a long swig.

Marshall: You double-crossed me, Liz. You promised the president's file. I'm extremely disappointed that neither you nor Daniela trusted me enough to confide in me.

He removes the blue file from his briefcase and tosses it across the table at Elizabeth.

Marshall: This is a piece of crap.

Elizabeth: I've learned not to trust when my life is in danger. Even you can't protect me from those monsters in the White House.

Marshall: Do you realize what you're doing? These people will stop at nothing to get the file. Your life is still in danger.

Elizabeth: The file is my only insurance to stay alive. When you tell the president that the file is forever safe, unless something happens to me, he'll back off.

Daniela: I'm afraid she has you by the balls, Marshall. I suggest you retreat with your testicles intact.

Marshall: You realize that regrettably I have to terminate all of my sexual relations with the Corsini sisters.

Daniela and Elizabeth turn to each other and cross their hearts.

Daniela and Elizabeth: Thank you, God.

Marshall: Cut it out. It's true. I can be an asshole.

The sisters nod their heads in unison in agreement.

Marshall: Liz, the president wants to see you in the Oval Office. Daniela, you're not invited.

Daniela: I always miss all the fun. I take my leave without further adieu.

Daniela gets up and exits. Marshall and Elizabeth follow and get into an FBI limousine parked outside the hotel lobby. The limo drives off.

Marshall: Those words were meant for Daniela. Not for you, Liz. I hope we can still see each other.

Elizabeth: I couldn't hurt Dannie any more than I already have.

Marshall: Not meant to be, I guess.

Elizabeth: Dannie and I were a little too hard on you. She's romantically in love with you, and I love you as a friend.

Marshall clutches Elizabeth's hand.

Marshall: I don't know what leverage you have, Liz. But my advice is to hang tough with Jason Smithies. He can deal cards out of every part of the deck.

The limousine arrives at the White House. Elizabeth gives Marshall a peck on the cheek. They are greeted by a Secret Service agent.

Secret Service Agent: This way, please.

The agent escorts them to the chief of staff's office.

49

HONOR AMONG THIEVES

The phone rings in the Hirsch household. Esther picks up and hits the speaker button.

Esther: Hello.

Kavorsky: It's Frank Kavorsky, Esther. I'm calling from a public phone at the train station. You and Dov need to hightail it out of the capital. Roger Arnold called to warn me before they hanged him in his apartment.

Dov interjects.

Dov: Those SOBs. Loyalty counts for shit.

Two men in shades come up behind Kavorsky. One wraps his arms around him, and the other slits his throat. Kavorsky groans as he falls to the ground.

Dov: Frank, are you there? For God's sake, answer me.

Dov turns to Esther.

Dov: They got Frank. We need to get the hell out of here. No time to pack. Grab your coat.

Esther: Maybe we should call Daniela.

Dov: No time for that. I never trusted her anyway.

Esther: I think we should call, Dov.

Dov: Okay, stop babbling. We'll contact her from the car. It's that damn psychiatrist's fault. She's the one who deserves to die, not Frank or Roger Arnold.

They rush out of the house and get into their car. Dov turns on the ignition and the car explodes.

50

POKER PLAYER

Marshall and Elizabeth are escorted into Jason Smithies' office.

Smithies: Marshall, you can leave now. I want to have a word with Dr. Corsini in private.

Marshall reluctantly departs. Smithies and Elizabeth sit.

Smithies: It's scotch, isn't it?

He pours a glass of scotch for himself and for her. She peers over the desk and notices the label on the bottle.

Elizabeth: Macallan 18. Out of my price range.

Smithies: Only the best for the best.

Elizabeth: I see you suit the job, Jason. You're well informed.

Smithies: I try to be. Daniela told us about the file in the Swiss bank.

Elizabeth: This isn't about the president's psychiatric file, is it? You know that I'll keep the file safe if you keep me safe.

Smithies: You're as shrewd as ever.

Smithies puts his scotch down and stares directly at Dr. Corsini. Michael and Gabriel fly into the room unseen. Smithies gets up out of his chair and cracks his knuckles. He then walks around his desk to Dr. Corsini and glares down at her just inches away from her face. He purposely spits as he scolds her.

Smithies: You know goddamn well what this is about. You had better get with the program or else.

Elizabeth removes a Kleenex and wipes saliva from her face. She calmly sips her scotch.

Elizabeth: Calm down, Jason. It's not good for your arteries. I presume you're referring to Code Name Daniel. Does the president know what you're planning?

Smithies: That's none of your concern if you want to live. You do want to live, don't you, Dr. Corsini?

Elizabeth: It was your miscalculation, Jason. You set up the sting on me by Esther and Dov Hirsch and my sister. It was a rather ingenious plot.

Smithies: That was our plan to get the president's file. Circumstances have changed since you now know about Code Name Daniel. That makes you an enemy of the state.

All this time President Macorley has been standing by Jason's door listening. The president enters.

President Macorley: This lady is very special, Jason. No threats, please.

Elizabeth: Malcolm, do you really need to be so ambitious? You had it all over Obama and Clinton, and you turned out to be a weasel.

President Macorley: Jason, will you excuse us? Let's take a walk in the White House Gardens, Elizabeth. The sun is out and not a cloud in the sky.

They walk in the gardens.

Elizabeth: We could have had the rainbow, Malcolm.

President Macorley: Still living in your fantasy world. Haven't you figured it out yet? Romance is for fools.

The president looks up at the perfectly clear blue sky.

President Macorley: You see? Not a cloud in the sky. It's an omen for us to make peace with each other.

Elizabeth: You can dispense with your false charm. I know you all too well. Remember? Malcolm, why not just be satisfied with being president?

President Macorley: You don't know me at all. The presidency is not enough. I won't curtail my ambitions until I'm ruler of the world.

Elizabeth: That's God's job.

President Macorley: God died a long time ago. Only the Devil exists within each of us. Keep up the good work, Elizabeth. You're actually helping me by keeping my file in Switzerland. And at the same time, you're protecting your own beautiful ass.

Elizabeth: I've made a lot of mistakes in my life, but unlike you I'm sorry for them. I'm doing what I think is right, even if it helps an egomaniac like you. I was in love with you, and now I pity you for who you really are.

Rain begins to pour down on them. While thunder echoes and lightning marks the sky, they seek shelter under a tree.

Elizabeth: A warning shot from the Divine. God will make sure that your narcissism will not be triumphant.

President Macorley: Nonsense! Though it is rather strange that the rain came without clouds.

Elizabeth: For those of us who believe, we call it a miracle. Of course you wouldn't know anything about faith.

President Macorley: You always did underestimate me.

The rain stops abruptly. They continue their walk.

Elizabeth: I fell in love with your charm and zest for life, but you don't have feelings. Your passion is only for your own ambition. You need to come back into therapy before you destroy yourself.

President Macorley: I always adored you for your beauty, honesty, and superior intelligence. It's rare to have all three qualities in a woman. That's what made you special.

Elizabeth: I know that I never meant anything to you, Malcolm, but for God's sake you need to help yourself before it's too late.

President Macorley: Destiny beckons, Elizabeth.

Elizabeth: How sad. How very sad.

President Macorley: I need your assurance that you will obliterate Code Name Daniel forever from your mind.

Elizabeth takes a few more steps and then stops.

Elizabeth: Okay, I'll cooperate, but only if you leave Daniela alone. If harm comes to her, then harm will come to you. Goodbye, Malcolm.

She shakes his hand and walks back to the White House by herself. He watches her familiar wiggle and yells out.

President Macorley: Don't forget to watch me on TV.

Elizabeth speaks without looking back.

Elizabeth: That's the only place I ever want to see you again.

The president's cell phone rings. It's the 666 number.

Leamas: I see you botched the operation. I can't allow so many mistakes, Mr. President.

President Macorley: Don't worry, Devil.

51

HEAVENLY WHITE HOUSE

J ason Smithies and the president are chatting about their present dilemma.

Smithies: What should we do about the Corsini sisters?

President Macorley: The fabulous Corsini sisters are untouchable unless we can recover my records. I want you to put pressure on the Swiss bank to have them surrender the file. Do it on the quiet.

Smithies: I'm way ahead of you, Mr. President. The Swiss are prepared to make an exception to their ironclad rules because of United States national security. As soon as we have recovered your file, I can order the hit on both sisters.

President Macorley: A pity, but they are sacrificing for a cause greater than themselves, as McCain was fond of saying. We'll done, Jason.

Meanwhile Michael and Gabriel stand in the Third Temple Sanctuary in Heaven, discussing the gravity of the situation with God, whose voice is heard in the chamber.

GOD: Daniel's prophecy in Babylon shall come to pass. The world will be fooled into a sense of complacency with President

Macorley. Horrific war against Israel will follow. It is then that I shall intervene. Mankind has written the script of history, but I shall write the ending.

Gabriel: How shall we proceed, Ancient One?

GOD: As I instructed you. And watch over the Corsini sisters. Even presidents can be weasels. I have a future mission for the sisters after the president's reelection campaign.

Michael: But the election is three years away.

GOD: I'm fully aware of the time differential, angel. Nevertheless the president will be reelected for a second term in 2020 with Satan's help. And Gabriel, take care of Dr. Corsini's problem at the Swiss bank.

52

NICKNAME

Elizabeth Corsini is riding in the White House limousine accompanied by the Secret Service agent.

Elizabeth: Do all the White House guests get this royal treatment?

Secret Service Agent: Only the ones that are special, Dr. Corsini. I guess it's a real honor to meet the president.

Elizabeth: That it is. What's your name?

Secret Service Agent: Kyle, ma'am.

Elizabeth: Kyle, I've heard via the grapevine that the Secret Service's nickname for President Macorley is "Messiah."

Kyle blushes.

Kyle: Can't say, ma'am. We receive our instructions when we're picked for this assignment.

Elizabeth: You needn't. Your behavior is very admirable. Most people in the real world love to gossip. Thank you for the lift. The hospital is just up ahead.

The limousine pulls up in front of the main entrance. Elizabeth gets out and enters through the lobby doors. Daniela is there waiting for her.

Daniela: You're not going inside your loony ward until you tell me everything. And I mean everything. You and I are heading back to the Four Seasons to down a bottle of scotch.

Elizabeth: Why not? I survived the president and Jason Smithies. You're a piece of cake, sis.

53

FRIENDS IN HIGH PLACES

The President smokes a Cuban cigar at his desk. Smithies barges into the Oval Office without knocking.

Smithies: I'm sorry for interrupting, Mr. President.

President Macorley: Get to it, man.

Smithies: The Swiss just called. There was nothing in Dr. Corsini's safety deposit box.

President Macorley: What the hell? Elizabeth is smart but not that smart. And not that stupid, either. She would never double-cross me. Oh, shit!

Smithies: What is it?

The president belly laughs.

President Macorley: I'll be damned. Maybe there's a God after all.

Smithies: I don't understand, Mr. President.

President Macorley: Private joke, Jason. Didn't you ever experience a miracle?

Smithies: Why, no! I'm not a believer, sir. Shall we kill the Corsini sisters?

President Macorley: You still don't get it, Jason. The Corsinis have friends in high places. Lay off them. Permanently!

* * *

The angels Michael and Gabriel in human form laugh and toast each other in a bar in Zurich.

Michael: I haven't had this much fun in years…watching you steal the president's psychiatric file from Dr. Corsini's safety deposit box.

Gabriel: You know that I rarely laugh, Michael. But it was pretty funny. Did you see the look on that Swiss bank manager's face when he saw that the box was empty?

Michael: At least the president can appreciate a good joke. The Ancient One will be pleased.

54

GODFATHER

A bottle of Macallan 18 scotch is on the table in the Four Seasons lounge, compliments of Marshall Lamster:

Daniela: I'm a naughty girl. I put this on Marshall's tab. He gets a huge discount because the hotel knows he's the FBI director.

The sisters kick off their shoes and raise their glasses.

Elizabeth: A toast to the sisters Corsini…and good riddance to men.

They clink glasses. Nearby Michael and Gabriel also clink glasses.

Gabriel: You've corrupted me, Michael.

Michael: Lighten up. All's well that ends well.

Daniela's mood becomes somber.

Daniela: I was shocked to hear about Esther, Dov, Kavorsky, and Roger Arnold. We can't prove it, but it was the work of Smithies' henchmen, probably untraceable foreign agents. He's a real bastard.

Elizabeth: Yes, the worst kind.

Daniela: Smithies kills without conscience out of absolute loyalty to the president. They were at Yale together and members of that secret society, the Skulls and Bones. Between sisters, Lizzie, is any of it true?

Elizabeth: Is what true? Oh, you mean about the president and me and our sexual escapades while I was seeing him as a patient? Yes, it's all true.

Daniela: Quit playing coy. You know it was me who provided Esther with Daniel's ancient dream. You and I both had the same religious training with the sisters. I'm talking about the president being a global leader and all that nasty stuff you and Esther concocted in interpreting Daniel's dream. That wasn't in the game plan.

Elizabeth: That was more Esther than me. She had quite the creative mind. If you're asking me whether Code Name Daniel will actually happen to make the president a global Messiah, I would answer you in the following way. Do you remember the Godfather movies?

Daniela: Of course. I've seen those movies over and over. I'm Italian.

Elizabeth: You always had a Sicilian streak in you.

Daniela: Get to the point.

Elizabeth: Kay Adams played by Diane Keaton says to the Godfather, Michael Corleone, played by Al Pacino, "Are you responsible for killing your sister's husband?" The Godfather responds, "OK, Kay, I'm going to tell you this one time." He pauses and replies, "No, I didn't murder Carlos."

Daniela: The Godfather obviously lied. I would have done the same in his place.

Elizabeth: My answer to your question is I would have to lie if I were forced to reveal the truth under oath.

Daniela: I'm not asking you to swear on the Bible, Lizzie. For Christ's sake give me a straight answer.

Elizabeth: My personal opinion is that Code Name Daniel is a myth based upon worn-out religious beliefs. On the other hand, the president really does want to rule the world. Is it true that Daniel's ancient dream is connected to the president's desire to be the Messiah? Only time will tell if both shall come true. What's your opinion, Dannie?

Daniela: Good will win out over evil in the end, even if Daniel's dream comes true at the hands of the president. God, it's a nightmare trying to extract a simple answer out of you in the midst of all the bullshit you fling.

The sisters get up from the table and give each other a hug. They depart the Four Seasons and head for Elizabeth's car. They stand by the car, talking.

Daniela: I'm meeting Marshall tonight to hash out what's left of our relationship.

Elizabeth: Go easy on him. You two can make a life together.

Daniela: I hope that I have the energy to keep up with him. I'll definitely need hormone replacement if I'm going to survive.

They both laugh.

Elizabeth: Will I see you this weekend? Abel and Sophia are coming over for dinner.

Daniela: How's the romance going?

Elizabeth: They definitely have the hots for each other. Sophia is smiling all the time, but she keeps her love life private.

Daniela: Don't worry. If Abel ever hurts her, he'll have me to deal with. He's fully aware of how I feel about Sophia.

Elizabeth: I just want her to be happy. If it takes a Jewish boy, then that's all I want. Sophia is pretty busy in her obstetrics residency at the hospital, so the time that they have is probably spent in bed. I'm hoping that he'll make an honest woman out of her. An engagement ring would be nice.

Daniela: See you for dinner on Saturday, Lizzie.

Elizabeth opens the car door, but before she can get in, they hear a voice.

Michael: See you in Heaven, Gabriel.

They look around, but there's no one there.

Elizabeth: Angels, Dannie.

Daniela: The nuns always told us that we were bad enough to have a divine encounter.

One more hug and the sisters part ways. The angels fly off into ethereal space.

55

NO FREE LUNCH

Leamas and the president are strolling in Anacostia National Park.

President Macorley: The Corsini sisters are still alive, but our plans for Gog and Magog are progressing. In another three years, we'll be out of Afghanistan, with the Taliban and Al Qaeda defeated.

Leamas: And Iran? We need to eliminate three large horns. Daniel's prophecy must be fulfilled if we are to proceed with Gog and Magog.

President Macorley: I'll settle for Yemen or possibly North Korea for a third horn. Iran keeps Israel on its toes, and we'll need Iran for the initial attack on the Holy Land.

Leamas: And of course this is all happening about the time of your reelection campaign. After you screwed up on the Corsinis, I have no intention of supporting you.

President Macorley: That's just dandy. My poll numbers are sinking, and if I can't count on you, Devil, I'll lose the election. We are family after all. I am descended from your blood. You raped Eve outside of the Garden of Eden, and you have reminded me more times than I care to enumerate that I'm from your seed. That my ancestor was the biblical Cain. Without your help I can't do this.

Leamas: I hate people who suck up to me with their phony compliments. I invented insincerity, and I am the evil inclination in you and every blasted human. So don't give me this blood is thicker than water shit. There's no free lunch.

President Macorley: I'm willing to do anything.

Leamas: Are you sure?

President Macorley: Yes!

Leamas: I want you to kill Sophia Corsini after you're reelected.

President Macorley: I'm sure you have your reasons, and that's good enough for me.

Leamas: Sophia Corsini is your biological daughter.

President Macorley shakes his head in disbelief. He always wondered where Elizabeth went after they broke up. She disappeared for a year. She said she was taking a sabbatical in Great Britain. Son of a gun!

Unfazed the president shows his true nature.

President Macorley: Absolutely, no problem, Devil.

56

2020

President Malcolm Yale Macorley and his son, Cain Arlis Macorley, are casually dressed in jeans and Yale sweatshirts, watching television in the White House.

The president, now in his early fifties, has not aged well. His handsome face shows evidence of permanent lines, and bags from sleeplessness are forming under his hazel eyes. Just about all his hair has turned gray, and he looks worn out. All presidents look the same after a few years in office. It's the nature of the beast.

In contrast, his son Cain, early thirties, is strikingly Hollywood beautiful. He has black eyes, with slick black hair parted down the middle, and he stands about six feet tall, the same height as his father. Cain rarely smiles, but when he does his pearly white teeth force you to stare in his direction.

Cain doesn't look at all like either of his parents, nor does he look Irish. Many a day since Cain's birth, the president has wondered where Cain came from, and he doubts that Cain belongs to him. The First Lady has never admitted to adultery. Yet the president has always sensed that she was bedded by Leamas. Although both Leamas and Cain are the same age, there is a striking similarity in appearance between them. The president is also baffled by the fact that Leamas, alias the Devil, doesn't age.

President Macorley: I love to watch Fox News and gloat. By the end of this historic night, I shall be reelected president.

Cain: MSNBC and CNN are already predicting your victory in one of the closest presidential contests ever.

President Macorley: And the congratulatory gift to my fellow Republican enemies will be a special announcement. You, Cain, will be my new chief of staff and my most trusted advisor. The youngest ever to serve in this capacity. The president's right arm.

Cain doesn't feel grateful. He perceives his father to be weak. Cain manages a smirk.

Cain: I continue to learn from you, Dad.

President Macorley: You ran a brilliant presidential campaign, Cain. You worked harder than even me. Quite an accomplishment.

Cain: Hold on! They are about to announce your carrying Florida.

President Macorley: The Jews vote Democratic no matter how I screw them and their Jewish state. Their sacrifices will make me the Messiah of the world.

Father and son turn their heads to the television. The Fox newscaster comes on.

Fox Newscaster: Florida can now be placed in the blue column. Macorley has won the Sunshine State in a dramatic come-from-behind victory over Senator James Laughton of Wisconsin. The differential seems to be less than two thousand votes.

The president is beaming.

President Macorley: I love it. This election is so close that my asshole is beginning to squeak.

Cain pulls a small tube of ointment from his pocket.

Cain: Here's the one percent hydrocortisone cream. I came prepared.

The president laughs.

President Macorley: Laughter extends your life.

Cain: Your hemorrhoids are calling.

Macorley takes the tube from Cain and heads to the bathroom. Cain grabs the remote and switches the channel to MSNBC. The announcer comes on as the president is listening from the bathroom.

MSNBC Announcer: Only two states remain—the Big Ten giants, Ohio and Michigan. We've got ourselves a football game. The president needs to carry only one of these two states to win.

* * *

Meanwhile in Sophia's apartment, Sophia and Abel are sipping red wine in crystal goblets, watching the election returns. It's odd that Sophia looks exactly like Eve from the Garden of Eden. She is wearing a diamond ring.

Abel: Shit, Sophia. Another four years of this egomaniac.

Sophia: The son of a bitch is going to pull it out with his testicles intact. I used my mother's Waterford crystal tonight because I thought he was going to lose.

Abel: Your mother told me that his nickname at the Secret Service is the Messiah. At the FBI he's Sly, the Gray Fox. Great balls of fire, it looks like Laughton has Ohio.

CNN Announcer: CNN can now project that Senator James Laughton has won Ohio, with 98 percent of the vote counted.

Abel and Sophia clap.

Sophia: Hooray for our side. Abel, have you told your parents that we're engaged, and with my obstetrics residency complete, we would like to set a wedding date?

Abel: As soon as they heard I was serious about dating a gentile girl, they wrote me off; so as far as they're concerned, I'm dead. They actually mourned me by sitting *shivah* for a full month.

Sophia: I want them at my wedding, Abel. I'm willing to convert. Do you have a rabbi who can help?

Abel: I'm good friends with Rabbi Zev Goren. We went to law school together. He's also a lawyer. I can ask him to set up your training, but it will be the whole megillah—a Jewish Orthodox conversion—mikvah and all.

Screams come from the campaign headquarters of President Macorley. Hundreds of balloons fly into the air, music plays, campaign workers dance, as there is general pandemonium in the room. The TV camera switches to the CNN announcer.

CNN Announcer: The state of Michigan belongs to Malcolm Yale Macorley. The president has grabbed the brass ring in this merry-go-round of an election. He has beaten the odds and has snatched victory from despair in a squeaker of an election. All the polls were wrong.

* * *

Someone else is watching the returns with interest. Elizabeth Corsini is sitting in her apartment with Muffin, nervously smoking a cigarette and getting drunk on vodka gimlets. She is thinking back to that one night a lifetime ago when she became pregnant by then Senator Macorley of Delaware. He doesn't know to this day that Sophia is his daughter, or so she believes. They are lying in bed together. Elizabeth is Cinderella and Snow White, and Malcolm is the handsome prince in the Disney fairy tales.

Elizabeth: Malcolm, you've already achieved celebrity status. Everyone knows you as the famous Delaware senator. Why do you need to be president?

Senator Macorley: You treated me in therapy. You of all people should know who I am.

Elizabeth: You're not God, Malcolm.

Senator Macorley: True, though I'm different from other humans, who can only achieve the possible. I can accomplish the impossible, like God. The presidency is only the first step in reaching my goal to become ruler of the world.

Elizabeth: You're the brightest man I know. I broke the doctor–patient relationship because I've never felt this way about any man before. I'm in love with you.

Senator Macorley: Elizabeth, I'm grateful to you for helping me in regressive therapy with my lack of parental love, but this is our last night together.

Elizabeth is totally taken back. She starts crying.

Elizabeth: What? I don't understand.

Senator Macorley: It's really very simple. I have to shed any traces of vulnerability in my past. Tomorrow I announce my candidacy for the presidency.

Elizabeth: Just like that. You're a callous bastard, Malcolm. You don't care about anybody but yourself.

Senator Macorley: Nothing can stand in the way of my ambition. Not even God. Emotional attachments make you weak.

Elizabeth jumps out of bed. She puts on her robe.

Elizabeth: Get the fuck out of here, Malcolm.

* * *

The scene shifts back to Abel and Sophia.

Sophia: My mother never speaks about it, but she once let it slip that she had an affair with then Senator Macorley.

Abel: Does Daniela know?

Sophia: Yes. About three years ago, my aunt and my mother were involved in a secret White House operation, Code Name Daniel.

Abel: I was privy to that operation. It had to do with the president's psychiatric file. He was a patient of your mother's when he was a senator from Delaware.

Sophia: That I didn't know. I hate secrets. Speaking of which, I can't marry you until you reveal yours to me, Abel. These past three years together have been wonderful, but you need to tell me everything. Have you done that, Abel? Or are you still hiding something?

Abel gets up off the couch and pours himself a glass of red wine.

Abel: I promise to tell you soon. There was one part of my mission that I told you I couldn't speak about.

Sophia: We're talking about marriage. There can be no secrets between a husband and a wife. I don't want to end up like my mother with a cancer in her memory. No lies, Abel. I can't bear lying or cheating.

Abel thinks back to cheating on his geography test and on the FBI admissions exam with Leamas.

Abel: I swear it on my Jewish Star of David.

57

ISRAELI EMBASSY

Abel carefully glances around, making sure that he is not followed as he enters the back door of the Israeli Embassy. After screening by security, he proceeds to the office of Ambassador Shlomo Katchalski. He sits down opposite the ambassador. They begin speaking in Hebrew and then later break into perfect English.

Ambassador Katchalski: Shalom, Abel. Prime Minister Duskin is very worried about the White House. Our intelligence indicates that the United States will soon activate Gog and Magog against the State of Israel. I have a letter for you from the prime minister. It's sealed. It arrived by courier this morning.

Abel takes the letter, opens it, and reads it.

Abel: Do you know the contents of the letter, Shlomo?

Ambassador Katchalski: Yes. The prime minister has informed me of your mission. He's a very careful and decisive man, and he wants you to destroy the letter in front of me now that you've read your instructions.

Shlomo hands Abel a match and an ashtray. Abel reads the message once more and without expression tears up the letter into small pieces. He places the pieces in the ashtray, lights a match, and they both watch the note burn completely to ashes.

Ambassador Katchalski: I'm afraid the president's reelection is not a good sign for Israel. He appears to be blessed with the luck of the Devil. It seemed like he was sure to be defeated. Even Charlie Cook had him losing, and the Las Vegas betting odds were soundly against him.

Shlomo's comments give Abel pause. He reflects on his encounters with the Devil and wonders if Leamas played any role in the president's victory.

Abel: I need to get inside Cain Macorley's head if I'm going to kill him. Cain will be the point man on Gog and Magog.

Ambassador Katchalski: Be careful, Abel. Cain is more demonic than his father, who at least has a rational mind. Cain is worse than a wounded animal. Totally unpredictable.

Abel: Is it a coincidence?

Ambassador Katchalski: What?

Abel: An Abel confronts a Cain in modern times

Ambassador Katchalski: You know that there are no coincidences when you believe in the Creator. Be very cautious, Abel. Cain will try to kill you before you kill him.

Abel gets up and shakes Shlomo's hand.

Ambassador Katchalski: Go out the back way; there's a car waiting for you.

Abel: Shalom, Ambassador.

58

FOREVER YOUNG

Abel is in the back seat of the ambassador's limousine. He doesn't realize that Leamas is the driver. Leamas is without the beard and mustache Abel saw him with several years ago when Leamas admitted him into the FBI. He looks exactly like the Leamas who was Abel's fourth grade geography teacher. He remains forever young.

Abel recognizes him when he turns around.

Abel: You keep your age very well, Leamas.

Leamas shows off by going into a diatribe of Hebrew conversation about the fate of the State of Israel and its relationship to God. He then switches into English.

Leamas: Hello, Abel. I've known all along that you are a double agent. But don't worry. I won't tell anyone as long as your God is watching. Do you believe that God will save you from my hands?

Abel draws his gun and points it at Leamas's head. Leamas laughs.

Leamas: I dare you to pull the trigger.

Abel pulls the trigger. The bullet goes directly to Leamas's heart, but nothing happens. Abel lowers the gun.

Leamas: You can't kill me, Abel. Only an angel, a peer, can do that. And I've beaten every angel I've faced in battle. Hey, don't be sad. You did well, Abel. I didn't think you had the balls to shoot.

Abel: Who are you?

Leamas: I told you when we met last. I'm the Devil. You have a date with destiny, but it's not with me. I'll inform Cain Macorley who you are so we can have a fair fight. You'll find that I play strictly by the rules. I never cheat.

Abel: What do you want?

Leamas: Your soul. You can trade your soul for the lives of the president and Cain Macorley. Say the word and they'll be dead. Isn't that what your prime minister asked you to do? You know, the note you just burned in front of the ambassador.

Abel: And in return?

Leamas: You must cross over to the dark side. I want you to kill Sophia Corsini, the beautiful Italian princess whom you love with all your heart and soul.

Abel: And this would be your test of my loyalty and devotion to you.

Leamas: Yes! You must destroy the most precious thing in the world to you. Then I'll be sure that you have surrendered your soul.

Abel: I need to think about it. Where is the driver, Abie?

Leamas: Oh, you mean Avraham. He's sleeping peacefully in the alleyway. I used a little bit of chloroform.

Leamas gets out of the limo and smiles, and Abel watches him disappear from view.

59

LIKE FATHER LIKE SON

President Macorley is standing behind his desk in the Oval Office deciding whether to flatter his son Cain, who is facing him. He lights up a Cuban Cohiba and then sits down in his cushioned Queen Anne chair. Cain mimics his father, but declines the cigar his father offers him.

The president has always had difficulty getting a read on Cain. His son rarely shares what he's really thinking.

President Macorley: Cain, nobody knows that it was your idea for the federal government to bail out GM and Chrysler. It was payback time, and the unions in Michigan went far and beyond their usual corruption to get me reelected.

Cain: If I've learned anything from you, Dad, it's that absolute power trumps both truth and hope.

President Macorley: I'd better get ready for my debut. The country is waiting. Will you excuse me, son? I have a congratulatory call coming in from James Laughton, the buffoon. He never conceded on election night, and I have to make nice even with dummies.

Cain bows and exits. President Macorley speaks aloud.

President Macorley: I'd better keep a personal eye on Cain now that Smithies has gone off to Wall Street. Cain has always been a bit strange, and I don't think he would hesitate to throw me under a bus.

President Macorley's private number rings. He picks up.

President Macorley: Hello, Senator. I was expecting your call… Oh, thank you for those nice words. I'm speaking in about a minute from the Oval Office. I'll catch you later.

The president combs his hair and is seated at his desk.

President Macorley: Thank you, America. It was a hard-fought battle, and I congratulate Senator Laughton for the good fight. My first action as your reelected president is to announce that my son, Cain Arlis Macorley, will be taking over as my new chief of staff. I want to pay tribute to Jason Smithies for his excellent service. Jason is leaving the White House to return to private life.

Cain Macorley, standing in his new office, switches off the television and looks around. The room is three hundred square feet and is tastefully decorated, courtesy of Jason Smithies. On the wall are an American flag and cheaply framed eight and a half by eleven picture of the president. Cain walks around the room, stops at the photo, and removes it from the wall. He then tosses the picture in the wastepaper basket.

Cain: I should be the one giving tonight's speech to the nation. My father's the one who's the buffoon.

President Macorley: We are safer now than ever before. Under my leadership we have secured Iraq and defeated the Taliban in Pakistan and Afghanistan. Al Qaeda and Yemeni terrorists have been rooted out of their caves, and the snake's head of Iran is hanging by a thread. For the first time in decades, there is real peace around the globe.

Abel and Sophia smile to each other after hearing the president on TV.

Abel: I wonder what planet he's living on. I think America is the one hanging on by a thread. There are more suicide bombings, and Iran has the capability of launching a nuclear attack anywhere in the world. The president is wearing blinders.

Sophia: I wouldn't mind if he'd stop lying to us. And how could it hurt him to once in a while give credit to his predecessors? I detest arrogant braggarts. I feel sorry for the president's children.

Abel: I'll remember that when we're married.

Sophia: Abel, I'm concerned about the dreams you've been having. Perhaps you should talk to my mother. She's pretty good at dream interpretation.

Abel: Maybe I should speak to your mother. I just feel kind of funny because of our relationship. After all I'm planning to be her son-in-law.

Sophia: Abel, I don't want to set a date until we visit your parents in Brooklyn.

Abel: I told them about your converting, and that's softened them up a bit, but they want to meet you, too. Sophia, I have something to tell you. It's that dark secret I've been harboring. Brace yourself.

Sophia: Nothing you could say would frighten me off.

Abel: I work for Israeli intelligence, the Mossad. I joined the FBI because we've suspected for several years now that the Americans were planning to lead an attack on the State of Israel. Have you ever heard of the wars of Gog and Magog? The wars are based on prophecies from the Hebrew Bible. And events happening right now suggest that Gog and Magog will soon be activated by the president.

Sophia: I haven't, but the nuns schooled both my aunt Daniela and my mother, so they probably are acquainted with the prophecies. Oh, my God, Abel, we can't tell either one of them. My aunt is big on loyalty, and she hates being played for a fool. My husband or not, you could wind up in jail. Shit! Pardon the expression. Now I have a damn secret to keep.

Abel: I have no choice but to continue my mission. Are you sure you want to go through with marrying me?

Sophia: I'm sure. I've always had this sixth sense, and I've felt the presence of God since my childhood. I know He's here now, and will protect the both of us. I'm getting strong spiritual vibes that there's something you and I have to do together, but I'm not sure what it is.

60

THE ANGELS EXPLAIN

Michael and Gabriel are standing near the incense altar in the sanctuary of the Third Temple.

Michael: I love the solitude in Heaven.

Gabriel: Me too. Do these humans understand the connection of Code Name Daniel to Gog and Magog

Michael: Only Satan comprehends the import of the three of the ten uprooted large horns and the little horn in Daniel's dream. The Hebrew prophets, Joel, Ezekiel, and Zechariah, spoke about the End of Days, but no human has ever made the connection to the seven remaining large horns on Daniel's beast. The seven horns represent the seven Islamic nations, which will attack the State of Israel in the first of three phases in the wars of Gog and Magog.

Gabriel: Yes, the seven nations comprising the Muslim governments of Libya, Turkey, Sudan, Somalia, Iran, the Russian Caucasus Mountain countries, and Syria. In the initial attack, these foreign enemy forces will land on Israeli soil, but will be repelled by the Israeli Defense Forces. However, the enemies of the Jewish people shall not be discouraged.

Michael: As prophesied in the Bible, seven will become seventy nations in the second phase of the wars. Virtually the whole world will smell blood and will join together to once and for all attempt to eliminate the heart of the Jewish people by destroying the Holy Land. The leadership of the war will by default fall to President Macorley and his son, Cain. The president, because of his foreign policy successes in Afghanistan, Pakistan, and North Korea, will be the global Messiah.

Gabriel: Yes, the European countries and the remaining Arab countries will be part of the attacking forces. The seventy nations shall reach the foothills of Jerusalem in this second phase of the wars of Gog and Magog.

Michael: In the third and final phase, the fall of Jerusalem will be followed by the Ancient One's divine intervention to destroy the enemies of the Jews.

Gabriel: Half the population of Jerusalem will be killed or captured, and then God will create an earthquake incredible even to Him. This will cause Mount Moriah to emerge from beneath the earth like a volcanic eruption.

The two angels visualize the Mount of Olives in East Jerusalem splitting in two in God's great earthquake. One half of the mountain is pushed north and the other south, creating a valley stretching twenty-five miles, with the city of Jerusalem displaced to the southern tip. At the north end, Mount Moriah emerges from beneath the earth and rises high above the valley. It is Mount Moriah where King Solomon's First Temple and the Second Temple were destroyed, and where the Third Temple will be erected into the mountain by the Messiah.

Michael and Gabriel hear God's voice.

GOD: I shall crush the enemies of My people for the thousands of years they have inflicted murderous death and persecution. All who survive my justice and mercy shall know Me, as the waters are of the sea. Those who don't survive will be subject to abhorrent punishment and shall vanish from life. I shall give man a new heart and a new spirit so that he shall no longer possess the evil inclination of Satan. Wars will disappear forever from the earth, and peace shall rule eternally. A higher form of evolutionary humans shall spring forth out of the ravages of Gog and Magog. I shall create miracles that are incredible even to Me. As prophesied in the Garden of Eden in the time of Adam and Eve, those who are deserving shall be resurrected from their graves to live again, no matter what their faith and no matter what their belief. I shall be the judge and jury and will determine who shall live for eternity and who shall not, as written in the Book of Daniel. All will face their Maker at the final Judgment Day. Every human was given a Divine Soul by My breath, through which I have kept the scorecard of man's moral choices. Man has written world history, but I shall write its ending at the *End of Days.*

Michael: Gog and Magog are in full bloom, Ancient One.

Gabriel: Satan and the Macorleys are cunning, and they will soon move ahead with the prophecies. The world is in great danger. I implore You, Master of the Universe, to act now.

GOD: I mourn the killing of any human being. It was difficult for me to destroy the ancient Egyptians during the Exodus, but it was a necessity so that my Torah could be given to the Israelites, imperfect as I knew they would be.

Michael: We tried to warn You years ago, Ancient One, not to give the Ten Commandments to the Jewish slaves. They were as corrupt as their Egyptian taskmasters.

GOD: Not only was my Torah a necessity, so was the imperfection of the Israelites. I have created imperfection in all human beings so that they shall understand perfection at the End of Days. Like good and evil, they are both sides of the same coin.

Gabriel: My humble understanding, Ancient One, is that the End Times can come about in two ways—either through the apocalypse of the prophecies of Joel, Ezekiel and Zechariah, or when humans merit the transformation to freedom from the evil inclination.

GOD: You underestimate Me, My angel. There is a third way for the Messianic Age to come about.

Michael: Have You found Your Prophet Messiah?

GOD: Yes, the yet-to-be-born son of Abel and Sophia. He is already inside the womb of Sophia and will be born from the egg and sperm of a Christian and a Jew.

Gabriel: Abel is in great danger, and so is Sophia. When Satan finds out, he will kill Sophia to destroy Your plan for humankind.

GOD: Satan serves Me at My pleasure.

Gabriel: Send me, Ancient One, and I shall destroy all evil in the world. I shall kill Satan in fair combat.

GOD: In due time, My angel. Satan expects Me to be on the defensive, but I have a surprise for him.

61

SURPRISE PHONE CALL

E lizabeth shuts off the TV and is about to get undressed when her phone rings.

Elizabeth: Hello.

Cain: My name is Cain Macorley.

Elizabeth holds her hand over the phone and mutters, "What the hell does he want?"

Elizabeth: Speak of the Devil. Sorry! That was a Freudian slip. It's a bit late to be calling, isn't it?

Cain: I know about my father's psychiatric file.

Elizabeth: Being blunt is not necessarily a virtue. Do you have anything else to say on your father's behalf?

Cain: "The wise man seeks counsel."

Elizabeth: I see you know some Bible. A quote from King Solomon's Book of Proverbs.

Cain: You'd be surprised by my talents.

Elizabeth: Let's get right to the point, Mr. Macorley. What can I do for you?

Cain: I wake up with migraine headaches.

Elizabeth: Plenty of people do the same. Have you consulted with a neurologist?

Cain: I toss and turn in my sleep and have this awful nightmare every night. I need an expert to figure it all out.

Elizabeth: Why me?

Cain: You treated my father. We'll meet at the Holocaust Museum. I'm not fond of Jews.

Elizabeth's brain momentarily focuses on her future son-in-law, Abel Slobodkin.

Elizabeth: What makes you think I can explain your sleeping patterns? I'm not Joseph, the Jew who interpreted the pharaoh's dreams.

Cain: I know exactly who you are. You're my father's whore. Oh, pardon me! That was a Freudian slip. Let's just say that you'll have a friend in the White House if you help me out with the interpretation.

Elizabeth: Your father once said those very same words to me. I was less than impressed by his actions when he tried to have me killed. Though he was, at least, well mannered. You're a boor.

Cain: Well, I'm nothing like my father. You can trust me.

Elizabeth: Noon. Inside the museum entryway. It will be good for your soul. That is, if you have one.

Elizabeth awaits a response. She hears a click on the other end. She breathes deeply. The phone rings again. Elizabeth picks up

Elizabeth: You're being a pest, Mr...

Sophia: Mom, it's me. Abel is standing right next to me. I need a favor.

Elizabeth: So sorry, darling. I had a crank call just seconds ago, and I thought it was him again.

Sophia: Abel and I were hoping to meet you for drinks. He needs your advice.

Elizabeth: Is everything okay?

Sophia: Yes, of course! Abel's been having some unusual dreams lately. He would like your help. He thought you might have some insight into their meaning.

Elizabeth laughs.

Elizabeth: They're not divine, are they?

Sophia: I haven't heard them yet.

Elizabeth: The Four Seasons Hotel, Friday night happy hour. I'll bring your aunt Daniela.

Sophia: Thanks, Mom. I love you.

Elizabeth: I love you, too. Bye, darling.

They hang up. Sophia and Abel chat.

Sophia: It's all set for tomorrow.

Abel: You didn't tell her about the other problem.

Sophia: Another time. I want us first to visit your parents. Can you get away?

Abel: Yes, we can drive up to New York on Saturday. My father would want me to go to services in the evening.

Sophia: Can I come?

Abel: Sorry, they separate the men from the women.

Sophia: I'll be stuck with your mother.

Abel: You're the one who wants to meet them. Besides she doesn't bite.

Sophia: I know. It's just that I feel like you're my buffer against them if they start discussing religion.

Abel: The services are at 770 Eastern Parkway in Brooklyn at the Chabad Lubavitch Center.

Sophia: I started my conversion classes, Abel. We're reading the Torah.

Abel: Are you having fun?

Sophia: Studying the Torah is not fun. It is fascinating, though. I really love reading about the personal stories of the patriarchs, Abraham, Isaac, and Jacob. Did you know that Isaac was married to Rebecca? Your parents are also Isaac and Rebecca. That's cool.

Abel: Yes. My parents are actually first cousins. And my paternal grandparents coincidentally were named Abraham and Sarah. The stories in the Bible actually foretell events to come in our future.

Sophia: What scared me most was when I read about Cain and Abel. You're an Abel, and President Macorley's son is a Cain. Is that also a coincidence?

Abel gives pause, knowing that the prime minister of Israel has instructed him to kill Cain. He looks into Sophia's innocent eyes and decides not to tell her about his mission.

Abel: That's all it is—a coincidence. Let's retire to the bedroom. I can't get enough of your voluptuous body.

62

SNAKES IN THE PARK

Leamas as the talking Serpent and President Macorley are sitting around a campfire at night in a wooded area of Anacostia National Park. Strange sounds, like those of coyotes or wolves, are heard in the distance. Leamas is munching on six live bullfrogs that he has caught in the meadow.

Serpent: I hope you don't mind my eating. I can spare one if you like.

The president is using all his willpower not to puke.

President Macorley: They look delicious, but I'm actually full from the White House chef's early dinner of roast beef and mashed potatoes.

Serpent: You have to watch the red meat, Mr. President. It's not good for your constitution. You need to eat more vegetables and fruit, like I do.

The Serpent shoves down another live bullfrog, while espousing the virtues of a vegetarian diet. President Macorley is looking on in disgust.

Serpent: This is my opportunity to defeat God.

President Macorley smirks in disbelief as if saying, "You're out of your fucking mind, snake." He thinks better of saying what he truly feels and gives an innocuous response.

President Macorley: How will you achieve your victory?

Serpent: By destroying His holy nation through the fulfillment of the prophecies of Gog and Magog.

President Macorley: But in those prophecies God saves the Jewish State when all seems lost.

The Serpent does a dance in different directions, displaying its confidence. It raises itself high above and across the fire, and its head comes to rest directly in front of the president's face. When the Serpent is eyeball to eyeball, it looks deeply into the eyes of the president, who cowers away, trembling in fear.

Serpent: Yes, but I have a surprise plan that even God is unaware of. Abel Slobodkin.

President Macorley: Who is Abel Slobodkin?

Serpent: If you stop interrupting me, I will tell you. Abel is my pet project. I was there at his birth. I egged him on to cheat on his fourth grade geography test. I admitted him into the FBI, even though I knew he cheated, and I have a survivor-like challenge in store for him. Abel is a double agent. He's Mossad, but that's between you and me. Abel has been instructed to kill Cain, but if Cain kills Abel, and you fulfill your end of the deal to murder Sophia Corsini, then God's plan will be thwarted.

President Macorley: I don't like all this talk of killing. I feel your breath under my shirt collar, Serpent. Am I safe?

Serpent: What? No sense of family loyalty? I just told you that your son is in great peril.

President Macorley: Cain is a survivor.

Serpent: Like father like son. It's time to activate Gog and Magog.

President Macorley: I've already cut the ribbon.

Serpent: Your grandson will be born to Sophia Corsini in eight months time. God has a plan to make the baby the Messiah. The emergence of a Messiah of any religion must be stopped at all costs.

President Macorley: I read you loud and clear. Why don't we kill Sophia now?

Serpent: Wasn't that your pledge to me in return for your reelection?

President Macorley: What else do I get out of it?

Serpent: Haven't I done enough for you? I've made you president.

President Macorley: Ever since I was a kid, I've wanted to be ruler of the world. You need to make that happen, Devil. Otherwise all bets are off.

The Serpent hisses and moves closer to the president. The president gasps, and as his mouth opens, the Serpent drops a bullfrog's leg into his mouth. The president chokes and vomits all over his clothes.

Serpent: I guess you weren't really hungry. A deal is a deal. One thing I can't stand is someone who doesn't own up to his part of an agreement. I draw the line in the sand on disobedience, particularly since I own your soul, Mr. President. I can easily replace you with your son Cain. After all he's from my seed, not yours. He looks like me, not you.

President Macorley: I always suspected that. Why?

Serpent: Why did I do it? Simple! I needed an heir—Cain—to kill Abel, just like the biblical Cain murdered his brother Abel. I'm recreating evil to defeat good. The building of the Third Temple in Messianic times is the redemption for the biblical murder of Abel. If I can do the same in modern times, then I shall hand God a double defeat.

President Macorley: And the First Lady? Did she voluntarily agree to sexual relations with you, Leamas?

Serpent: She did when I told her about all the affairs you've been having during your term in office.

President Macorley: I've only had one affair. You know that. It was with a campaign worker, and it was only oral sex. Women are constantly throwing themselves at me.

Serpent: So I embellished a little, but it was enough to turn her rage into lust. Besides, who wouldn't want a thirty-year-old stud like me? I never age, and you're getting old and soft in the belly, Mr. President. You need to start working out.

President Macorley: I'll do what you ask, Leamas. But you'd better damn well make me the global Messiah.

Serpent: So long, King Macorley.

President Macorley departs.

Serpent: Why do I have to deal with these human fools who think they can outsmart Satan?

63

HOLOCAUST MUSEUM

E lizabeth and Cain walk through the Holocaust Museum and look at the horrifying scenes of Jews in the concentration camps. Cain breaks the silence.

Cain: This is the last time I'll visit this place full of wretched souls. They allowed themselves to be led to the slaughter. They deserved what they received.

Elizabeth's instincts as a psychiatrist are begging her to talk about the lack of compassion and mercy in Cain, but thinking she wants to spend as little time as she can with this despicable creep, she gets right to the point.

Elizabeth: Tell me about your dreams.

Cain: I'm over seven and a half feet tall, and I'm fighting a much smaller youth, who only possesses a slingshot and a small *rock.*

Cain envisions an ugly giant of a man dressed in full body armor, except for his lips, nose, and eyes. The giant has a shield in one hand and a sword in the other hand. He wears sluggish heavy metal boots laced to his shinbones.

Underneath the face mask, one can vaguely get a sense that the man's features in the dream are those of Cain, while the handsome youth is that of Abel Slobodkin.

The youth pulls back on his slingshot and fires a small rock at the giant. The stone hits the giant's lips but misses his forehead. The giant tilts backwards slightly, but doesn't lose his balance. He immediately slices the youth with his sword. The boyish, wounded, slingshot warrior falls to the ground. The giant lifts his right foot and crushes the skull of the youth with his metal boot.

Cain has a smile on his face, and he licks his chops at the remembrance of the youth's brains squashed on the ground.

Elizabeth: You're reliving the story of David and Goliath.

Cain: Except that I'm victorious. I crush the little fellow without mercy.

Elizabeth: If you've won, why is the dream bothering you?

Cain: Because there is more to the dream. Immediately after the battle, I see this young girl, named Eve, being raped by this man who resembles me. I'm in a strange place, somewhere in a tent in the forest outside a beautiful garden.

Cain drifts off. Satan, identical to Adam and Leamas, is raping Eve in the tent in the biblical forest outside the Garden of Eden. Cain watches at the entrance of the tent but doesn't go over to help Eve. Satan looks back at Cain, winks, and laughs while he continues to rape Eve.

Elizabeth: Are you sorry that you didn't help the girl?

Cain: I enjoyed her being raped. I get sexually aroused in my dream, and my blood vessels expand. The migraine comes in the morning when I wake up.

Elizabeth is dismayed and decides to go with her gut feelings.

Elizabeth: You have a sadistic streak in you, Cain. The dream tells me that you enjoy other people's suffering. I can't help you.

Cain angrily turns beet red. He raises both hands in a strangling motion and then realizes where he is. He drops his hands to his sides and then storms away, mumbling to himself. Elizabeth's eyes carefully follow him until he exits the museum. She speaks aloud.

Elizabeth: Daniela was right about Cain. He's a nut job.

* * *

That evening, Elizabeth is relaxing when she hears a knock. She opens the door partially, with the chain intact.

Elizabeth: It's almost midnight. You're the last person I expected to see after the stunt you pulled.

Cain: I came to apologize. May I come in?

Elizabeth hesitates.

Elizabeth: No, you may—

Cain pushes the door with his shoulder, breaking the chain. His eyes are wildly darting around the room as he grabs her arm and rips off part of her blouse. He smacks her hard across the face. She pulls away and rushes to the phone, but before she can dial, he pushes her down onto the carpet. She tries to scream, but cannot.

Cain: I'll take what my father took.

The unseen angels, Michael and Gabriel, enter the apartment. Before Cain can throw himself down on top of her, he trips over Michael's invisible foot. Cain falls flat on his face next to Elizabeth. When she sees Cain isn't getting up, Elizabeth regains her composure, stands up, runs out of the room into the hallway, and screams at the top of her lungs for help. Gabriel releases Cain, and he rises to his feet. He then runs out of the apartment after her. He watches Elizabeth get into the elevator, and he runs in the same direction toward the exit sign. Cain rapidly descends the stairs and beats the elevator to the ground floor. The elevator opens, and she spots him running toward the front door of the apartment building. She screams again.

Elizabeth: Help! Help! Stop that man!

The doorman, Louie, hears Dr. Corsini yell and takes out his cell phone. Cain rushes past him, and Louie freezes as Cain exits through the outside doors onto the street.

Elizabeth: Cancel the call, Louie.

Louie: Don't you think you should report this incident to the police, Dr. Corsini?

Elizabeth: I'm okay. I doubt if he'll be back, Louie. Please have the handyman come up tomorrow morning and repair the door. The chain is broken.

Louie: What happened?

Elizabeth: That man tried to rob me.

Louie: I'm sorry, Dr. Corsini. I don't know how he slipped into the building.

Elizabeth: Not your fault, Louie.

She walks back to the elevator and pushes the button. She rubs her arm and touches her face, where she was slapped by Cain. Inside the elevator she speaks her thoughts.

Elizabeth: I wish Muffin was here tonight. He would have protected me. Oh, well! At least, he's watching over Sophia in her apartment.

Elizabeth doesn't realize that God has sent His angels to protect her.

64

ABEL'S DREAM

Elizabeth and Daniela drink strawberry mango margaritas and eat scrumptious pastry hors d'oeuvres in the Four Seasons lounge. They are waiting for Abel and Sophia to arrive. It's Friday night happy hour.

Elizabeth: Cain Macorley paid me a visit last night.

Daniela: I'm never going to lose weight this way. I'm going to complain to the management.

Daniela stuffs in a couple of flaky cocktail hot dogs and a couple of mussels.

Daniela: Now, what did you say again? Cain Macorley paid you a visit. Why on earth would he do that? You're a trifle old for him.

Elizabeth: To tell me his dreams.

Daniela: Here we go again. What happened?

Elizabeth: He tried to attack me, and if he hadn't tripped over his feet, he might have raped me. I had the feeling that there was someone else in the room. It was just a feeling. Maybe angels!

Daniela: That's quite a compliment.

Elizabeth gives her sister one of her looks. Daniela reacts quickly to cover up her blunder.

Daniela: I don't mean about a younger man wanting you. I mean about your guardian angels.

Elizabeth: You were always fast with your mouth, Dannie. I'm not that old.

Daniela: I'm not going near that one, because I'm older than you, sis. What were Cain's dreams about?

Elizabeth: David and Goliath, followed by a second dream about a biblical rape scene he was observing in a tent in a forest. He was getting off on it.

Daniela: I told you he was a weirdo. Every time I meet him, he strikes me as a misfit. Not human, if you know what I mean. There's an evil about him, like he was born from the Devil. Sounds crazy, I know.

Elizabeth: Not at all. Your instincts are usually right on. I had the same feeling. Shush! There's Sophia and Abel. I wonder what Abel's dream is about.

Sophia and Abel greet the sisters.

Sophia: Hello, Auntie. Hello, Mom. What happened to your face? I see a bruise under your makeup.

Sophia gently touches her mother's face. Elizabeth winces in pain.

Elizabeth: You were always so damn observant, darling. There's nothing I can hide from you. I banged myself stepping out of the shower.

Abel: Hello, ladies. You're way ahead of us on the hors d'oeuvres.

The waitress comes over. Abel orders margaritas.

Abel: Two of the same for my fiancée and me.

Elizabeth examines Sophia's ring.

Elizabeth: Abel, you must be working two jobs to afford such a beautiful diamond ring.

Abel gulps, knowing Dr. Corsini has accidentally struck a true chord. Only Sophia knows that he is a double FBI/Mossad agent.

When he looks over at her, she shrugs her shoulder as if saying, "I didn't tell my mother anything." He quickly recovers.

Abel: I've never been a big spender. I was able to save money from odd jobs over the years, waiting for the right time to dip into my nest egg. I would spend every penny I had and go to the ends of the earth for your daughter, Dr. Corsini.

A huge smile lights up Elizabeth's face.

Daniela: You damn well better take care of my niece, or I'll have your balls, Abel.

Elizabeth: Hmm! Now that we all understand each other, tell me about the unusual dream that Sophia mentioned you were having. It wasn't about David and Goliath, was it?

Abel: Oh, my God! How could you possibly know?

Daniela looks at Elizabeth in amazement.

Elizabeth: It was just a hunch. Describe your dream, Abel.

Abel: I'm David in the dream, and I'm using my slingshot to hurl a small stone into Goliath's right eye. He's covered in armor and stands about eight feet tall. When the stone hits his eye, he falls on his back and drops his sword. I run over, pick up his sword, and drive it through his unshielded mouth, deep into his throat. I hear him groan, and then all sounds disappear. There's no movement.

Elizabeth downs her own margarita. She then takes Daniela's drink and downs hers as well. Sophia is staring at her mother.

Sophia: What is it, Mom?

Elizabeth: Abel, did you pull off the mask from the giant?

Abel: Yes, I did.

Elizabeth: Who did the giant look like?

Abel: It sounds crazy. It can't be.

Daniela: Nothing's crazy, Abel.

Sophia: Go on, Abel. Hurry up and tell us.

Abel: The giant had the face of Cain Macorley.

Elizabeth gasps.

Elizabeth: Yesterday Cain came to me with his dream about David and Goliath, but in Cain's version Goliath slays David. It's remarkable that you both had the same dream with different endings.

Sophia: I'm frightened.

Daniela: Even I'm spooked. And nothing usually fazes me, because I've seen it all. What does it mean, sis?

Elizabeth: It's a forecast for future events. My belief is that Abel must fight Cain Macorley to the death.

Daniella: Son of a bitch! A modern-day Cain will clash with a modern-day Abel. It has to be some kind of divine destiny.

Sophia is sobbing. Elizabeth puts her arm around her daughter and soothes her.

Elizabeth: I'm full of nonsense, and your aunt has too active an imagination. We're both getting old. All of this is just a coincidence. Not to worry, darling.

Sophia stops crying, but she doesn't smile.

65

PEARLS OF WISDOM

Abel and Sophia knock on the outside door of his parents' house on Eastern Parkway in Brooklyn. Isaac Slobodkin cracks the door and then shuts it. Abel knocks again. His father opens the door wide this time.

Isaac: I can't let you in, Abel. Your mother doesn't want to see you.

Abel: Papa, this is my fiancée, Sophia Corsini. I told Mama that Sophia is undergoing an Orthodox conversion to Judaism. We're going to be married, and we want you and Mama to come to our wedding.

Isaac hears Rebecca shouting from inside the house. He doesn't acknowledge Sophia, who politely says hello to him.

Rebecca: If it's a solicitor, Isaac, shut the door. I don't like *solicitors.*

Isaac: It's your son.

Rebecca: I have no son. He's dead. I sat shivah for him.

Before Isaac can close the door, Abel sticks his foot inside. Isaac yields and lets them in.

233

Isaac: I'm letting Abel in, Rebecca.

Rebecca: Wait, I'm coming to the door. Is the shiksa with him?

Sophia blushes at the reference to her gentile origins. Rebecca comes to the door and sees Abel and Sophia. She breaks down crying. Abel goes over and hugs his mother.

Abel: Hello, Mama. Sophia and I want you and Papa to come to our wedding.

Rebecca: Will you be married by a rabbi?

Sophia: Yes, Mrs. Slobodkin.

Abel: You remember Zev Goren from my college days. He became a rabbi after law school.

Isaac: That no-goodnik became a rabbi?

Isaac looks up at the ceiling, holding his hands up as if seeking an answer to his question.

Isaac: Please, God, tell me how that's possible?

Rebecca: Why are we standing here at the door? Come in. We have to seal your engagement with schnapps. Abel, what's the matter? You don't love your mother. I never hear from you.

Abel: But, Mama, I thought you didn't want to see me again.

Rebecca: For a lawyer you're not very smart, Abel. You still don't understand women. The secret is that you're not supposed to understand us. You're just supposed to love us, while we're supposed to understand you. Isn't that right, Sophie?

Sophia: Correct, Mrs. Slobodkin. My name is Sophia.

Rebecca: You name yourself what you want and I'll call you what I want. Sophia is not a Jewish name. Sophie is.

Abel: We'll have it changed for the wedding, Mama.

Isaac: Will you join me at the Chabad Center, Abel, for the Shabbat service?

Abel: Of course, Papa. It will be like old times.

Rebecca: Why don't you two men run along, and Sophie and I will have a nice chat?

Sophia gives Abel a don't-leave-me look. Abel looks back at Sophia, utterly helpless. Abel kisses Sophia on the cheek. The two men depart. They approach 770 Eastern Parkway and enter the Chabad Lubavitch Center.

Isaac: Shall we dance together, Abel?

Abel: It's been a long time, Papa.

The ground floor is filled with Orthodox men in black coats and black hats, all with long, scraggly beards. Women and children are upstairs looking down over the rail at the men. Jewish music is playing, and all the men are dancing together. After about twenty minutes, Isaac and Abel take a glass of kosher wine and a piece of sponge cake. Isaac has a concerned look on his face.

Isaac: Abel, it's too dangerous for you.

Abel: I couldn't say no, Papa. The orders came from the highest source in the Israeli government.

Isaac: Prime Minister Duskin?

Abel: Yes. You're Mossad, Papa. You understand.

Isaac: It was different in my day. The Americans were always on our side, and the world wasn't facing an apocalyptic ending.

Abel: Gog and Magog, Papa.

Isaac: Does Sophia know what's going on?

Abel: I've told her that I'm a double agent. It's complicated, because her aunt is my boss at the FBI. She has no knowledge of Gog and Magog. I'll have to tell her soon.

Isaac: What's your assignment?

Abel looks around the room to make sure no one is listening.

Abel: I've been ordered to kill Cain Macorley.

Isaac almost chokes on his sponge cake.

Isaac: Are you crazy? He's the president's son. How will you do it?

Abel tries to calm his father down.

Abel: I don't know. Sophia's aunt, Daniela Corsini, the deputy director of the FBI, is my mentor. She thinks I'm ready to be the FBI liaison to the White House. I'll be meeting with Cain Macorley, the chief of staff, on a regular basis. Our first appointment is scheduled next week. I'll get a better feel for an operational plan once we meet.

Isaac: Let's go home. Your mother has dinner waiting. We've been married for forty years, and if there's one thing she loves, it's to mentor a novice like Sophia in the culinary art of Jewish cooking. I'm sure she has gone over every minute detail of how she prepares for the Sabbath. Abel, I'm worried. You need to be extremely careful. You're holding a hot poker in your hands. You can get burned at any time. You must anticipate the unexpected.

Abel: I promise, Papa. I will be overzealously alert.

Abel and Isaac enter the Slobodkin home.

Abel: Are you having fun, Sophia?

Sophia: Oh, yes! Your mother was showing me your childhood pictures. You were so cute. If we had met as children, I would have fallen in love with you back then.

Rebecca: I don't know how I'm going to teach Sophie how to cook if you live in Washington, Abel. You'll have to ask for a transfer to New York.

Abel: First things first, Mama. We need to marry. Will you come to the wedding? You haven't said whether you would or not. We're planning the ceremony now. It will take place in the Israeli embassy. Papa's old friend, Shlomo Katchalski, is the Israeli ambassador to the United States.

Rebecca: Of course we'll come to your wedding. I'm the mother of the groom. Papa will have to buy me a new dress. I haven't worn a new dress in ten years. It's time.

Isaac: Charge your glasses. A toast to our son and his bride.

They all clink glasses and down the red wine. Sophia laughs.

Sophia: Deliciously sweet. Why does it burn so much?

Everyone laughs.

Isaac: The burning symbolizes our desire to seek out the divine in life. The sweetness is our reward if we do.

Sophia: How beautiful an analogy, Mr. Slobodkin.

Isaac realizes he has a captive audience.

Rebecca: Now you got him started. I talk about cooking, and he talks about the soul.

Sophia: Jewish wisdom is fascinating. Can you tell me more? Judaism seems different than Christianity, but I'm not sure I understand the differences.

Isaac: Well, for starters both religions believe in the Original Sin of Adam and Eve in the Garden of Eden. In Christianity, the Original Sin was of such magnitude that only Jesus, who died for the sins of all Christians, can atone for mankind. The way to Heaven is thus through Jesus. In Judaism the Original Sin was also great, but Jews believe that each individual has to atone for his sins directly to God; that it's possible to defeat the evil inclination within us, the Satan inside of us, in our lifetime. The Jews look at the expulsion of Adam and Eve from the Garden of Eden as God teaching his children that we must each be accountable for our actions; that life is about improving one's character by making good moral choices.

Sophia: And how does that apply to a husband and wife in a marriage? Do you and Mrs. Slobodkin live your morality?

Isaac: It's impossible to have a perfect marriage, Sophia, because God created humans imperfect. After the expulsion from the Garden of Eden, both good and evil were part of what Chabad calls the animal soul of all human beings. God also breathes into every human at the time they are born and gives them a Divine Soul. When you do good things in life, you activate your Divine Soul, and the good of the Divine Soul finds the good in your animal soul.

Sophia: And if you do bad things?

Isaac: Then your Divine Soul does not get activated, and good doesn't find good. Instead you activate the bad of your animal soul. Some people are evil, even demonic, and their Divine Soul gets buried under the rubble. God is no longer available to them.

Sophia: Like Satan!

Isaac: In a manner of speaking, yes, Satan. The Book of Genesis in the Hebrew Bible talks about Satan having descendants. So, yes, there are very bad people in the world we live in. Some of them even become leaders.

Sophia: I hope that we can continue to talk, Mr. Slobodkin, when I'm back in Washington. I love to listen to you. Do you have one pearl of wisdom for our marriage?

Isaac: Yes! You don't have the right to hurt each other.

66

EVIL HURTS GOOD

A bel and Sophia are wondering around the Washington Zoo. They are in front of the chimpanzee cage.

Abel: Who's the monkey? Them or us?

Sophia smiles at one of the two chimps. The chimp smiles back. She takes a banana from her purse, and the monkey comes scrambling over. The monkey takes the banana, peels it, and the second monkey lets out a screech. Amazingly the first monkey splits the banana in half and hands half to its companion spouse.

Sophia: We're definitely the monkeys.

Abel: Did you have a good time at my parents?

Sophia: I really liked them both. You come from good stock, Abel Slobodkin. I like the ring of my new name, Sophie Slobodkin.

Abel: Sophie?

They both giggle and embrace and just as they begin to part, a loud noise is heard. The bullet strikes Sophia. Abel holds Sophia up in his arms, and awkwardly draws his gun out of a holster strapped to his belt. He sees a man running from the zoo area; he fires, but the bullet misses and the man escapes. There is a trickle of blood coming from Sophia's chest, close to the heart. Abel applies pressure as an ambulance arrives at the scene almost immediately. Abel holds Sophia in his arms as she gazes at him.

Sophia: I don't want to die, Abel. I'm pregnant. I'm carrying your baby.

Abel: Oh, Sophia, I love you. You're going to be okay.

Sophia: Why me, Abel?

Two emergency medical technicians place Sophia on a stretcher, and the ambulance races to Washington General Hospital with sirens blazing. A policeman on a motorcycle escorts the ambulance. Abel jumps in the back and holds Sophia's hand. Sophia opens her eyes and looks at Abel, and then falls into an unconscious state. Abel is cursing himself.

Abel: My father just warned me to anticipate the unexpected. I fucked up royally. I paid no attention to my surroundings when I should have been alert.

Abel is in the surgery waiting room of the hospital when Elizabeth and Daniela Corsini storm by him and head to the nurses' station. No word yet on Sophia's condition. The doctors are working feverishly to save Sophia's life.

Elizabeth: I'm Dr. Elizabeth Corsini from Psychiatry. My daughter, Sophia Corsini, is in surgery. Who's on duty?

Head Nurse: Dr. Kent Fowler.

Elizabeth turns to Daniela.

Elizabeth: Thank God! Kent is one of the best trauma surgeons in the capital. He's had many years of experience and is very well thought of in medical circles.

Head Nurse: A young man, Abel Slobodkin, was with your daughter when she came in. He's sitting in the waiting room. He described what happened to your daughter at the zoo. They were enjoying the day when an unknown assailant fired a bullet. The man escaped.

At that moment inside the operating room, Dr. Kent Fowler is extracting the bullet from Sophia's chest.

Dr. Kent Fowler: I've got the bullet. I'm closing now. Readings, nurse?

The surgical nurse looks at the monitor.

Surgical Nurse: Normal, Dr. Fowler.

Dr. Fowler is about to step away. The machine starts to blip. The monitor readings go flat.

Surgical Nurse: Oh, my God! We're losing her.

Dr. Kent Fowler: Quick! Epinephrine. I'll inject directly into the heart.

The surgical nurse hands Dr. Fowler the syringe, who aims it for Sophia's heart. Nothing happens. They try to shock the heart through electrical stimulation, but still nothing. Gabriel, invisible, enters the room.

Dr. Kent Fowler: We've lost her.

Gloom sets in the operating room. Dr. Fowler removes his mask and just stares at the body. As he turns to leave, Gabriel places his hands on Sophia. The monitor starts recording, and Sophia's vitals come back to life. There is a cheer in the operating room. Sophia is going to be okay. Dr. Fowler leaves the room, heads down the hall, and spots Elizabeth. Gabriel follows.

Dr. Kent Fowler: She's going to be alright, Elizabeth. It was a close call.

Elizabeth: Thank you, Kent, for saving Sophia's life.

Dr. Kent Fowler: Don't thank me. A miracle took place in that room just a few moments ago. Miracles cannot be explained by science. She was dead on the table, Elizabeth, and she came back to life.

Daniela: Our guardian angels. They're still with us, Lizzie.

Dr. Kent Fowler: Angels. I buy that. They can operate with me anytime.

The head nurse comes rushing over and hands Dr. Fowler a note.

Dr. Kent Fowler: The blood analysis came back. Sophia is one month pregnant. We didn't see any discharge from Sophia's vagina. Another miracle! The baby also survived.

Daniela crosses her heart. Abel has been listening to the conversation from a short distance away. He slowly approaches with tears in his eyes.

Abel: I was holding her in my arms when she told me she was carrying our baby. I didn't know until then. I'm so sorry, Dr. Corsini, that this happened. It was my fault. I should have paid more attention to the environment around us. God, I wish I had taken the bullet instead of Sophia.

Elizabeth goes berserk and starts pounding Abel's chest.

Elizabeth: You asshole! The bullet was meant for you. Why would anyone want to harm a beautiful innocent girl like my Sophia? I don't give a flying fuck if you are the father, you fucking stay away from my daughter.

Everyone is frozen and embarrassed, including Dr. Fowler. Abel is visibly crying.

Abel: But we were planning to marry soon.

Elizabeth: Over my dead body. Get out of her life, Abel.

Abel turns and leaves. Daniela shakes her head.

67

STEAM ROOM

Abel is jogging around the indoor track at the Capital Gymnasium. Rabbi Zev Goren catches up with him. After a few more laps, they go downstairs and skip rope. Abel then goes through his weight strengthening program.

Abel: We have a problem.

Rabbi Goren: I know. The Americans are trying to squeeze us, and this time they may be successful.

Abel: There's a personal issue.

Rabbi Goren: Shush! Follow me.

They walk through the men's locker room. They undress, wrap towels around their waists, and proceed to the steam room. Rabbi Goren and Abel sit on benches.

Rabbi Goren: Ah! The beautiful Italian rose.

Abel: With your help she was supposed to become a Jewish orchid. I need to tell her what's going on; that is, if her mother will ever let me see her.

Rabbi Goren: You can't tell her. You'll compromise your mission.

Abel: Was the bullet meant for me or her? You would think that an assassin would be sure of his target. I tend to feel that it was Sophia that was supposed to be killed. Why? There's no reason as far as I can determine.

Rabbi Goren: The hit on Sophia seems to have come from the White House. What doesn't make sense is that our agents learned today that Sophia is the daughter of President Macorley.

Abel: God! Does Sophia know? Wait a minute. When I first met Sophia, she told me that she didn't want to know who her father was, even though her mother, Dr. Corsini, was going to tell her.

Rabbi Goren: The other unknown is whether the president knows he is the father. If he is Sophia's biological parent, it seems unlikely that he ordered the hit.

Abel: But the president must have known about it. Nothing that goes on in the White House would escape his attention.

Rabbi Goren: Unless it was Cain Macorley who ordered the hit.

Abel: It's all convoluted. I need to come at this differently. Einstein said that you can't solve a problem at the level at which the problem is created. I'm still also wondering about this Leamas character, who doesn't age. He claims he's the Devil, and I wonder if he's the one pushing the president's buttons. The president could have sold his soul to the Devil for the promise of absolute power. The president has always wanted to rule the world. It still makes no sense how Sophia is involved. I need to confront Leamas. I'm getting stronger, and I'll be ready for him the next time we meet.

68

THE SQUEEZE

Abel and Daniela are waiting for FBI Director Marshall Lamster to return. The director was called out of his office to meet with Cain Macorley, who has paid him a surprise visit.

Daniela: Sophia's feeling better each day. My sister took her home yesterday. She's been asking for you.

Abel: And your sister?

Daniela: It was a natural gut reaction in the hospital. I would have done the same. My sister wants you to stop by and visit with Sophia. The baby's fine by the way. You're going to be a father.

Abel: I can't blame Dr. Corsini. I should have been on top of it and prevented Sophia from being hurt. Do we know anything at this point about the gunman?

Daniela: Funny you should ask. We just got a tip from the Mossad, of all people, that the hit was meant for Sophia. It was ordered by someone in the White House and doesn't make sense. You could be next. So be careful.

Abel: I will. Do we know anything else?

Daniela: Not about Sophia's assassin, but something new just came up that might interest you as a Jew.

Abel perks up and waits for Daniela to speak.

Daniela: We're getting leaked information that the foreign appropriations allotment to the State of Israel is being held up.

Abel: By Congress?

Daniela: Our sources tell us that the four billion dollars in foreign aid is being held up in committee by the committee chair, Senator Lucius Craywalter.

Abel: Craywalter is a publicly admitted anti-Semite.

Daniela: That he is. He's also Cain Macorley's lackey. It's likely that the chief of staff is blocking the usual commitment of arms and aid to Israel. Cain claims he doesn't have a prejudiced bone in his body, but that's a total lie. Cain is calling the shots. I wonder what sinister plot he's concocting right now with Marshall.

Abel: So Cain Macorley wants more time to study the request. Does that sum it up?

Daniela: Yes.

Abel: This has never happened before. Where's the usual pressure from the Israeli lobby?

Daniela: It's there, but Craywalter is very powerful in Congress, and with Cain's backing it may be impossible to break the impasse on funding. It looks like a squeeze on our only true ally in the Middle East. Iraq turned out to be a dud after all the blood we spilt. The world is sure fucked up.

Marshall Lamster enters his office, grumbling under his breath.

Marshall: That Cain Macorley is a real prick.

Daniela: What's up, honey?

Marshall gives Daniela a look that could kill and then throws his hands up in frustration.

Marshall: Macorley doesn't trust anyone and wants us to put a tail on our own agents. He suspects that we have a mole inside the FBI.

Daniela: How ridiculous.

Marshall: Nevertheless, Abel, I want you to set up an investigation without anyone knowing here at the Bureau.

Abel: Yes, sir. Might I ask, sir, what your gut feeling is about the block on Israeli foreign aid? Israel depends on the aid and the friendship of the United States.

Marshall: That pisses me off, too. I'm Jewish.

Daniela: Marshall, you never told me.

Marshall: Didn't you ever notice that my penis was circumcised?

Abel blushes. The conversation continues.

Daniela: Yes, but goyim do it for health reasons. My father, God rest his soul, was circumcised. Now that you've told me that you're Jewish, why did God make a covenant with Abraham through the circumcision?

Abel holds his hand up. Daniela and Marshall give him the nod to speak.

Abel: The covenant with Abraham was for spiritual reasons. God gave us pleasure through the penis, but we were meant to think with our brains and not our sex organs. The removal of the foreskin was a reminder of that. The Orthodox Jews bury the foreskin in the ground to get rid of any evil in the newborn and purify the baby.

Marshall: Shit! Why didn't my parents explain that to me? I can't keep my dick in my pocket.

Daniela: Oh, Marshall, I love everything about you, especially your penis.

Marshall: Can we get back to the topic at hand? I realize that Abel will soon be family, so there were no holds barred in this pornographic conversation.

Daniela: And when are you going to make an honest woman out of me?

Marshall: When the Devil appears?

Abel chuckles.

Marshall: My feeling on the block of foreign aid to the State of Israel is that it's part of a bigger picture to cause panic in the country; to destabilize our ally in the Middle East by causing a run on the Israeli shekel.

Abel: But why?

Marshall: The ostensible excuse is that the United States has been spending its way out of the economic recession, and we can't afford the foreign aid.

Abel: How naïve I've been. I thought it would be the United States' foreign policy in Iran that would lead to Israel's downfall. What's the real reason for the United States abandoning a friend?

Marshall: The president for some reason is very much pro-Muslim. He sees the future of our country with the Islamic countries, particularly the Arab countries, and not with Israel.

Daniela: You're so smart, Marshall.

Marshall: Daniela, cut the bullshit and get back to work. And Abel, you have a meeting with Cain Macorley on Thursday. You're our new liaison to the White House. I need Daniela for the important stuff, not the political shenanigans that go on at the White House.

69

MARK OF THE BEAST

Abel is in Rabbi Goren's study, deeply concerned with what the FBI director spoke about yesterday in his office.

Rabbi Goren: I communicated your concerns to Ambassador Katchalski, and he has forwarded the intelligence on to Prime Minister Duskin. We have contacted all our friends in the Israeli lobby, and we are turning the tide on Lucius Craywalter and Cain Macorley. The prime minister deeply appreciates your efforts, Abel. I see your wheels are turning. What's troubling you? Have you found another Einsteinium solution to a problem?

Abel: I always look for the nuances in life. The director alluded to the president's pro-Muslim policies, and that got me thinking. Are we nearing Armageddon? I thought we'd do a calculation, Zev.

Rabbi Goren: You know as well as I do that we Jews do not believe in a Beast with the Mark 666.

Abel: Humor me. I'm marrying into a Christian family.

Zev takes out his blackboard and chalk from the closet.

Abel: Write Malcolm Yale Macorley on your blackboard.

Rabbi Goren: You have to be kidding. Abel, you have a warped sense of humor.

Abel: I'm dead serious.

Zev assigns Hebrew numerical letter values to the president's name.

Rabbi Goren: I'll be unorthodox and count each letter, including variants of the same sounding letters. That's not the usual practice, but as I look at the president's name, it's the only way we'll get close to a value of 666. Bear in mind that we are manipulating the actual Hebrew translation of the name.

Abel nods in agreement.

Rabbi Goren: The numerical equivalent for Malcolm is 160, if we use the "M" at the beginning and the "m" at the end, totaling 80. Similarly the "l" has to be counted twice, giving us 60. The "c" can be counted as "20," and the "o" won't be counted as its sound is pronounced more like a vowel.

Abel: The middle name, Yale, is next.

Rabbi Goren: The "Y" at the beginning is ten, and the "l" is 30, giving us a total of 40. Macorley starts with an "M," which has a value of 30. The "a" is a vowel, and we can count the "c" as 20. A true "o" has a value of 6, while the numerical equivalent of "r" is 200. Let's assign a ten to the last "y." So let's see. What have we got?

Abel: 306 for Macorley. Plus 160 for Malcolm, and 40 for Yale totals 506. I'm disappointed, Zev.

Rabbi Goren: We can do one more manipulation. If we count the "c" in Malcolm and the "c" in Macorley as 100 each, then we need to add an additional 160 to the 506.

Abel: Yielding 666. I'm not following, Zev. You changed the value of the "c" from 20 to 100.

Rabbi Goren: You forgot your Hebrew, Abel. The "k" sound can either be a "kaf" for 20 or a "koof" for 100. If it's the latter, you need to add 80 points for each "c" in the president's name. Please use caution, Abel, in interpreting our findings. I've manipulated the Hebrew letters so that the value of the name yields 666.

Abel: Nevertheless 666 is the Mark of the Beast in Christianity. Let me ask you a question. If you took any name out of the hat, what are the chances of a person's name translating to a numerical value of 666?

Rabbi Goren: Good question, for which I don't have the answer. My statistical guess would be that it would be one in a thousand or perhaps one in ten thousand.

Abel: Can we take your calculation one step further?

Rabbi Goren is puzzled by Abel's request. Then he realizes where Abel is going.

Rabbi Goren: You want a calculation on Cain Arlis Macorley. Correct?

Abel: Correct.

Zev cleans the blackboard and writes down Cain's full name.

Rabbi Goren: We'll use the "kaf" for the "C" of Cain, a 20. The "n" has a value of 50. The sum of 20 plus 50 is 70. The "a" and "i" are not counted, as they are vowels. For Arlis, we have a 200 for the "r," a 30 for the "l," and a 60 for the "s."

Abel: That's 360 altogether for Cain Arlis. Plus our previous calculation of 306 for Macorley. Holy Mother Theresa! The son, like the father, is 666. Can this be a coincidence?

Rabbi Goren: I believe in divine providence.

Abel: Do you believe in the Devil?

Rabbi Goren: Certainly! There is a place called Hell. In Hebrew we call the fiery furnace *Gehinnom*. It's where the evil souls are sent to face their punishment. As an Orthodox rabbi, I hold the belief that the Devil exists. I don't know if there ever was a Fallen Angel named Satan. Satan goes by many names. He is the Angel of Death, Samael. Some call him Lucifer. Others have referred to him as Beelzebub. All of them are the Devil, who is the evil inclination within each of us. We battle the Devil every day.

Abel: This ageless man calls himself Leamas. He was emphatic about being the Devil. Could the Devil really be alive?

Rabbi Goren: A horrifying thought, but as we discussed the other day, it's possible according to the Book of Genesis. Wait a minute. Leamas can be spelled L-e-a-m-a-s. If you spell the name backwards, you have S-a-m-a-e-l. Samael, the Angel of Death.

Abel: Shit! He's alive, and he's right here in the capital. My hunch must be true. The Devil has bought the soul of the president and probably Cain Macorley as well. God told the Serpent that it would have descendants, and His prophesy is coming true in modern times.

Rabbi Goren: Be very careful, Abel. The biblical Cain killed the biblical Abel.

Abel: I can't worry about myself, Zev. I'm concerned for the safety of Sophia. I still don't know why the White House wanted her dead. I'm going to see her right now. Her mother forbade me from being with her in the hospital. I miss her so much. She means more to me than my own life.

70

THE VOICE

Abel is alone with Sophia, who is recovering in her mother's apartment. Dr. Corsini has gone to the hospital for a couple of hours to see some recently admitted patients. Abel is gently hugging Sophia, who is still sore from the surgery.

Abel: You're so beautiful, my love. You've made a remarkable recovery. I think you're ready for an evening out of dinner and dancing.

Sophia: I've always had a great immune system. I feel great, and I'd love to go dancing. I have these red satin high heels that I've been wanting to break in. It's been so long since I wore anything but the comfortable soft shoes for my medical practice.

Abel: I need to come clean with you, Sophia.

Sophia: Was the bullet meant for me?

Abel: Yes, actually it was. Someone in the White House ordered your murder, but for the life of me, I don't know who or why.

Sophia: It was the president, wasn't it? I also need to come clean with you, Abel. Many years ago I found some correspondence between my mother and the president, and it was obvious that they were lovers. My mother made a separate entry in a hidden notebook, which I fortuitously discovered and peeked at one day out of curiosity. I know it was wrong, but there it was in black and white. The president is my father.

Abel: Does he know, and does your mother know that you know?

Sophia: My mother thinks that I don't want to know who my biological father is. She's actually right. It was just a fluke that I found out. I'm not sure whether the president is aware that he has a biological daughter roaming around the capital under his nose.

Abel: I've been racking my brains. It makes no sense.

Just then, a gentle deep assertive voice is heard in the apartment.

GOD: The baby growing inside your womb is the key to the future of humanity.

The voice is gone. Abel and Sophia hug.

Sophia: The Voice of God. Oh, Abel, we heard a miracle.

Abel: Yes, my darling. Now we know why they tried to murder you. Sophia, my assignment is to kill Cain Macorley.

Sophia: Please, Abel, I don't want to hear anymore. You need to live to be a father to our son.

Abel: Don't worry! I plan to be around for a very long time. I love you so much, Sophia.

71

DEVIL'S DESCENDANTS

Cain is strolling in the Rose Garden smoking a cigar. It's almost dusk. His cell phone rings and he picks up. Leamas is on the other end.

Cain: How did you get my private number, and who the hell are you?

Leamas: I get that question a lot, and my standard answer is, I'm the Devil, of course.

Cain: Funny! I thought I was.

Leamas: No, you and your father are my descendants.

Cain: And your name, Devil?

Leamas: You can call me Leamas.

Cain: I'm all in, Leamas. Lay down your cards.

Leamas: For starters it has always been my intention that the son shall betray the father. Does that bother you?

Cain: I'm listening.

Leamas: Gog and Magog must be activated immediately. Your father keeps screwing up simple tasks, so I decided that it's time to work directly with you. Your father has unfortunately become expendable.

Cain: Only my father and I knew about Gog and Magog. Did my father share our secret plan with you, Leamas?

Leamas: No, I told you. I'm the Devil. I just know things.

Cain: Why activate the operation now?

Leamas: Because God has created your nemesis. His name is Abel Slobodkin. And you must kill him so I can destroy God.

Cain: Where is this mysterious Abel?

Leamas: You have a meeting with him tomorrow.

Cain: He's not on my calendar.

The human Leamas turns into a Serpent. The phone falls to the ground. The Serpent speaks close to the phone.

Serpent: Shit! It's dusk. Damn God for this evil curse He placed upon me.

The Serpent slithers away.

Cain: Hello! Hello! Shit! Nobody's there. What the fuck happened?

Cain pushes some buttons on his cell phone. He mutters to himself.

Cain: Nope! No Abel Slobodkin. Leamas must either be CIA or a nut job. There are so many whackos walking around this town.

He stomps out his cigar, momentarily looks up at the sky for a sign, and then turns toward the White House.

72

PROTECTION

Abel walks through the checkpoint of the Israeli Embassy and on to the ambassador's office. He is paged in by the secretary and sits down opposite Shlomo Katchalski. They speak in Hebrew.

Ambassador Katchlaski: You look like you just woke up, Abel. What's bothering you?

Abel: I need round-the-clock protection for the Corsini family—my fiancée, Sophia, her mother, Dr. Elizabeth Corsini, and the sister, Daniela Corsini.

The ambassador gives Abel a quizzical look.

Ambassador Katchalski: The FBI can't protect its own?

Abel: You know the stakes, Shlomo. We're dealing with unscrupulous men with zero morals: the president of the United States and his son, Cain. And there's the third man.

Shlomo immediately perks up.

Ambassador Katchalski: You never mentioned a third party before. Are we discussing a foreign agent?

Abel: You'll think I've gone off my rocker, but there's an unknown evil force walking around the capital. The Mossad is completely unaware of him.

Shlomo is completely baffled by Abel's information.

Ambassador Katchalski: That's impossible.

Abel: He goes by the name of Leamas, but he's actually the Devil. He has angelic powers and can appear and disappear at will. He is very strong—he once lifted me up as if I was light as a feather. I've been furiously working out, trying to gain body strength to prepare for our next encounter.

Ambassador Katchalski: Consider it done for keeping watch over the Corsini family, but how will I convey the business of the Devil's existence to Prime Minister Duskin?

Abel: Jacob Duskin is a man of the Bible. He'll understand. Oh, one more thing. Leamas doesn't age. He's taken a special interest in me since I was born. I didn't just get admitted into the FBI on my own. It was Leamas who presided over the entrance exam, and it was Leamas who ensured my entry.

Ambassador Katchalski: Do you have any proof of the existence of this Leamas? Has anyone else seen him?

Abel: No, except I'm sure he's familiar to the president and his son. My gut tells me that the Devil has bought their souls, and I wouldn't be surprised if the Devil is directing Gog and Magog.

Ambassador Katchalski: I'm overwhelmed by this information. Is there anything else you can tell me?

Abel: He's immune to bullets fired by human beings. I shot him once and nothing transpired. It happened when I left you last time. Leamas knocked out your driver and was sitting in the driver's seat of your limousine when I got in. I shot him at point-blank range, and he walked away unharmed. You have to believe me, Shlomo. I'm not crazy.

Ambassador Katchalski: Let's say for the moment I believe you. How do we counter such a force?

Abel: This too will sound nuts. But God and his angels are also here, helping us. We need to rely on divine providence.

Ambassador Katchalski stares at Abel, trying to decide whether to pull him from his assignment.

Ambassador Katchalski: I hope you understand, Abel, that I have to run all of this craziness by the prime minister.

Abel: Of course! Do it soon, Shlomo. I have a meeting in the next couple of days with Cain Macorley. Cain believes there is a mole at the FBI. At this point I can keep things under control, because FBI Director Marshall Lamster has put me in charge of sniffing out the traitor.

Ambassador Katchalski becomes alarmed.

Ambassador Katchalski: You weren't followed, were you? Did you take precautions?

Abel: Rest easy. I was careful.

Ambassador Katchalski: Go out the back way. Our new driver, Eli, will drop you.

Abel: My father and mother will be coming down for the wedding. I'm glad you'll be able to attend, and thank you for allowing the marriage to take place at the embassy. It will just be a small group. Rabbi Goren, one of our own, will officiate. I'm hoping the prime minister will be able to attend. I understand he'll be in Washington.

Ambassador Katchalski: Your father and I were in the Mossad together. We are still the greatest of friends. I can't believe they are letting you marry out of the faith. And yes, the prime minister would like to come to your wedding, if at all possible.

Abel: It took some serious conversation to convince my parents. Sophia hit it off with my mother, who was teaching her the art of Jewish cooking, and my father was only too happy to explain the parallels and differences of Judaism and Christianity. He still gives her lessons on the phone. But the clincher was Sophia's willingness to undergo an Orthodox conversion. Before the assassination attempt on her life, she was doing pretty well. Her only problem was the mikvah bath. Sophia isn't fond of the ritual.

Ambassador Katchalski: I'm very happy for you, Abel, and I'll do everything I can to ensure your safety and that of your bride. As you know our intelligence discovered that the hit on Sophia came from the White House. Perhaps the bullet was meant for you and not for her. I can't understand why they would come after Sophia.

Abel decides not to reveal anything further about what he knows: that the bullet was truly meant for Sophia. The two shake hands.

Abel: Shalom, Ambassador. And thank you.

Ambassador Katchalski: Shalom, Abel. Godspeed.

Abel slips out the back door of the embassy. Just in case, he draws his gun as he enters the limousine parked at the back door.

73

SPORTS EVENTS

Abel addresses the driver. He is paranoid about his last meeting with Leamas. He recalls shooting Leamas at point blank range to no avail.

Abel: I know it's you, Leamas.

Eli, the driver, is dumbfounded.

Eli: Is there a problem, sir?

Abel breathes a sigh of relief.

Abel: I'm sorry, Eli. I'm just a bit shaky. There's no problem. Drive on.

As the car moves, Abel puts his gun away. In Star Trek fashion, Leamas suddenly appears in the car next to Abel. Leamas has a gun pointed at Abel. When Eli sees Leamas appear in the backseat, he loses control of the wheel, and almost hits the car in front of him. He brakes hard and barely avoids an accident. Leamas orders Eli to continue driving. Abel is thrown to the car floor, but Leamas hasn't moved one square inch from his position.

Leamas: Drive on, Eli. I have a gun next to Mr. Slobodkin's head.

Leamas addresses Abel.

Leamas: Hello, Abel. Do you mind if I grab a lift with you?

Abel: I'd rather you didn't.

Leamas: Pretty funny. I like your sense of humor. I'll take your gun, Abel. Remove it slowly. It's of no use to you anyway. You can't kill me.

Abel reaches for his gun and hands it over to Leamas. Leamas stuffs Abel's gun in his trousers.

Leamas: Eli, drive to Anacostia National Park. And Eli, no funny stuff unless you want a corpse in your back seat.

Leamas pulls out a flask and takes a swig.

Leamas: From Heaven's winery.

Leamas offers the flask to Abel.

Abel: No, thanks. I'm kind of picky over who I choose to drink with.

Leamas: You don't know what you're missing.

Leamas takes another snort.

Abel: Is that your home? You live in the park?

Leamas: Temporarily. Until I can take over Heaven.

Abel: And how do you expect to do that?

Leamas: You certainly ask a lot of questions for a condemned man. Wounding Sophia was just a preliminary warning. I know about the baby, and I promise you that your son will never see the light of day. Killing you would mean a complete defeat for God. I should pull the trigger right now.

Abel: But you're not going to do that, are you?

Leamas: I haven't decided if I'm going to kill you myself or let Cain Macorley have that privilege.

Abel: I prefer Cain Macorley, because I've been ordered to kill him.

Leamas: God would love that. Reverse the biblical history and have a modern-day Abel kill a modern-day Cain. Tell you what, Abel. Are you a gambling man?

Abel: I play penny ante poker once in a while.

Leamas: Good! I'll give you three chances to defeat me in any sport of your choosing. Of course that's an impossibility for you, since I'm the Devil. Oh, we're here at the park. I took a shortcut.

They arrive at Anacostia National Park. Leamas directs Eli to an isolated clearing.

Abel: And if I defeat you?

Leamas: I'm an honorable man. Everyone knows that. The keys will be in the car, and you can drive away. You can face Cain in a fair fight.

Abel: And the driver?

Leamas: He'll drive back with you.

All three men get out of the limousine. Abel is directed to walk a step ahead, while Eli is beside Leamas. Leamas pulls out Abel's gun from his pants and promptly shoots Eli in the head. Eli collapses dead on the ground. Some of the spattered blood reaches the back of Abel's shirt. Abel is horrified at Eli lying there. He is about to swarm Leamas, but Leamas anticipates his movements.

Leamas: Don't try it, Abel, or you'll never live to see Sophia and your son-to-be.

Abel: You goddamn fucking bastard! You broke your word. You lying piece of shit.

Leamas: Careful! You're taking the name of the Lord in vain. I'm just a cold-blooded killer like you, Mossad agent.

Abel: No, I'm not like you. I kill evil. You killed an innocent man who never did a damn thing to you.

Leamas starts clapping.

Leamas: Bravo! Bravo! Your God granted humans with the gift of free will. I simply changed my mind. What's your first sport?

Abel doesn't answer. He glares at the Devil.

Leamas: Answer or I'll kill you right now, although it would be more fun to have you explain how you shot Eli. Nobody would believe your cockamamie story of a Devil shooting the driver. I don't exist.

Leamas cocks the trigger of Abel's gun. Abel responds.

Abel: Horseshoes.

Sand pits appear out of nowhere, with metal poles at each end sunk into the ground. Abel gazes in wonder at the power of the Devil.

Leamas: I was a top angel in Heaven until God kicked me out for insubordination. It was more than that. I wanted to depose Him. For years I was the devoted Angel of Death, Samael. And what did I get for all my dedication and loyalty? The Archangels Michael and Gabriel ensured that I would be the famous Fallen Angel. I was booted out to become a human by day and a Serpent by night on this ghastly planet, collaborating with a couple of goons, the ambitious Macorleys. By some stroke of luck, Heaven screwed up and left me with some of my angelic powers.

Abel: Why tell me all this?

Leamas: The Macorleys are evil, and I need to spend time with good people. I'm really not choosy who I kill, but I find I feel more rejuvenated when I'm with one of God's disciples. My descendants are boring, and they drain me.

Abel looks over and sees gold and black horseshoes.

Leamas: In case you're wondering, the black are mine. They're made of onyx, while yours are constructed of the finest eighteen-carat gold. Your rules, Abel.

Abel ponders and realizes that no matter what rules he institutes, he won't get a fair shake. He looks over at the Devil and wonders if he could take his gold horseshoe and crush his skull. He remembers what the Devil had told him. That he could not be killed by the hand of a human, only by a peer angel. He thinks back on his biblical studies, and it clicks that only one angel will duel with Satan. Gabriel, the Angel of Fire and War, will have that honor.

Leamas: I'm asking a simple question, Abel.

Abel: Game is fifteen. One point for closest horseshoe to the pole. Two points for a leaner and three points for a mucker. I'll keep score.

They pick up their horseshoes.

Leamas: Sinners first. Oops! Private joke. It was me that started your life of cheating on that fourth grade geography test. You cried like a baby. You haven't changed. You're still a wimp.

Abel throws first. It's a mucker around the pole. Leamas counters with a three-point cancellation mucker. Abel's second toss is a leaner. Leamas's second shot falls short.

Abel: Abel, two. The Devil, zero.

Leamas is not happy. They continue playing as each settles in. They match each other point for point until the Devil seizes an opportunity and ties the score at twelve to twelve. It's the Devil's turn. Abel pipes in.

Abel: Since you go first and have the advantage, why don't we change the rules to further benefit you?

Leamas makes eye contact with Abel, thinking Abel is trying some kind of trickery. He looks hard at Abel, but is unable to see why Abel is being so kind. Of course he doesn't trust Abel.

Leamas: Very sporting of you, old chap. You wouldn't try to put one over on the king of trickery, would you, Abel?

Abel laughs.

Abel: How can anyone best you? You're the Devil.

Leamas: I hate people who suck up to me, but somehow I think you're holding an ace up your sleeve. Alright, I'll throw both my black shoes. Boy, I feel the pressure.

Leamas follows a mucker with a leaner and realizes why Abel wanted him to go first.

Leamas: Shit! You tricked me. You can easily knock away my leaner.

Abel throws his first gold shoe and knocks the black leaner away, while his gold horseshoe becomes a mucker. Abel knows that all he has to do is safely throw another ringer, and he wins. He focuses and makes the double mucker; but when he looks again, the Devil now has two muckers and magically, one of his muckers has unwrapped itself from the pole and rolled away.

Abel: I won, Devil, fifteen to twelve. Fair and square. You cheated.

Leamas: Isn't that what you've been doing all your life, sport? Remember the FBI entrance exam? New sports challenge, Abel. I can't wait for your next choice.

Abel looks at the Devil smirking and sees no hope. He might as well carry on the charade and prolong his life. His mind drifts to Sophia, and he sees himself embracing her and kissing her lips. The smell of her breath spurs him on.

Abel: Eight ball.

Leamas: And the rules?

Abel: Fifteen numbered balls have to be hit in the pockets in numerical order, except for the eight ball, which you knock in only after you hit the fifteen ball into the pocket. All shots have to be called. Any ball going into a pocket randomly is pulled out and placed on the dot. If before all fifteen balls are in the pocket, you scratch the eight ball—that is, the eight ball goes into any pocket—that person loses. It doesn't matter how many balls you knock in, it's only the eight ball at the end that counts. If you scratch the white shooter ball, you forfeit your turn.

Leamas: Let's make it interesting. One game for all the marbles. I love your choices. I may let you go, because even if you lose, you're so unexpectedly original.

A professional billiards table appears. The players chalk up their cues.

Abel: You break, Devil.

Leamas: Why thank you, Abel. I'll remember your kindness when I kill you.

Leamas breaks. The nine ball goes in the pocket and gets pulled out. Able runs the one, two, three, but misses the four. The Devil makes the four, five, six, and seven, but it looks like he will lose, as the eight ball heads for the side pocket. The Devil takes a deep breath and blows against the eight ball so that it stops shy of the pocket. Whoever makes the fifteen will surely win the game by tapping in the eight ball.

Leamas: Your rules didn't specify anything about blowing on the balls.

Abel: You have to be kidding.

Abel plays it safe on the nine ball and so does the Devil.

Abel: What's the difference? You're going to win anyway.

Abel does a trick shot and calls the nine ball in the end pocket. It goes in.

Leamas: What a terrific shot. You'll have to teach me how to do that. I don't know how you got the nine in. It was completely blocked by the eleven.

Abel has a long shot down table, but he knocks in the ten ball and uses English to bring his shooter ball back to set up a perfect shot on the eleven. Abel miraculously makes the twelve, thirteen, and fourteen.

Leamas: Don't you ever miss? You're a hustler, Abel. Minnesota Fats in living color. You'll never make the fifteen.

The fifteen ball is right up against the rail. There is only one way to make this virtually impossible shot, but it is certain to leave the shooter ball at the wrong end of the table to make the eight ball. Abel barely touches the fifteen, and the ball goes scooting along the rail into the pocket. Abel plays it safe on the next shot, and so does the Devil. Abel surveys the table.

Leamas: I dare you. Try banking it off the back wall and have the shooter ball knock the eight ball into the side pocket. You'll need to pull a rabbit out of your hat.

Abel looks at Leamas and smiles. Leamas doesn't smile back. Abel does exactly what the Devil says, and his shooter ball taps the eight ball. As it heads for the pocket, Leamas causes the eight ball to divert slightly, so it hits the corner of the pocket without going in, as it was certain to do.

Leamas: Too bad, Abel. You were on a hot streak.

Leamas taps the eight ball into the pocket.

Leamas: I win. Last chance, Abel. What will it be?

Abel: Arm wrestling. I want to give you every opportunity, Devil.

Leamas: That's not giving me the advantage. That's sheer stupidity. I was curious about what your last choice would be, and you didn't disappoint me, but you know my strength. Tell you what. I don't usually do this, but for the sake of God, choose another sport.

Abel: No! It's arm wrestling or nothing.

Leamas: I'm going to miss you. And the rules?

Abel: Blindfolds that you can't see through. Left arms.

Leamas: Aren't you the clever one? You miscalculated, however, as I'm ambidextrous.

A table with two chairs appears, and Abel and Leamas take up their positions. Abel goes on the offensive, but he cannot budge the Devil. Leamas starts to wear Abel down, and his arm starts to give way. Leamas has Abel's arm halfway down to the table, but Abel in a burst of strength forces the Devil's arm back to its original vertical position. Then shockingly to the Devil, Abel starts to bend the Devil's arm downward. Leamas struggles to hold his arm up.

Leamas: I see you've been training. I commend you.

Just then Leamas places his right hand over his left arm and pushes as hard as he can, forcing Abel's arm almost to the table.

Leamas: The rules only talk about not using the right arm, but you didn't say anything about using the right hand.

While all seems lost, Gabriel is invisibly hovering about. Abel feels an angelic force within him, and begins to raise both of the Devil's arms. Leamas cannot believe the incredulous strength of Abel.

Leamas: What's going on? It's impossible. You're cheating again, Abel.

Abel: Fuck you, Devil. Cheating is your middle name.

Abel forces the Devil's left arm almost to the table. Leamas pulls his arm away before Abel can claim victory. Leamas stands up and towers over Abel.

Leamas: Arm wrestling is for amateurs. Your biblical ancestor, Jacob, wrestled his evil brother's angel and defeated him.

Abel: And the rules?

Leamas: You can only win by pinning your opponent. Fair, Abel?

Abel: You don't know the meaning of the word.

Leamas belly laughs.

Leamas: You gotta love this guy. I brought the perfect outfit for you.

With a snap of the Devil's fingers, they find themselves in T-shirts, shorts and sneakers. Leamas's shirt has a picture of the Golden Calf. Abel's has an imprint of Moses holding the Ten Commandments. A circular mat appears on the ground.

Both men take up their positions. The match ensues, with nobody scoring a takedown. After several minutes of sparring, Abel flips Leamas and has him in a position where the Devil's shoulders are pinned against the mat. Abel starts the count-down, as the Devil squirms to release Abel's hold.

At the count of two, Leamas disappears and is now standing over Abel. He pulls out his gun and bops Abel gently on the head. Abel falls over onto the mat. The Devil quickly thrusts himself on top of Abel, and counts one, two, three.

Leamas: I win. You're too dangerous to keep alive. I can't afford to leave you to face Cain Macorley in a fair fight. If he's anything like his father, he'll lose to you. Sorry, Abel, I've enjoyed our time together, but it's time to say goodbye.

Leamas cocks the trigger of the gun and points it at Abel's head.

Leamas: Last words?

Abel: And I shall love the Lord with all my heart, with all my soul, and with all my might.

Leamas can't believe what he is hearing.

Leamas: The Shema prayer. Totally unexpected. Terrific ending, Abel, to a glorious afternoon.

Leamas laughs uncontrollably. He dances in a circle around the mat, tapping his mouth with his hand in a Native American-like gesture.

Leamas: Wah, wah, wah! Your God can't help you now.

Abel is still on the ground. From out of nowhere, a slingshot with a rock shaped like a Jewish Star appears in his hand. Abel looks up to Heaven. As he fires the rock, he calls out to Leamas.

Abel: You remember the story of David and Goliath.

Leamas turns toward Abel, but the stone is already flying toward him. The rock hits Leamas on the forehead, knocking him down. A permanent imprint of the Jewish Star of David appears on Leamas's head. Abel rushes over and removes the guns from Leamas's belt. Leamas feels the imprint on his forehead and curses God. For the first time, Abel sees Leamas tremble.

Abel: Your friends at the White House are going to have a field day mocking you and making fun of you when they see your permanent Jewish Star. They're both anti-Semites.

Leamas suddenly disappears. Abel looks around the area, but Leamas is gone. He puts Eli's body in the limo and gets in the driver's seat. He has bested the Devil and has survived. He looks at Eli's cold body and cries.

Abel: I've got to get back to Sophia. God, I hope she's alright. And I have that meeting with Cain Macorley tomorrow.

The same deep assertive voice is heard in the limousine.

GOD: Sophia is safe. Satan shall not bother you again. I shall protect you, Abel.

The voice disappears. Abel calls out.

Abel: Thank You, Lord.

74

CAIN AND ABEL

It's the next morning, and Abel enters the office of the chief of staff, Cain Macorley. The secretary is busy on her computer. She looks up and greets Abel.

Secretary: May I help you?

Abel: I'm here for the FBI appointment with the chief of staff. My name is Abel Slobodkin.

The secretary hits the intercom. Cain responds. Abel hears Cain's voice.

Cain: Send in Agent Corsini.

Secretary: I'm sorry, sir. I have Agent Abel Slobodkin to see you.

Cain: Ask him to wait a couple of minutes. I'm just finishing up a document.

Cain speaks quietly to himself.

Cain: Leamas is the Devil. He knew about Slobodkin.

Cain opens his desk drawer and pulls out a tape recorder. He checks it and returns it to its place. The office still has the look of the former chief of staff, Jason Smithies, except that a framed picture of the Devil, bearing a remarkable resemblance to Leamas, hangs on the wall. A couple of minutes pass, and Cain buzzes the intercom.

Cain: Send in Agent Slobodkin.

Abel opens the door and enters Cain's office.

Cain: Coffee, Agent Slobodkin? Or is it more appropriate to call you Abel? Please call me Cain.

Abel: No to the coffee and yes to Cain and Abel.

Cain: I like a man who's direct. Do you know your Bible?

Abel: Yes, I'm a student of the ancient text.

Cain doesn't miss a beat.

Cain: Then you believe in history repeating itself?

Abel: I believe in the power of God.

Cain: I don't, but I believe in the almighty Devil.

Abel glances at the distasteful picture of the Devil hanging on the wall.

Abel: I like your painting.

Cain: Why, thank you.

Abel: Did you purchase it at auction?

Cain: No, it's a family heirloom. A gift from my father, when I was thirteen. Kind of like a bar mitzvah present. I just decided to hang it up today in honor of your visit.

Abel: We don't seem to have anything in common, Cain.

Cain: Can I give you a hypothetical?

Abel: You called the meeting.

Cain: If you were to fight to the death, what would be your choice of weapons?

Abel laughs, thinking about his recent battles with Leamas. The scenes are replayed in Abel's mind.

Cain: Is my question that funny?

Abel: Sorry! I was just thinking about my recent encounter with a Devil of a person. My answer to your question is American Revolutionary pistols.

Cain is surprised. He wonders how Abel was able to read his mind that pistols were also his preference.

Cain: I can see that you're a true patriot. Excellent choice.

Cain excuses himself, and goes over to his desk to buzz the intercom.

Secretary: Yes, Mr. Macorley.

Cain: Have my limousine brought around.

Cain goes to a glass cabinet and removes a beautiful inlaid cherry wood box. He picks up the case by its leather handle.

Abel: What's in the box?

Cain ignores the question.

Cain: Follow me.

They exit Cain's office, enter the limousine, and drive off through the White House gates. Abel makes chitchat. Cain is not interested in idle conversation.

Abel: It's a nice day for a drive in the country.

Cain: Some other time.

The limo pulls up in front of the FBI building.

Abel: You're dropping me off. Thank you.

Cain: I'm testing your skills.

Cain opens the inlaid box. There are two magnificent American Revolutionary pistols inside.

Abel: Flintlock pistols. The firing range is in the basement.

They get out of the limo and head to the sub-basement. No one seems to be around.

Cain: Your choice. There's one lead ball bullet with black powder in each gun.

Abel reaches for the pistol farthest away from him.

Abel: I'm superstitious. I'll take this one.

Abel removes the gun from the box. He puts on his head gear. Cain does the same. Abel sets the target distance.

Cain: You first.

Abel remembers the game of horseshoes, where he convinced the Devil to throw both his shoes before Abel threw his. He smells a rat, but accedes to Cain's wishes. Abel fires his shot and brings the target forward. A bull's eye to the center of the forehead.

Abel: Your turn.

Cain takes his stance and then turns to Abel. He points the pistol at him.

Cain: I could kill you right now.

Archangel Michael flies into the area and touches Cain's Adam's apple. Cain coughs and is momentarily distracted. Abel quickly takes Cain's pistol and places it against Cain's head. Cain's eyes close, and he trembles with fear.

Abel: Even the Devil likes it when a man stands him down. Are you the Devil, Cain?

Abel removes the bullet from Cain's gun and hands both pistols back to Cain.

Cain: Are you a double agent, Abel?

Abel: My loyalty is to the president, but if you threaten my life, then I'm going to take yours.

Cain: My bullet would have been dead center. Yours was a couple of millimeters off. Adieu, until we meet again.

Cain exits.

Abel: I just met the epitome of evil.

75

RED MOON

That afternoon Abel and Sophia are walking around the Lincoln Memorial. The sun is shining, and no one would expect an eclipse on such a beautiful day. Lovers are wistfully strolling hand in hand.

Sophia: How did your meeting go with Cain Macorley?

Abel: I don't think we took to each other. You look one hundred percent better, Sophia. You're the prettiest girl in the capital. More important, you're my girl, Dr. Sophia Corsini. And you'll soon be Sophia Slobodkin. The name has a nice ring. Don't you think?

Sophia: It takes a while to get it out, but yes, I like the sound of it.

Sophia looks down at her diamond engagement ring. The ring is sparkling in the sun's rays.

Abel: We're getting closer to Armageddon, Sophia. Your father will adopt his son Cain's plan to destabilize the State of Israel. They will then destroy it in a war that biblical prophets referred to as Gog and Magog.

Sophia: What happens in this war, which was predicted so long ago?

Abel: Unimaginable devastation never seen in the history of the planet.

Abel's mind wanders to Jerusalem. The Western Wall with Chassidic rabbis praying is blown up by enemy forces that have attacked Israel. The entire city of Jerusalem is under siege and burning. Smoke is everywhere, and buildings, cars, and homes are in flames.

Abel: Even our most holy site, the Western Wall of the Temple, may be destroyed. Jerusalem will be in ruins.

Sophia looks up in the sky and sees a wondrous sight. There is an unexpected eclipse of the sun. Abel is fascinated by the darkening of the sky, and everyone at the Lincoln Memorial is looking upwards in awe. Abel and Sophia sit, just gazing at the light transforming into utter darkness. Sophia clutches Abel's hand.

Sophia: I want to make love to you. Let's go back to my apartment.

Abel: We'd better wait a little while until the eclipse passes. Hey, we could make love right here in public. Nobody would bother us in the dark.

Sophia: Okay, wise guy. I could call your bluff. But I'll be a nice girl and let you get harder in anticipation.

The eclipse eventually passes, and Abel and Sophia depart. They return to Sophia's apartment and hop into bed. They finish making love, and Abel rolls over and looks through the bedroom window at the sky. He rubs his eyes, gets up out of bed, and goes outside onto the terrace. The moon is blood red. He calls excitedly to Sophia, who joins him. Abel turns to her and clasps her hands tightly.

Abel: "And I shall place portents in the sky. The sun will darken and the moon will turn to blood."

Sophia: What?

Abel: God said that He would place signs in the sky at the time of the Messianic Age. The eclipse of the sun and the moon turning blood red on the very same day.

Sophia: Abel, it's so beautiful. I'm so grateful to be alive to witness this magnificent event. And our son is here, too.

Abel's private line rings on a special electronic phone. He responds to the message of the caller on the other end.

Abel: Yes, I understand.

He turns to Sophia.

Abel: That was the Israeli ambassador, Shlomo Katchalski. Israel is starting to call up its men in anticipation of an attack by Muslim nations.

Sophia: Oh, my God, Abel. World War III.

* * *

Meanwhile President Macorley and Cain also are awake, staring at the red moon in the sky.

Cain: A freak of nature.

President Macorley: Have a shot of Macallan 18 with me, Cain. I need to calm my nerves.

The president fills two glasses of scotch and hands one to Cain.

President Macorley: The blood-red moon is the work of the Hebrew God. It's a sign of the End Times.

Cain: Then we had better get cracking on Gog and Magog.

The president lights up a Cuban.

President Macorley: Yes. It's time to jolt the Israelis.

Cain: I hate God, and I hate His Chosen People.

President Macorley: We have to prevent God from fulfilling his plan for humanity: the Messianic Age and the elimination of evil. I can't imagine a world without evil. It would be a boring place that I wouldn't care to live in. If it happens I hope that the Angel of Death takes me.

Cain: Do you know a man named Leamas? He claims that he's the Devil.

The president chokes on his cigar.

President Macorley: Smoker's cough. No, I can't say that I do.

Cain: He knew about Gog and Magog, and he told me I'd meet Abel Slobodkin today. He was right on both counts. I had an encounter with Slobodkin this morning. Abel and I have been instructed to kill each other, I by Leamas, the Devil, and Abel by the Israelis, I think. I can't prove it, but I believe Abel is Mossad, a double agent working at the FBI. Leamas said that destroying Abel would destroy God. It seems like some kind of prophetic destiny,

President Macorley: Wait a minute. If you spell Leamas backwards you get Samael.

Cain: Brilliant of you to figure that out, Dad. What the hell does it mean?

President Macorley: I don't have many fears, son, but I fear Samael. While in Heaven, Samael served God as the Angel of Death, the supreme poison. Samael is another name for the Devil.

Cain: Then he really is the Devil. I'd like to meet him.

President Macorley: You have a half sister, the daughter of Dr. Elizabeth Corsini, my old flame. Sophia, your sister, is carrying Abel's child.

President Macorley has a change of heart.

President Macorley: I hope you'll forgive me for not telling you sooner, but I lied earlier. I do know Leamas. He helped get me elected in my first presidential run, and somehow he did the same for my reelection. I sold my soul to the bastard, and he's been squeezing me ever since. He was the one who told me about Sophia being my daughter. He even ordered me to kill her. Now I see that it must have something to do with the fetus that Sophia is carrying. Abel's messianic child.

Cain: We need to kill them both. I'm a chip off the old block, Dad. I'm just like you, except that I have no regrets. You've always been too soft on Elizabeth Corsini. Deep down, you really dug her. Am I right?

President Macorley: When she was younger, nobody could come close to her. She was more beautiful than Sophia. I just couldn't let romance stifle my lust for power. Your mother didn't make demands on me. I wanted to rule the world. I still do. You're right, I have some regrets. We need to be careful of Leamas. He has his own devious interests. He's doing all this for his own ambition to destroy God. He wants to occupy God's Throne of Glory.

Cain: You always taught me that God doesn't exist.

The president laughs.

President Macorley: That was before the Devil showed up in my life, and now yours. The only thing that the Devil can't accept is that he doesn't exist without God. His ego won't allow it. The fucker is ageless, while I'm aging geometrically being the president. Even my charm is dissipating. I'm getting old, and I'm still a young man in my fifties. This is a cocksucking job.

Cain: Easy, Dad. I'll pass the word along to our friends to prepare for an attack on the Jewish State.

President Macorley: Yes, tomorrow the Jewish Festival of Sukkoth begins, the time when Armageddon is prophesied to take place. I'll go on international TV to assure the Jewish American population and Jews everywhere that I'm their savior.

Cain: That's the spirit. Don't you worry; I'll take care of Abel Slobodkin and Sophia.

President Macorley: Not Sophia. She's our blood.

Cain: Of course, Dad. We'll spare Sophia, but the unborn son has to go since he is destined to be the Messiah. We need some type of accident to occur that causes her to lose the baby.

President Macorley: Fine, but I don't want to know about it. I'm afraid, Cain, we'll both suffer the wrath of God for our actions. There is no turning back and there is no repentance.

Cain: You really are a believer. I feel sorry for you.

Cain exits. The president's private phone rings.

President Macorley: We're raising the alarm tomorrow night when I speak before the American people.

Leamas: There can be no more screw ups, Macorley. I want to give Heaven a jolt. By the way I was only kidding to get your goat. Cain is your biological son.

President Macorley: Thank God, I never told Cain about our ancestry.

Leamas: Why should he know or care that your great-grand-father was a Muslim?

President Macorley: Remember our bargain.

Leamas: Haven't I made you famous enough? After this you'll rule the world.

President Macorley: And you'll occupy God's Throne. There will be no more good in the world. How delicious!

76

THE ATTACK

Abel and Sophia are with Elizabeth and Daniela watching the TV in the lounge of the Four Seasons Hotel.

President Macorley: Our intelligence has learned that the governments of Libya, Turkey, Sudan, the Russian Caucasus Mountain countries, Somalia, Iran, and Syria have attacked the State of Israel. The United States condemns this cowardly attack. We are working feverishly with our partners in the Security Council of the United Nations. We need to put an immediate halt to these provocative actions, which are creating an untenable position for the United States and its friend and ally in the Middle East, the State of Israel. Let me assure Israel and the Jewish people throughout the globe that America stands with you.

Sophia: My father is a bloody liar.

The Corsini sisters, especially Sophia's mother, are completely surprised.

Daniela: You're an unbelievable slut, Lizzie. I know you went to bed with the asshole, but getting pregnant?

Elizabeth remains silent. Abel tries to put a good spin on the disclosure of Dr. Corsini's secret.

Abel: A beautiful person came out of a mismatch of innocent lovers. Dr. Corsini was very young and in love when it happened. Daniela, if it hadn't happened, you wouldn't be an aunt to this beautiful girl, Dr. Corsini wouldn't be a mother, and I wouldn't have the chance to spend the rest of my life with her.

Sophia smiles at Abel. She looks into her mother's eyes.

Sophia: I'm sorry, Mom. I was snooping one day when I saw the entry in your notebook. Do you forgive me?

Elizabeth: I should be the one asking for forgiveness. Malcolm Yale Macorley doesn't love me or you, Sophia, because he can't feel. He's lost in his own ambition and power, and there's no room for anything else.

Elizabeth starts crying. Daniela hands her a tissue.

Elizabeth: I was in love with him, and I foolishly believed that he was in love with me. It was a long time ago, and I feel nothing for him now. He's a stranger to me.

Sophia: I never told you, Mom, but I've had this curiosity for years, what it would be like if he and I met. But when Abel told me that the White House tried to have me killed, there was no want or need left in me.

Daniela: Is this true about the White House? Why didn't you tell me, and where did you get your information? I need you to be honest, Abel. Your life depends upon it.

Sophia: No, Auntie, Abel mustn't.

Abel kisses Sophia on the cheek.

Abel: I can't lie to the family any longer, Sophia. I was recruited by the Mossad long before I was an FBI agent. You can do anything you want with me, but please let me finish my mission. I've been ordered by the prime minister of Israel to kill Cain Macorley. Cain has activated Gog and Magog. It's his plan that the president is following, and father and son are being directed by the Devil.

Daniela: I'm going to have you check into my sister's psychiatric ward, Abel. You're insane.

Elizabeth: Why can't it be true, Daniela? We've had angelic experiences. So why not the Fallen Angel, Satan.

Sophia: We, too, Mother.

Daniela: This whole family belongs in the loony bin. What does the Devil look like? Let's pick him up and bring him for questioning. Maybe we should kill him.

Abel: Only his peer, another angel, can do that. I tried shooting him, but there was no effect. He goes by the name of Leamas. Leamas spelled backward is Samael. And Samael is the Angel of Death. It was actually Leamas who ordered the president to murder Sophia.

Sophia: Because I'm one month pregnant with Abel's child. And the child will grow up to be the Messiah.

Daniela: Shit! Now I can't incarcerate you, Abel. We have to have a shotgun wedding to get my niece married.

Elizabeth: I'm so happy for you, darling. You found true love. And a new baby in the family. How wonderful!

Sophia: I was going to tell you, Mother, when the attempt on my life occurred. I was waiting for the right time.

Daniela breaks out laughing.

Elizabeth: What's so funny, sis?

Daniela: I'll be able to call you Grandma in public. Abel, don't breathe a word of any of this outside the family. When this is all over, you'll need to find a new line of work.

Abel receives a private call. He leaves the table and comes back after a few minutes.

Abel: The Israeli prime minister called Ambassador Katchalski, and the message was relayed to me. The prime minister felt confident that the Israeli Defense Forces would prevail in the initial attack of Gog and Magog.

Elizabeth: Daniela and I know our Old Testament. Israel will not survive the second and third waves when all the nations of the world join in to destroy the Holy Land and the Jews once and for all. It's on the third try that half of the population in Jerusalem will be captured or killed, and then the city will fall.

Daniela: God will intervene and perform miracles incredible even to Him. He shall destroy all the enemies of His Chosen People for the centuries of Jewish persecution.

Abel: Chosen not because the Jews are special, but because the Jews were supposed to be a nation of priests charged with bringing God's Commandments to the rest of the world. I'm afraid we failed to do this over the centuries. Human beings were born imperfect since the time of Adam and Eve in the Garden of Eden.

Daniela: Just to set the record straight, in Christianity Gog and Magog is not the End of Days. Jesus is resurrected to fight the Beast with the Mark 666. Jesus will destroy the Antichrist. Maybe Sophia is carrying Jesus in her womb. Anything is possible, right?

77

OFFENSE OR DEFENSE

Michael and Gabriel are talking in the sanctuary of the
Third Temple in Heaven.

Michael: There are new developments on Earth. Gog
and Magog is in full bloom.

Gabriel: Satan and the Macorleys have initiated the terrorist
Muslim attack on Israel.

Michael: The evildoers will lose in the end.

Gabriel: But even if they lose, they win. They will have brought
Israel to the brink of disaster, and humanity as we know it will no
longer exist.

Michael: The Ancient One mourns the killing of any human
being, even His enemies. Remember the biblical Egyptians. God's
Ten Commandments must be preserved at all costs. Evil must never
triumph over good.

The angels hear God's voice in the sanctuary.

GOD: I am saddened by today's events on Earth. Humans do
not pay attention to history. The Bible clearly describes the wars
of Gog and Magog.

Gabriel: Send me, Ancient One. I shall destroy Satan.

GOD: Not yet, Gabriel. It's time for Me to once again take My place on the public stage as I did back in biblical days. Satan expects Me to be on the defensive. I have a surprise in store for him and the Macorleys. Sometimes the best defense is a good offense, or have I got the quote reversed? No matter! The world will feel My omnipotence, and all humanity will know their God, as waters are of the sea.

78

DIVINE MIRACLES

Daniela and Elizabeth are on their third scotch in the Four Seasons Hotel lounge.

Daniela: Did Sophia call?

Elizabeth: Yes. She and Abel are in her apartment. He's drinking beer, and she's sipping milk. She told me that she was feeling nauseous. I told her that I was planning her wedding.

Daniela: I'm afraid it won't be a church wedding with all the trimmings. But you'll still be maid of honor.

Elizabeth: My assignment is to be the designer of the flower arrangement covering the *chuppah.*

Daniela: Will you please stop this Jewish thing and speak English? You mean the wedding canopy. Besides we gentiles can't pronounce the "ch." You have to reach from the back of your throat when you sound it out. Marshall can do it, and I'm mad at him because he never told me that he was Jewish. Would you ever have guessed that Lamster was a Jewish name? I thought he was Irish, especially the way he drinks. He probably has more alcohol than water in his blood.

Elizabeth: Speaking of which…

Daniela interrupts.

Daniela: No, he hasn't proposed. But he damn well better, or no more nookie. I've drawn the line in the bed.

Without warning loud noises, which the ear can barely tolerate, come roaring inside the hotel. Chandeliers shake, and glasses slide across the bar. The sisters hold onto their scotch and duck under the table. Windows break as the wind pushes through the hotel, claiming anything not solidly fixed. Daniela's purse flies through the air. Another patron in the lounge yells that it's coming from outside. The sisters crawl on their hands and knees to the entrance of the hotel. They stand and make their way outside, where pandemonium and panic sweep the streets.

Cascades of lightning bolts are shooting across the sky, unchecked by alternating waves of clamorous thunder. Small sulfurous fires and pillars of smoke are everywhere, and cars are flipped on their sides or backs. Torrential rains are striking the pavement of the capital, and people on the streets are running like decapitated chickens. Miraculously, no one is hurt.

Daniela and Elizabeth turn to see the lights in the hotel blink and then darken. The thunder and lightning abate, and a generator kicks on to restore light at the Four Seasons. The sisters survey the damage and return to the lounge. The television comes on and the weatherman appears. It's probably his greatest moment in his dull life. He seizes the opportunity and takes center stage.

Weatherman: Good evening, America. At 8:00 p.m. the United States was struck by unknown forces that may have been initiated by aliens from outer space. We now turn to our MSNBC newscaster, Jim Smith.

Jim Smith comes on the air totally disheveled. He hasn't shaven and his tieless shirt is wrinkled. His usually impeccable coiffure, for which he pays two hundred dollars, is nowhere to be seen, and he looks like someone who has just arisen from bed.

Jim Smith: Hello, America. Pardon my appearance. We have breaking news. The Pentagon has informed us that there is no evidence of an invasion. What we do know is that this weather pattern is happening simultaneously in every country in the world except Israel. We have pictures from all over, which we would now like to show you.

The TV flashes similar pictures in New York, Los Angeles, Caracas, Toronto, Vancouver, Fairbanks, Lima, London, Paris, Reykjavik, Berlin, Oslo, Stockholm and Madrid. The weatherman comes on again.

Weatherman: Towns and rural areas are experiencing the same lightning fires and torrential rains. This is a worldwide phenomenon with no apparent explanation. Back to you, Jim.

Jim Smith: It's a miracle, folks. No one has been injured or died, although there is considerable property damage. Is this a sign from the Supreme Being? Is He sending us a warning?

Elizabeth: A sign from Heaven. It would be nice if the president stepped up and mentioned divine providence.

Daniela: Well, he won't take any blame. That's for sure.

Elizabeth: I must call Sophia to see if she's okay.

Daniela: Hopefully she's in Abel's arms making love.

Elizabeth and Daniela hear voices coming from the TV. They turn their heads to see what's happening. Jim Smith is speaking.

Jim Smith: The president of the United States is in the Oval Office and will be addressing the American people momentarily. We hope that he'll try to calm everyone's nerves. Here's the president.

President Macorley: As President Franklin Delano Roosevelt once said, "The only thing we have to fear is fear itself." There is no cause for alarm. The unprovoked attack by the seven Muslim nations against the State of Israel has been repelled, and Israel has not retaliated except to exercise its right to defend itself. This Holy War has nothing to do with these unusual weather patterns, which appear to be nothing more than a freak of nature. I would suggest—

Just then flashing lightning and tumultuous thunder are seen and heard in the sky. Once again fires break out, followed by rain and hailstones the size of golf balls.

All of Washington, DC, loses its power, and the capital plunges into pitch-black darkness. Generators activate and the picture on the television comes back on.

Jim Smith: The whole country went into darkness exactly one minute ago. We're getting word that the blackout is happening all over the world, even in countries in different time zones where it is currently broad daylight. I stand corrected. Only the tiny country of Israel is lit up and has not been affected. It's as if God is repeating the plague of darkness before the Exodus from Egypt.

Elizabeth and Daniela smile.

Elizabeth: That was quite a leap of faith for Jim Smith, an espoused atheist,

Daniela: The old expression comes to mind, "There are no atheists in foxholes."

Elizabeth: I doubt if President Macorley will have the guts to come back on.

Daniela: He's had enough embarrassment for one night. He'd look like a fool in front of the American people. What would he say? That an act of God just happened?

Elizabeth's cell phone rings. Sophia is calling from her apartment.

Sophia: Mom, are you alright?

Elizabeth: I'm with your favorite aunt. We're at the Four Seasons.

Sophia: Where else would you be in a crisis? You and Auntie drink too much.

Elizabeth: Is Abel with you?

Sophia: Yes. He's on the phone with Shlomo Katchalski.

Elizabeth: Israel is the only country not affected. Your aunt is beginning to feel that the nuns didn't tell us the truth about the Jews. They really seem to be the Chosen People. You know how devout a Catholic she is.

Daniela leans over and speaks into the phone.

Daniela: And you're not, Grandma?

Sophia laughs and then tells her mother to hang on for a moment. She comes back on.

Sophia: Abel says to look at your TV in thirty seconds.

Jim Smith: I wish I was in Jerusalem right now. There's a whole lot of shaking going on, to quote the rock star Jerry Lee Lewis. Look, America. And observe the work and handicraft of the Creator of all creatures and all things.

Milk is flowing from the hills around the golden city of Jerusalem, and red wine is pouring down the Mount of Olives. Israelis of all ages are dancing and singing in the streets. The Israeli Philharmonic Orchestra has assembled under the direction of its conductor, Zubin Mehta, and is playing the theme from the movie *Exodus.*

Jim Smith: An unbelievable sight. We have an exclusive for you. Prime Minister Jacob Duskin of Israel wishes to address the American people.

TV cuts to a live image of Prime Minister Duskin.

Prime Minister Duskin: Good to be with you, Jim.

Jim Smith: We see the celebration in Israel. Can you tell us what's going on?

Prime Minister Duskin: First, I want to express Israel's sorrow for damages throughout the globe. From what we understand, no one is hurt, and for that we praise God. The weather we are experiencing, and the milk and wine flowing in Jerusalem, are signs from God that were described in the Hebrew Bible thousands of years ago. God's Hebrew prophets, Joel, Ezekiel, and Zechariah, warned the Jews back then of a time in the future when the wars of Gog and Magog would lead to the apocalypse. There would be horrific destruction accompanied by miracles. It seems God has brought forth the miracles, but has preempted the cataclysmic devastation Israel was supposed to undergo during the second and third phases of the war against our country.

Jim Smith: Prime Minister, does that mean that no further attacks will occur on the State of Israel? That the world will not mass together to destroy the Holy Land in these wars of Gog and Magog? The second and third phases, as I understand it, were supposed to follow shortly.

Prime Minister Duskin: I must compliment your biblical knowledge, Jim. You are exactly right. By stopping the war with His miracles, the Holy One is kind and merciful. He has saved hundreds of thousands of people who would have died by His hand had they joined the initial seven Muslim nations in the Gog and Magog attack. God has performed miracles that are incredible even to Him, and there will be no further attempts to destroy Israel. We have entered the Messianic Age, Jim. I hope, as the Bible states, that the world can beat their swords into ploughshares so that we can have a lasting and just peace.

Jim Smith: Before we let you go, Mr. Prime Minister, I want to thank you for sharing your biblical knowledge. On a personal note, this reporter will no longer be a disbeliever. Thank you again, Prime Minister Duskin. It's a time for the entire world to be grateful.

Both sisters are crying with tears of joy.

Sophia: Mom, are you still there?

Elizabeth: I'm so moved, Sophia. I feel more alive now than I've ever felt before.

Sophia: And I feel I want to do something meaningful for God.

Elizabeth: You are, my darling. The baby, remember! Bye, Sophia. Give my love to Abel. Your aunt and I are just getting started. She's ordered another round.

They hang up.

* * *

The scene shifts to the White House. Cain Macorley sits alone in his office mumbling to himself and shaking his head.

Cain: It's all over. We're ruined. Good has defeated evil. The damn Hebrew God has gained the momentum. Operation Gog and Magog is dead, finito, caput!

His cell phone rings. It's the 666 number.

Cain: Is that you, Devil? I have a headline for you. It will appear in tomorrow's *Washington Post.* "God Trumps Devil." I'm calling it in myself. How do you like them beans?

Devil: All is not lost if you hear me out. I instructed you to kill Abel Slobodkin, but what you didn't know is that directly from Prime Minister Duskin's mouth came the order to kill you because of your plan for Gog and Magog. If you can kill Abel, we can still be successful. God's plan to reverse the murder of the biblical Abel by the biblical Cain in modern times will have been thwarted. If you kill Abel, the Third Temple cannot be built since its construction is to atone for the biblical murder. Without a Third Temple on Earth in Israel, there can be no Messianic Age. Evil in the final battle will have defeated good. To hell with God's miracles. I have a few tricks of my own. When our mission is complete, the world will only know the Devil.

Cain smiles for the first time.

Cain: We can still win.

Devil: Your father has become expendable, Cain. His belly is soft. And you will need to kill Abel in a "fair" fight, if you know what I mean.

Cain: Destiny calls for us all. I choose pistols.

Devil: I'll act as your second. I suspect that the angel Gabriel will be Abel's second. He and I must also fight to the death, as God must destroy me in order to eradicate the evil inclination in humankind. After you kill Abel, you will kill Sophia Corsini and her messianic child.

Cain: Agreed! Where shall our duel take place?

Devil: A most appropriate place. Arlington National Cemetery, tomorrow. Godspeed. Oops! A slip of the tongue.

79

LEAMAS/SAMAEL

That night we find President Macorley sitting alone at his desk with a loaded revolver beside him. He picks up the gun and places it at the side of his head. He shakes and is unable to pull the trigger. He puts the gun back down on the table and pours himself a drink of scotch. He then lights up a Cuban and stares at the door, knowing that the Angel of Death is coming for him.

Leamas is dressed all in black and carries a small dropper bottle. The president knows that the bottle contains untraceable poison not of this earthly world.

President Macorley: I've been expecting you, Angel of Death. Can I finish my drink, Leamas?

Leamas: I'll have one with you, Mr. President. Under the circumstances I prefer to be called Samael.

Samael removes a barrel glass from the cabinet, pours himself a drink, and they clink glasses.

Samael: Excellent scotch, Macallan 18. You need to be taken out of your misery, Mr. President. Your dream to be ruler of the world will, unfortunately for you, pass on to your son. By the way Cain didn't bat an eyelash when I told him that you had become expendable.

President Macorley: Cain was always more evil than I. He's in the demonic category, like you. I found true love once, and I stupidly let it go. Cain has never had that pleasure. Contrary to the beliefs of my psychiatrist, Elizabeth Corsini, I do feel. I have feelings for her.

Samael: Confessions are good for the soul. I've had a few women in my time, but the absolute best was Adam's wife, Eve, outside the Garden of Eden. I raped her. I still look exactly like Adam. That was God's gift to me, and these thousands of years living as a human have been His plan for me all along. Call it divine providence if you wish. The only change will be that I shall defeat Him in the end.

President Macorley: You're a fool, Devil. You only exist at God's pleasure. You're nothing but a lackey for God.

Samael goes into a rage. His face and neck turn purple.

Samael: Enough. Last words, Mr. President.

President Macorley: "The Lord is my shepherd. I shall not want. He maketh me—"

Samael bangs his head against the office wall.

Samael: You're the worst kind, a closet believer. Damn you and damn your God.

Samael stretches out his hand, and the president convulses uncontrollably in his chair. Samael approaches. The president gasps. Samael takes a dropper full of the liquid in his bottle and places it in the president's mouth. He forces the president to swallow by holding his nose. The president slumps in his chair and keels over, falling to the floor. His cigar and glass of scotch fall out of his hand. Samael picks up the president's cigar and puffs on it, while feeling his pulse.

Samael: Cuban cigars. Long live the false Messiah. He was a man of taste. Too bad he had to die.

Samael dials Cain's private number. Cain answers.

Samael: What's done cannot be undone.

For the first time in his life, Cain exhibits a little emotion. A single tear forms at the corner of his right eye.

Samael: Your father, I'm sad to say, was a believer all along. He fooled everyone, including me.

Cain: It was you who brought that out in him, Devil.

Samael: Me! What did I do?

Cain: The Devil doesn't exist without God.

Samael: Et tu, Brutus? Shakespeare's Julius Caesar reference to betrayal. We'll see who's standing at the end of the day. Au revoir until tomorrow, Cain.

The Devil hangs up. He realizes that the original curse by God has disappeared. It's past midnight, and he's still human.

* * *

Cain: I shall avenge my father's death. After I kill Abel, I'll obliterate the Devil.

Cain takes out his cell phone and dials. Abel and Sophia are sleeping. Abel picks up, thinking it's the ambassador.

Abel: Hello, Ambassador.

Cain: No, it's me, your worst nightmare.

Abel quickly wakes up.

Abel: Couldn't wait until morning?

Cain: In the morning you'll be dead. Pistols at dawn.

Abel: Where?

Cain: Meet me at the Tomb of the Unknown Soldier, Arlington National Cemetery.

Abel: I commend you on your choice of location.

Cain: You can congratulate me after you're dead. I intend to dig up the Unknown Soldier's grave and bury you in it.

Abel: I'll be there.

Cain hangs up. Sophia is groggy and speaks.

Sophia: Who was that?

Abel: No one. Go back to sleep. I have to leave early tomorrow morning. I'll see you for dinner.

Sophia has fallen back to sleep. Abel sits up with his eyes wide open, biting his nails. A voice is heard in the room that only Abel hears. It's as if Sophia's ears have been stuffed with cotton.

GOD: I shall be with you. Fear not!

Sophia continues sleeping. Abel strokes her hair and smiles.

80

NO EXPECTATIONS

Michael and Gabriel are in the Third Temple discussing the situation on Earth. They are eating black seedlings from the Tree of Life in the Garden of Eden.

Michael: We have our own Garden of Eden in Heaven. Eating manna is like eating caviar at the Ritz. Manna is the secret to eternal life. The Ancient One was prepared to offer the manna to Adam and Eve, before they ate figs from the Tree of Knowledge of Good and Evil.

Gabriel: Had the Israelites not sinned with the Golden Calf, the manna they ate during the Exodus from Egypt would have sustained them for a hundred and fifty years.

Michael: When the opportunity is right in front of you and you don't take it, your life is full of shallows and miseries, as Shakespeare wrote.

Gabriel: Satan is expecting me at dawn.

Michael: I relish your challenge.

Gabriel: Satan never plays fair.

Michael: Good! You have no illusions. You can't expect a sinner of the highest order like Satan to have a smidgeon of integrity. He's expecting you to act as Abel's second.

Gabriel: And I shall. I wish I could warn Abel about Cain's deception. Abel expects a fair fight, but he won't get one. The Ancient One has instructed me not to mention anything to Abel. He wants Satan and Cain to dishonor themselves so that He will have no mercy on them when the time comes for their demise.

Michael: Satan has never lost in battle. God has restored all of Satan's angelic powers, so be careful.

Gabriel: The clash of the Titans.

Michael: I'll be there in invisible form, observing the duel. We'll toast your victory at the Ritz tomorrow night at happy hour. Free hors d'oeuvres…and the drinks are on me.

81

DUEL AT ARLINGTON

It's dawn and both Cain and Abel walk through Arlington National Cemetery's hallowed graves of American military soldiers. They approach the Tomb of the Unknown Soldier from different directions. Satan is there waiting for them. Satan is wearing a white suit with a black bandanna covering the Jewish Star imprint inflicted by Abel's slingshot. In Satan's outstretched arm is a gold box covered by a black silk cloth.

Abel: Hello, Leamas. Or should I call you by one of your other names?

Satan: I use different names appropriate to different settings. I'm in a somber mood among all these dead people, so today you can call me Satan. After today, of course, you won't be able to call me anything. You'll be lying quietly in a grave of your own.

Cain: Where is your second?

Gabriel, dressed in his blue biblical robe, suddenly appears from behind the Unknown Soldier's tomb.

Gabriel: I'll stand for Abel.

Abel seems perplexed. He didn't know that there would be others at the duel.

Abel: Who are you? I don't know you.

Gabriel: A friend to you and an enemy to Satan. I am Gabriel, the Angel of Fire and War. It was I who was unseen and repaired your dislocated shoulder, inflicted by Satan at the time he admitted you into the FBI. It was I who was there when you were born. I have been sent by God to ensure a fair fight between you and Cain.

Satan: Hello, Gabriel. I didn't know that you were meddling in my affairs. It gives me all the more reason to kill you. How long has it been since the time of the Garden of Eden?

Gabriel: It's been 5,780 years. You seem to have remained youthful and look in splendid shape.

Cain: This is all very interesting, biblical friends meeting and all, but I'd like to get started. I'm hungry and haven't had my breakfast.

Satan pulls off the black silk covering, opens the golden lid, and reveals Cain's two American Revolutionary pistols.

Satan: Abel, you were challenged by Cain. Therefore you have your choice of weapons.

Abel this time picks the gun closest to him.

Abel: And the rules?

Satan smirks. He usually asks that question.

Satan: Until only one of you is standing. Ten paces back to back, turn and fire. One bullet only, just like in days gone by. Oh, I'm going to cry. I'm so sentimental.

Gabriel: May I see both guns?

Satan: I'm shocked. You don't trust me, Gabriel?

Gabriel's turn to smirk.

Gabriel: Would you trust you?

Satan laughs. He hands over Cain's pistol. Gabriel inspects Cain's gun and then hands it to Cain. He examines Abel's pistol to make sure its firing pin is in proper working order.

Satan: Shall we begin, gentlemen?

Cain and Abel stand back to back, and Satan gives the signal to start walking. Satan begins the countdown.

Satan: One, two, three, four, five, six, seven, eight…

Cain has already turned before the count of eight, and Gabriel has anticipated the treachery by turning into an angel on the count of six. He appears at Abel's back, who wonders why he hasn't heard the remainder of the count. Abel turns to see Cain firing. He hears the sound of Cain's gun and sees Gabriel catch the bullet aimed at his heart. Cain is stunned at what has transpired. He rubs his eyes in disbelief and looks for Satan, but Satan is nowhere to be seen.

Neither Cain nor Abel or Gabriel realize that the moment Gabriel changed to angel form, Satan transformed himself into the Serpent from the Garden of Eden. In seconds the Serpent has slithered along the ground, and it bites Abel's heel. Abel winces in pain as he falls toward the ground. He looks up at a stunned Cain. Still holding his pistol, Abel aims at Cain's head and pulls the trigger. Cain's skull is blown apart. The Serpent scurries over to Cain's body and angrily hisses a sound unknown to the human ear.

In the meantime Gabriel injects a potion into Abel's heel. Abel momentarily looks up into Gabriel's eyes and falls into an unconscious state.

Gabriel: God's prophecy from the Book of Genesis has been fulfilled. Abel has pounded on Cain's head, and the Serpent has bitten Abel's heel.

Serpent: There is no prophecy for your death. Will you allow me to change costumes one more time for a fair fight?

Gabriel nods in the affirmative. The Serpent switches into his formidable form from when he was an angel in Heaven. Satan, the black angel, has six brass toes and six wings with crawling tarantulas. He now sports six eyes instead of two, and his eight-foot body takes on an Incredible Hulk shape. Gabriel also transforms himself into his angel form, with his two wings and his eight-foot height.

Gabriel: Your true colors. Six eyes, six wings, and six toes. The Mark of the Beast—666.

Satan: And six daggers to destroy you.

Gabriel: God has made an exception this one time. We are angels with human bodies. We can bleed and die.

Satan: When you bleed, God will die.

Satan throws all six knives, but they are deflected by Gabriel. He and Satan make a circle of about fifteen yards and then simultaneously fly at each other head on at full speed. They collide and both do a back flip and land on their feet. Satan jumps on the Unknown Soldier's tomb and flings fire from his nostrils. They bump again and roll on the ground, each unable to gain an advantage. They begin circling each other; then both stop and assume a martial arts stance.

Gabriel: We'll see what all your training has produced.

Satan: My kung fu will destroy your tai chi.

A martial arts battle ensues in the air and on the ground, with both angels trading deadly blows. They draw their swords and joust. The battle continues, but neither can strike a final mortal blow. They land on the ground facing each other and transform back to completely human form.

Gabriel: Pistols, Satan?

Satan: You are a dead man, Angel of Fire.

Gabriel picks up Abel's pistol, and Satan takes the gun from a dead Cain's hand. Each adds fresh gunpowder to his pistol and a black lead ball that they remove from their cloaks.

Gabriel: Ten paces. Can I trust you, Satan?

Satan: Like I'm your very own brother. We'll count off together.

Gabriel: For once in your life, fight with honor.

Satan: Die, knowing that I shall destroy God.

They face back to back and count off the paces as they walk.

Gabriel and Satan: One, two, three, four, five, six...

They both turn at the same time, as Gabriel has anticipated Satan's untrustworthiness. Satan gets his bullet off a split second faster than Gabriel, and Gabriel's tai chi movements barely avoid the bullet. Multiple copies of Satan appear, all wearing black bandannas, but only the true Satan has the imprint of the Jewish Star on his forehead inflicted by Abel's slingshot. Satan's magic cannot duplicate the Divine Star. Gabriel fires his pistol, striking the real Satan in the heart. Yellow bile gushes out of Satan. His face ages six thousand years. The impostor Satans vanish.

Satan and Cain suddenly turn into two piles of dirt. God's voice is heard.

GOD: From dust have I made you and to dust you shall return. Gabriel, see to Abel.

Gabriel: And when shall the Messianic Age begin?

GOD: In eight month's time, when Sophia delivers.

Gabriel: And the earthquake?

GOD: On the day of the baby's birth, all inhabitants will leave the area, and I shall create the splitting of the Mount of Olives to further demonstrate my powers. The geography of Jerusalem shall change, and the city will lie twenty-five miles south of Mount Moriah, which shall emerge from under the rubble of the earth. Abel will build the Third Temple on Mount Moriah, the site of the First and Second Temples, to redeem the sin of the biblical Cain who murdered his brother, Abel.

Gabriel: And the child?

GOD: When he is old enough, he shall take his place as king of Israel. The sperm of a Jew, Abel, and the egg of a Christian, Sophia, will produce My offspring. Eternal peace and harmony will follow for all those admitted into the Messianic Age. Now tend to Abel. And stop all this nonsense with Michael. I'm referring to your drinking binges.

Gabriel looks disappointed.

GOD: Well, maybe this one last time for your celebration at the Ritz. Be careful of the caviar. Your digestive system is only used to manna.

Gabriel smiles and changes to angel form. He gently picks up Abel and they fly away.

82

AFTERMATH

Abel lies in a hospital bed at Washington Central. Sophia is in her doctor's white coat and is holding his hand. Dr. Corsini enters.

Elizabeth: What are you doing in my neck of the woods, Abel? And speaking of woods, how did you get that wound on your heel?

Sophia: He stepped on a rusty nail, Mom.

Dr. Corsini is holding Abel's medical chart.

Elizabeth: Your chart indicates snakebite. Someone administered anti-venom and saved your life.

Sophia: No secrets, Abel.

Abel tells a half truth, omitting Satan and Gabriel.

Abel: You're right. Cain Macorley and I had a duel with pistols at dawn this morning at Arlington National Cemetery. I think I killed him. Out of nowhere a snake appeared and bit me on the heel.

He pauses.

Abel: That's all I remember.

Elizabeth: Turn on the television. I think you'll both find the news interesting.

Sophia turns on the hospital TV. Jim Smith is speaking.

Jim Smith: President Malcolm Yale Macorley is dead at age fifty-four. He was found in the Oval Office having apparently died of a heart attack. There was no evidence of any prior coronary heart disease. Nor was a suicide note found.

Sophia hugs her mother and cringes. Abel is surprised by the news.

Elizabeth: Thank God, Sophia. Malcolm was evil from his youth, God rest his soul.

Sounds emanate from the television.

Jim Smith: We have an Associate Press news alert. Cain Arlis Macorley, the president's son, has been deemed a person of interest in the possible murder of his father. I have FBI Deputy Director Daniela Corsini standing by.

Daniela: Hello, Jim.

Jim Smith: Can you tell us, Deputy Director, the status of the case?

Daniela: The froth on the side of the president's mouth suggests a seizure. Our analysis at the FBI lab indicates an unidentified substance in his bloodstream.

Jim Smith: And the whereabouts of Cain Macorley?

Daniela: He seems to have vanished.

Jim Smith: Sorry, Deputy Director, but we have to cut to the White House. Vice President Karen McHugh is about to speak. Our first female president will be sworn in later today.

Sophia turns off the television. Mother and daughter look at Abel.

Abel: Don't look at me.

Dr. Corsini takes out her cell phone and dials Daniela.

Elizabeth: Hello, Dannie. We just caught your act.

Daniela: Sis, I'm famous.

Elizabeth: I'm in Abel's hospital room. We have you on speaker.

Daniela: Abel, you have to be careful. The capital is full of snakes.

Abel: Daniela, have you checked out Arlington National Cemetery?

Daniela: Yes, nothing but two unusual piles of dirt close by the Tomb of the Unknown Soldier. We've taken samples from each pile, just in case.

Elizabeth: I'll see you later, Daniela.

Sophia: I don't want to wait a moment more than I have to. I want to marry you, Abel. I need you.

Abel: We have the Israeli Embassy booked. I'm waiting for Shlomo to let me know when the prime minister will be in Washington. He's promised to attend our wedding.

Elizabeth: Speaking of the ambassador, he's outside in the hall, anxiously waiting to see you. We'll let you two talk. C'mon, Sophia, I'll buy you some lunch. You need to eat for the baby, too.

Dr. Corsini and Sophia kiss Abel on the cheek and depart. Abel sounds his thoughts aloud.

Abel: Am I living a nightmare? Did all this happen to me? Satan and Gabriel. Who would believe my story?

Shlomo Katchalski enters Abel's room.

Ambassador Katchalski: Shalom, Abel.

Abel: Hello, Shlomo.

Ambassador Katchalski: How are you holding up?

Abel: Someone else killed the president. I think I shot Cain in the head, just after a snake bit me on the heel. Sounds a bit like the prophecy in the Bible, doesn't it?

Ambassador Katchalski: Our Mossad agents were at Arlington ahead of the FBI. They removed the only sample that had a drop of blood from one of the two dirt piles. The blood sample matches Cain Macorley. Congratulations, Abel.

Abel: And the other pile?

Ambassador Katchalski: Nothing. Plain dirt, although it had a strange unidentified yellow mucous substance on it.

Abel: It's just a hunch, but I'm wondering if that pile belongs to Satan. Gabriel must have killed him.

Ambassador Katchalski: You need some time off, Abel. You're hallucinating. By the way our intelligence has discovered a well-kept secret. President Macorley's paternal great-grandfather was a Muslim. Maybe that's why the president was never a real friend to Israel. Do you see any connection to Gog and Magog?

Abel: I keep thinking about it. Maybe your information will allow me to decipher God's intentions. God always had His Hebrew prophets speak in riddles.

83

WEDDING

The *chuppah*, the Jewish wedding canopy, is decorated beautifully with white and yellow long-stemmed mums. Abel stands under the *chuppah* holding Sophia's hand, who is beaming with pride at her man. Rabbi Goren holds a prayer book. Elizabeth is maid of honor, and Abel's father is best man.

The guests at the Israeli Embassy include the Corsini sisters, Isaac and Rebecca Slobodkin, Marshall Lamster, Shlomo Katchalski, and Prime Minister Jacob Duskin.

Rabbi Goren: Abel, do you take Sophia to be your wife under the laws of Moses and Israel?

Abel answers in a loud voice.

Abel: I do.

Everyone laughs. Abel then says the prayer in Hebrew.

Rabbi Goren: Sophia, do you take Abel to be your husband?

Sophia: I do.

Rabbi Goren hands Sophia a silver chalice of wine.

Sophia: With this wine of God, I seal our marriage.

She passes the cup of wine onto Abel.

Sophia: Oh, it's so sweet.

Everyone laughs, including the invisible angels at the back of the room.

Rabbi Goren: Honored guests. I give you Mr. and Mrs. Abel Slobodkin.

Abel breaks the wrapped light bulb under his feet. Everyone claps while Michael and Gabriel clap silently. Abel lifts Sophia's veil and kisses her passionately. They all kiss and hug one another, then proceed into another room where a table is set up with kosher food.

The glasses clink, and Abel and Sophia kiss. The party goes on for a couple of hours. At one point music comes on, and a drunk Marshall Lamster gets up and toasts Daniela. They all clap as Marshall and Daniela start dancing. Isaac and Rebecca join in, and the ambassador and the prime minister take turns dancing with Elizabeth. Abel and Sophia sit at the table, watching the dancing and holding each other tightly.

Abel: You're the four Jewish matriarchs wrapped up in one, Sophia. You have such wonderful, special qualities, and I'm so lucky and grateful that you are my wife and soul mate. I'll love you, forever.

Sophia: And you are mine until the end of time and beyond, Abel.

Prime Minister Duskin yells out over the music.

Prime Minister Duskin: I must leave you for my meeting with President McHugh. Abel, will you walk me out? Please continue without me. I've had such a good time being here at Abel and Sophia's wedding.

84

GOG & MAGOG EXPLAINED

Abel and the prime minister step outside the embassy, where Jacob Duskin's car is waiting to take him to his meeting with President McHugh. The prime minister looks directly into Abel's eyes, searching his soul.

Prime Minister Duskin: Abel, before I go. Have you been able to figure out God's real meaning of Gog and Magog?

Able: I have an interpretation based upon President Macorley tracing his roots both to Islam and Christianity. His great-grandfather was a Muslim, and his mother's ancestry seems to be purely Christian. Through the Hebrew prophets, God spoke about punishing those who persecuted the Jewish people over the centuries. Both Christianity and Islam were guilty of killing innocent Jews, as were atheist dictators such as Hitler and Stalin. There are so few Jews in the world compared to Christians and Muslims, when their numbers should be equal. There has been so much killing over the centuries. Men are truly beasts.

Prime Minister Duskin: Yes, the Jewish people have been demolished, but Judaism has survived the onslaught.

Abel: I don't really comprehend anti-Semitism and hatred. The world would be such a better place if all people, no matter their beliefs, would live and let live.

Prime Minister Duskin: Who, then, is Gog?

Abel: The alphabet letters, g-o-g, are an acronym for "God of gentiles." Thus, President Macorley and his son, Cain, were Gog. They led the governments of the seventy gentile nations into battle against Israel in the second and third phases of the wars of Gog and Magog. Seven Islamic nations in the first phase became seventy nations in the second and third phases.

Prime Minister Duskin: And who are the seventy nations?

Abel: Seventy is a metaphor for the governments of the whole world trying to destroy Israel and the Jewish people. This was all foretold in the Bible almost five thousand years ago. Noah had three sons, Ham, Japheth, and Shem. From the descendants of these three sons came the seventy nations. Israel and the Jews were descended from Shem, but Israel is not counted among the seventy nations.

Prime Minister Duskin: And who or what is Magog?

Abel: Again an acronym. The letters m-a-g-o-g stand for "male ancestry God of gentiles."

Prime Minister Duskin: Of course the president's male ancestry is from Islam. His great-grandfather was a Muslim.

Abel: Our biblical sages missed this interpretation, because we needed to be looking for a leader who was of both religions. The president fits the bill. Gog was more likely to be the president, but he may also have intended to be his demonic son, Cain. There is a suggestion in the Bible that Gog dies before the wars are complete, so that also seems to be true.

Prime Minister Duskin: We are so fortunate that divine providence has intervened in the wars. The amount of devastation and death would have been beyond our wildest imagination. Both the Old and New Testaments speak about the horrifying nature of the apocalypse.

Abel: Only the Almighty has the power to change the prophecies, and He has done so through His miracles. In the end good has finally conquered evil.

Prime Minister Duskin: Abel, I've arranged for you to be Shlomo Katchalski's special assistant in the Israeli Embassy until the Messianic Age hits its full stride. I've had Shlomo clear the air with Daniela Corsini. She suggests that it would be best if it was your choice to leave the Bureau. You need to draft a letter of resignation. Nobody will suspect your choice for a new line of work, and the Americans will be grateful to have a former FBI agent inside the Israeli Embassy.

Your appointment to the Israeli Embassy won't happen for at least a month so that things can quiet down. Consider this your opportunity to go on a honeymoon with Sophia. Now I must leave for my meeting with Karen McHugh. Abel, what we spoke about must never reach anyone else's ears. Not a word of your interpretation of Gog and Magog to anyone. The secret must die with us.

Abel: I'll seal the book, as did the prophet Daniel, concerning the time of the end in the Book of Daniel; and as did the patriarch Jacob, who on his deathbed was about to reveal the exact end time to his twelve sons, the Twelve Tribes of Israel.

Prime Minister Duskin: I can't emphasize the point enough. Our discussion is only for your ears and mine.

Michael and Gabriel are standing beside Abel and Jacob Duskin. They were privy to the entire conversation.

Michael and Gabriel: And for ours!

The prime minister looks puzzled.

Abel: Angels, Mr. Prime Minister.

Prime Minister Duskin: Ah! The Divine! Shalom, Abel.

The prime minister gets in his car and the limo drives off. Abel takes in the awe of the moment.

85

TIME TO SAY GOODBYE

The angels are standing with Abel outside the Israeli Embassy.

Abel: Will you do me the honor this one time? It will be your wedding present to me.

The angels appear to Abel in angelic form, wings and all. Abel looks up at Michael and then the eight-foot-tall Gabriel.

Abel: Can you tell me why God has selected me?

Michael: Moses once asked God why He chose to help sinners like yourself. God's response: "I shall help whomever I please, even if it's the worst sinner."

Gabriel: The Ancient One's thoughts are not human thoughts. His ways are not human ways. God has instructed us to tell you that for whatever His reasons, He has selected you to build His Third Temple in Jerusalem. When completed people of all colors, races, religions, and beliefs will visit the Temple on the Holy Days of Passover, Shavuous, and Sukkot. Shavuous was the time when God delivered the Ten Commandments to the Israelites on Mount Sinai. And the holiday of Sukkoth will be the annual celebration of the redemption of humankind.

Abel: You still haven't answered my question. Why me?

Michael: All we can tell you is that God chooses those with damaged pasts, as this creates humility in men with the potential to rise to greatness. Even Moses was impure, and so was King David. All humans have checkered pasts.

Abel: What you're telling me is that I'll never know why.

Michael: God works in ways that even His angels are not privy to. Be content that you heard His voice, and you can live your life in bliss with Sophia.

Gabriel: Michael, you still owe me that drink at the Ritz.

Michael: We mustn't forget the caviar.

The angels become invisible. They speak in an echo from miles above the earth.

Michael and Gabriel: Shalom, Abel. Godspeed.

The angels are gone. Abel says goodbye.

Abel: See you again soon.

Abel then mouths the words to the song of the Swedish group, ABBA.

Abel: "I believe in angels..."

He then sings the most beautiful and saddest song he has ever heard.

Abel: "Time to say goodbye!"

Abel hears the voice.

GOD: Not goodbye, Abel. It's just the beginning.

Abel walks through the doors of the Israeli Embassy, picturing Sophia in his mind. There is an incredibly awesome glow in his face. He has been touched by the Hand of God.

ABOUT THE AUTHOR

Dr. Jerry Pollock is a Bachelor of Science and Master of Science in Pharmacy from the University of Toronto. He obtained his PhD in biophysics at the Weizmann Institute of Science in Israel in 1969, and then went on to New York University Medical Center for four years as a postdoctoral fellow and assistant professor in the department of microbiology. In 1981, at the age of forty, he became professor of oral biology and pathology in the School of Dental Medicine at the State University of New York at Stony Brook. He retired as professor emeritus from Stony Brook in July 2006.

He is a transplanted Torontonian to New York by way of Israel, and a transplanted New Yorker to Florida, where he now resides with his wife, Marcia. Dr. Pollock combines his scientific background with his spirituality. *Gog & Magog* is the author's third book. Like his other two books, *Messiah Interviews* and *Divinely Inspired*, Dr. Pollock writes to share his faith, trust, and love of God. All three books represent his humble attempt to give back to the Creator for the gifts of divine providence that have been bestowed upon him.